SIMON WHEELER, DETECTIVE

Mark Twain at Tuxedo Park, New York, August 1907

title: # Simon Wheeler, Detective...

By

MARK TWAIN

Edited with an Introduction

By

FRANKLIN R. ROGERS

New York

The New York Public Library

Library of Congress Catalogue Card Number: 63:18140

Judge and Mrs. Samuel D. Levy Memorial Publication Fund

A perpetual trust established by the sister of

Dr. HENRY W. and Dr. ALBERT A. BERG

for publications based upon

books, manuscripts and autograph letters

in the Berg Collection of The New York Public Library

PUBLICATION NUMBER TWO

Table of Contents

*   *   *

List of Illustrations

Acknowledgments

I am deeply indebted to the late Mrs Clara Clemens Samossoud and the Mark Twain Estate for permission to publish this edition of *Simon Wheeler, Detective*. I am also indebted to the Harvard University Press for permission to quote extensively from the *Mark Twain-Howells Letters* (1960); any work, large or small, concerning itself with either Mark Twain or William Dean Howells and written since 1960 must owe a substantial debt to that collection. I am grateful to Harper & Row, Publishers, for permission to quote from Albert Bigelow Paine, *Mark Twain, A Biography* (1912) and to the Henry E. Huntington Library and Art Gallery for permission to quote from *Mark Twain to Mrs. Fairbanks* (1949).

I wish to thank Mr Henry Nash Smith, editor of the Mark Twain Papers, who made available to me the resources of the Mark Twain Papers and generously offered any assistance I might need. For valuable aid in meeting various editorial problems, I wish to thank Mr Frederick Anderson, assistant to the editor of the Mark Twain Papers. Obviously, this work could not have been completed without the support and aid of the curator and the staff of the Henry W. and Albert A. Berg Collection, The New York Public Library. To Mr John D. Gordan, Curator, and to Mrs Lola L. Szladits, his assistant, I owe a substantial debt of gratitude.

My friend and colleague Mr Frank M. Collins was kind enough to read carefully a draft of the introduction, to criticize freely, and to offer his suggestions for revision. Much of the strengthening of the final draft of the introduction is owing to him; the errors and weaknesses remain my own. My special thanks go to Mrs Mary Ann Rogers, who prepared the manuscript, aided in correcting copy and reading proof, and exhibited a considerable amount of patience with my inconsistencies and vagaries.

F. R. R.

Introduction

EARLY in *A Connecticut Yankee* when he is setting the stage for his first miracle, Hank Morgan realizes he has made a mistake which to any reasoning being will reveal him for a "humbug." He worries over his error and its possible consequences for some time and berates himself for his heedlessness. "But finally," he asserts, "it occurred to me all of a sudden that these animals didn't reason; that *they* never put this and that together; that all their talk showed that they didn't know a discrepancy when they saw it. I was at rest, then" (*CY*, p 44).[1] Hank's estimate of man's ability or rather inability to use his reasoning powers is clearly Twain's own, for it is one which pervades a substantial portion of his writings. But the realization left Twain, unlike Hank Morgan, rarely if ever at rest.

No one who reads at any length in Mark Twain's works can escape noting his interest in ratiocination, especially when the process depends upon one or two minor and seemingly irrelevant bits of evidence. Such a quality may seem incongruous in a man whose relationships with friends and business associates were often marked by impulsiveness and frequently brought to an end by a pyrotechnic display of temper touched off by uninvestigated rumor, unsubstantiated suspicion, or at best a thorough misinterpretation of evidence. The list of such ruptures or eruptions in Twain's lifetime is impressively long, but equally long is the list of complete works or major episodes in his fiction obviously designed to stand as monuments to one man's reasoning powers and to exhibit by contrast the limitations of the great majority of men. One thinks immediately of the exoneration of Father Peter, in *The Mysterious Stranger*, when Wilhelm Meidling calls attention to the dates on the coins in question; or Pudd'n-head Wilson's unravelling of the murder mystery with the aid of fingerprints; or Tom Sawyer's penetration of Jubiter Dunlap's disguise and his consequent solution of the murder in *Tom Sawyer, Detective*. The list grows longer when one turns from major episodes and complete works to minor events where, nevertheless, the outcome hinges on a bit of evidence shrewdly interpreted by a character: for example, the leaves and twigs which Jim observes on the raft and uses to expose Huck's deception.

Twain's interest appears in a number of other works and episodes which are satiric attacks upon or direct denunciations of perverted reason, among them "The Stolen White Elephant" and "The Double-Barreled Detective Story" in the lighter vein and the more serious and extended treatment of the fault in the trial of Joan of Arc. The unfinished novel, *Simon Wheeler, Detective,* falls within this category. The story owes its genesis to the series of books written by Allan Pinkerton during the 1870s and 1880s, books based upon actual cases handled by Pinkerton's agency but sometimes so considerably embellished as to make massive demands upon one's willingness to suspend disbelief. As one glances through these books, the reason or reasons for Twain's satirical outburst become fairly clear. Certainly in a number of instances that capability and godlike reason of which Hamlet spoke are notably lacking in Pinkerton's detectives. But it seems equally certain that something else is involved in Twain's reaction. The pattern of evidence and analysis exhibited in what may be called the ratiocinative episodes in his works shows that Twain was a devotee of the C. Auguste Dupin school of detecting. He came to Pinkerton's accounts with a literary stereotype in mind and found the usual routine of police investigation and pursuit both colorless and disappointing.

I

"What a curious thing a 'detective' story is. And was there ever one that the author needn't be ashamed of, except 'The Murders in the Rue Morgue'?" [1a] So Twain wrote in his notebook in 1896 at a time when he was closely involved with two, possibly three, detective stories. In that year Harpers brought out a new collection of stories, the chief of which was *Tom Sawyer, Detective,* written a year or so earlier. On the day Twain made the notation, he sketched out "an extravagant romance," according to a letter to Livy, which had occupied his thoughts "for many years" and seemed now on the verge of taking form. [2] That the "extravagant romance" was a detective story is clear from the notebook entry; that it may have been "Tom Sawyer's Conspiracy," a Tom and Huck story he left unfinished, is suggested by the appearance in the notebooks from this point on of suggestions for that story. That it may have been another reworking of the Simon Wheeler story appears from the fact that Twain apparently used or considered using Si Wheeler's dream visit to heaven as part of his lecture-tour program [3] and from the fact that sometime after 1895 Twain reread the Simon Wheeler manuscript, made a number of minor corrections, and jotted in the margin at least one suggestion for revision. [4]

xii

The very extent of Twain's involvement in detective stories or tales of detection, despite his confession of shame, attests to the fascination which the genre and the ratiocinative process held for him. The history of Simon Wheeler furnishes further testimony. This amateur detective and his antics remained fairly close to the center of Twain's interests throughout the major portion of a long career, that is, from the mid-1870s to the late 1890s, despite Twain's declaration at one stage in the history of the story that he lacked the "faculty" for writing detective stories and that the adventures of Simon Wheeler appeared to him "dreadfully witless and flat."

The first complete surviving version of the story is a play which Twain wrote and revised in a tremendous burst of enthusiasm and energy between June 27 and July 11 1877. But there are several indications that the idea was somewhat older. In reporting his first day's work on the play to William Dean Howells, Twain wrote that he was deep in a comedy he had begun that morning, "principal character, that old detective." His report of work done that day indicates that his tank was full: he had outlined the first act and written the second, in all fifty-four pages of manuscript.[5] The reference to Simon Wheeler as "that old detective" implies what is clearly stated in a later letter to Howells describing an interview with Dion Boucicault. Twain read passages of the Simon Wheeler play to Boucicault, who then pointed out a curious fact: Boucicault was revising a play about a character named Simon Wheeler "which he wrote & laid aside 3 or 4 years ago. (My detective is about that age, you know)." [6] According to this statement the idea for the Simon Wheeler story had its inception in 1873 or '74. But it most likely did not reach paper until sometime in 1876 when he sent what was probably an outline of the plot to Charles Reade, apparently seeking encouragement to turn it into a play for production in London by Reade. The only record of this transaction is a note from Reade dated August 6 1876 warning him not to rely entirely on acting: "I beg to acknowledge your detecting plot. It is full of brains but improbable on the stage and not popular. The public want to see the plain realities of life reflected on the boards. All on acting is a bad card. Put in a story." [7]

The idea possibly reached paper even earlier, in late 1875 or early 1876, as a contribution to *St. Nicholas*, Scribner's magazine for boys and girls, in the form of a skeleton plot to be filled out by the readers of the magazine. On February 8 1876 Mary Mapes Dodge, editor of *St. Nicholas*, rejected a contribution, using various descriptive terms which point toward such a possibility: "I fear that this particular MS can't be made available for St. Nicholas. The idea is a good one, but the skeleton story you give, though just as full of fun as can be, & capital for grown-ups, is not one that I like to ask the children to fill out. The absurdity & humor of the thing would not be recognized by them — but they would set out to work by hundreds to write a bloody & sensational novellette that would out-do the dime novels. . . . As I know by experience, they would take the idea literally, quite overlooking the comic-burlesque undercurrents. . . ." [8]

If the *St. Nicholas* contribution was the Simon Wheeler plot, Mary Dodge's rejection did little to dampen Twain's regard for his brain-child, as the later exchange with Charles Reade shows. Nor was he long deterred by Reade's rebuff, for in the autumn of 1876 during a conversation at the St James Hotel in New York, he outlined the story to Chandos Fulton, a producer-director, who encouraged him on the spot and in a note dated March 12 1877 again urged him to build it into a complete play: "Was that a fanciful coinage of your imagination the plot which you sketched to me one autumn afternoon last year at the St. James' Hotel? As I told you then there was the germ of a good acting play, especially as the plot would be so new. I want a piece for two comedians. It strikes me there was the material there, — one the detective, the other the man of disguises." [9]

Fulton's encouragement was sufficient to send Twain to Quarry Farm, his summer retreat near Elmira, New York, brimming with enthusiasm and anxious to begin work. The Clemens family left Hartford for Elmira on June 6 1877; after the arrival at the Farm, Twain's first task was to complete the installments of "Some Rambling Notes of an Idle Excursion," which he had promised to Howells for the *Atlantic*. As soon as he finished the last of these on June 26, he turned the next morning to the composition of the Simon Wheeler play. When he was working on *Roughing It*, he had described himself as writing with a "red-hot interest"; between June 27 and July 11 1877, his interest in Simon Wheeler seems to have reached a white heat, if his progress reports to Howells are any indication. On July 4 he reported the completion of the first, second, and fourth acts to his satisfaction, a total of 151 pages of manuscript. He allotted two more days for the completion of the third act and gloated that he had written over thirty pages a day since he began on June 27.

"Never had so much fun over anything in my life — never such consuming interest & delight." [10] This letter had not yet left his work table
before he had further news to relate. In a post-script dated July 6, he
announced the completion of the play, a four-act comedy "conceived,
plotted out, written & completed in 6½ working days of 6½ hours
each; just a fraction under 250 MS pages besides the pages that were
torn up & the few pages of odds & ends of notes, such as one sets
down in the midst of his work for future reference. . . ." [11] But to
Twain, as to many other writers, the statement that a work "is finished" meant that he had turned out the last page of his rough draft.
The task of revision and polishing occupied the next five or six days.
On July 11 he wrote to Howells to gloat again over the size of his accom-
plishment: "It's finished. I was misled by hurried mis-paging. There
were ten pages of notes, & over 300 pages of MS when the play was
done. Did it in 42 hours, by the clock; 40 pages of the Atlantic. . . .
Those are the figures, but I don't believe them myself, because the thing's
impossible." [12]

The energy generated by his enthusiasm had not yet been dissipated.
The day after he finished revising he drew up an exhaustive synopsis to
be sent with a title-page for a copyright application. The copyright certificate for *Capn' Simon Wheeler, The Amateur Detective. A Light Tragedy* was issued July 29 1877.[13] Within a day or so of his application for
copyright, Twain left for New York to find a producer, but first he had
to visit Hartford to investigate reports of burglars around his house. In his
diary, the Reverend Joseph Twichell, a friend and neighbor, recorded
Twain's arrival at Hartford on the evening of July 16, "bringing a new
comedy 'The Amateur Detective' in his pocket." [14] On that and the following evening Twain read the entire play to the Twichell family. Twichell
expressed himself incapable of judging the merits of the piece as a play,
but thoroughly enjoyed Twain's reading of it. Mark Twain, detective,
settled the matter of the "burglar" by discovering that the man in question was the lover of one of the housemaids. All in one day, July 17, Twain
collared the man, forced him willy-nilly to marry the girl, celebrated the
nuptials with an impromptu feast, finished reading the new comedy to
Twichell, and — both his sense of propriety and his vanity satisfied —
dashed off the next morning to New York to peddle his play and revise
Ah Sin, the play on which he and Bret Harte had collaborated, for its
New York début.[15]

Before leaving New York on August 2 after attending the first two performances of *Ah Sin,* Twain approached Dion Boucicault, John Brougham, and Augustin Daly, but curiously enough not Chandos Fulton, with his new play. Brougham thought the play had marvelous potentialities, but declined to get involved with anything which promised to make no money. Boucicault, according to Twain's statement to Howells, said it "was ever so much better than Ah Sin; says the Amateur detective is a bully character, too." [16] When one recalls the tremendous flop of *Ah Sin,* this is certainly damning with faint praise. When Twain was writing the detective play, he had for the title role envisioned Sol Smith Russell, who had portrayed Colonel Sellers in the dramatization of *The Gilded Age.* Hearing of the play from Daly and Henry Wall, Russell wrote to Twain about it; there was an exchange of letters. Apparently Russell examined the manuscript, but nothing resulted.[17]

If the reception given the play by the professional dramatists, producers, and actors dampened his spirits at all, they were soon revived by William Dean Howells, who visited Twain in Hartford in the latter part of October, read the play or listened to Twain read it, and counseled turning it into a story or novel. After returning to Cambridge, Howells wrote on October 31 that after further thought it seemed best to him to make Simon Wheeler as much like Captain Wakeman as Twain could make him: "Why not fairly and squarely retire an old sea-dog, and let him [take] to detecting in the ennui of the country? This is what you first tho't of doing, and I don't believe you can think of anything better. I want the story for The Atlantic." [18]

Acting upon Howells' advice, Twain apparently began turning the play into a novel almost immediately, but he still had not given it up as a play. On November 12 1877 he commented in a letter to Thomas Nast that he was occupied with a book which he could have ready for the printers and the dramatist "(for I want it dramatized)" by the end of January.[19] Since Twain began the composition of *The Prince and the Pauper* some time in the winter of 1877–78, it is possible that the comment refers to that novel — but not probable, because Twain's notebook entry for November 23, which outlines the basic plot for *The Prince and the Pauper,* suggests that he was still in the process of planning and had not yet begun writing it.[20] The reference is more probably to the novel mentioned in his February 5 1878 letter to Mrs Fairbanks. After describing *The Prince and the Pauper,* which by then was under way, he added,

"Of course I am doing some bread-&-butter work. . . . To-wit, a novel of the present day — about half-finished. A talented young fellow here is dramatizing it from my MS (I have just finished hurling a few sentences into his 1st act here and there, this afternoon.) I expect to put the play & the chief character, into the hands of Sol Smith Russell." [21]

The novel in question appears to have been *Simon Wheeler, Detective* not only from the reference to Sol Smith Russell but also from the available information concerning the "talented young fellow" who was dramatizing it. Twain seems to be embellishing a bit on the functions of the young fellow, for the traces of his work still surviving in the Mark Twain Papers point toward the role of amanuensis instead of dramatist. The young man apparently took up his duties sometime before December 10 1877 and retired from the scene sometime after February 5 1878. Several routine letters and notes signed "Saml L. Clemens, per F. C. H." dated December 10 and 11 1877 remain. He seems to have taken over the task of making remittances to Twain's brother, Orion, for Orion, annoyed at receiving communications signed by a secretary, wrote Twain on February 5, "Please accept my thanks for the $42 drafts — three — and give my acknowledgements to your secretary for her autograph." [22] Orion apparently mistook the sex of the secretary on the evidence of the handwriting, which is rather full, rounded, and careful, and might easily be mistaken for a woman's. The secretary's major task seems to have been making an amanuensis copy of the Simon Wheeler play from Twain's manuscript. Such a copy, in the same hand as the notes and letters, is preserved in the Mark Twain Papers. A collation of the amanuensis copy against the manuscript reveals a number of minor revisions, never more than a sentence or two in length. The evidence pretty clearly indicates that the secretary was copying Twain's play manuscript with occasional aid from Twain on minor revision, not constructing a play from the text of the novel as Twain produced it. Something of the sort is suggested by Howells' choice of words in a reference to the young man in his letter to Twain dated June 2 1878: "I have had a very pleasant letter from your cub-dramatist in Hartford, renouncing — or rather disclaiming — all right and title to Clews [an alternate title for the Simon Wheeler play]" (*MT-HL* i 232–233). Twain may initially have invited the cub-dramatist to transform the novel into a play (thus the question of renunciation), but the task degenerated to the production of an amanuensis copy of Twain's play (thus the disclaimer).

Twain probably abandoned his first attempt to construct a novel from the play shortly after his February 5 letter to Mrs Fairbanks. In his letter he states the novel is "half-finished"; since throughout his life he clung to the notion that eight-hundred manuscript pages were necessary to complete a one-volume book, this statement would mean he had written about four-hundred manuscript pages by February 5. The surviving manuscript preserved in the Berg Collection of The New York Public Library consists of 541 pages and thirteen pages of notes. It shows evidence of extensive revision and expansion, but reflected in renumbered pages is a slightly earlier manuscript which contained at least 414, possibly as many as 451 pages. The text covers less than half the plot as it appears in the play; the expansion was achieved by retaining most of the detective nonsense, adding the feud-love story, and inserting two extensive episodes: the run-away horse episode midway in chapter 4, based upon a near-tragedy at Quarry Farm in the summer of 1877,[23] and Si Wheeler's dream visit to heaven in chapter 10.

Although Twain often reverted to Simon Wheeler in his thoughts during the next twenty years and tinkered with the manuscript already written, he never apparently carried the story much beyond that point reached before he abandoned it sometime after February 1878. The frequent returns to the story indicate that the abandonment did not result from loss of interest, although at no subsequent time does he exhibit the intense enthusiasm of 1877. The stoppage resulted instead from the preparations for the trip to Europe which was to result in *A Tramp Abroad*.[24] The writing of the travel book proved to be such a troublesome burden that he was often thrown into frenzies of frustration. For diversion from his troubles he apparently turned to *Simon Wheeler, Detective* from time to time during his European sojourn, but, perhaps jaundiced by his struggles with *A Tramp Abroad,* he was unable to recapture his former enthusiasm. Finally he gave up. On January 21 1879 he wrote Howells, "I have given up writing a detective novel — can't write a novel, for I lack the faculty; but when the detectives were nosing around after Stewart's loud remains, I threw a chapter into my present book in which I have very extravagantly burlesqued the detective business — if it is possible to burlesque that business extravagantly. You know I was going to send you that Detective play, so that you could re-write it. Well I didn't do it because I couldn't find a single idea in it that could be useful to you. It was dreadfully witless & flat. I knew it would sadden you & unfit you for work." [25] The interest in Simon Wheeler had, however, like Tom Sawyer, died only temporarily. Returned from Europe, ensconced in his study at Quarry Farm, his travel book at last almost finished, Twain regained at least a portion of his former optimism: his spirits revived and with them, Simon Wheeler. A suggestion from a now unidentifiable friend that he collaborate on a broad comedy caused him to write to Howells on September 15 1879 asking him if he wanted to join in writing a play with "old Wakeman (Amateur Detective)" in it.[26]

Except for minor deletions or additions of a word or two and marginal notes in pencil or black ink, the text was written in the gorgeous violet ink which Twain used at Hartford and in Europe from the mid-70s to June 1880. The greater part of the manuscript is on Crystal Lake Mills paper, with only a few leaves of "P & P" paper, both varieties used during the same period as the violet ink. Thus the evidence of paper and ink shows that nothing significant was done with the manuscript after Twain abandoned the project in 1878. But during the 1877–78 period of work the novel went through several sub-stages in its development. The earliest sub-stage may be called the "Charley" version because in it Dexter's given name is Charley, as in the play. Only after Twain had written thirty or so pages did he decide to make Dexter a visitor from Kentucky and to rename him Hale. Another sub-stage or possibly other sub-stages are represented by the expansions of the run-away horse incident and of Hale's conference with Judge Griswold after Hugh's "death." These revisions are revealed by the shuffling and renumbering of pages.

Although Twain never actually added any further text to his manuscript, the survival of his interest is clear from the fact that at some time or times substantially later in his career he returned to the manuscript long enough to review it, make some minor corrections, and project the conclusion outlined in Group C of the notes (see Part II below, p 162–166). Preserved in the Mark Twain Papers is a specimen of tablet paper matching that used for the Group C notes. This specimen is dated May 28 1889 in Twain's hand; other samples in letters and manuscripts indicate the paper was used extensively in the late 1880s and early 1890s. Such evidence suggests strongly that Twain's last major effort to complete the novel was in the period 1885–95. If this conclusion is correct, two notebook references point to the probability that the work was done in the early '90s. Some time shortly after May 29 1891 Twain jotted in his notebook, "Gave Mr. Hall 'The Californian's Story' to be [typed] & kept. Also

xix

gave him the Wheeler detective story." [27] The use of the phrase "the Wheeler detective story" would seem to indicate a reference to the novel, not the play. And although the reference is fairly cryptic, one logical inference is that Twain was placing his literary valuables in safe-keeping. In other words, the Simon Wheeler novel was no longer just another incomplete manuscript in the files, but one which gave promise of "completing itself," as Twain would say, and therefore was worthy of special treatment. Certainly, a later notebook entry from this period indicates a recent review if only to salvage the useful portions of an otherwise useless manuscript. Just before departing on his around-the-world lecture tour, Twain canvassed his memory and his works both published and unpublished for possible readings to be used for the various programs. One of the suggestions listed under the date of November 4 1894 is "Si Wheeler's arrival in heaven." [28]

If the projection for the conclusion were made in the period 1885–1895, one must then postulate an additional review and some minor revision in the latter half of the 1890s on the basis of a penciled note in the top margin of MS p 433: "Gillette's SS speech." The reference is apparently to William Gillette's play *Secret Service*, produced in 1895. In the last act, in his major speech of the play, Captain Thorne, who faces a dilemma analogous to Dexter's, expresses emotions similar to those described in that portion of the manuscript where the note appears. Twain apparently noticed the similarities and made the note to remind him of a way to heighten the melodrama of Dexter's situation. But since Twain probably did not see *Secret Service* until its London run in 1896 with Gillette, Twain's friend and former protégé, in the role of Captain Thorne, one must conclude that the related work on the novel was done in or after 1896.

In all probability, the note on MS p 433 and the related minor revisions were not made until after August 16 1898. On that date Twain made his last surviving reference to the novel in a letter to Howells from Kaltenleutgeben, Austria:

> In 1876 *or* '75, I wrote 40,000 words of a story called "Simon Wheeler" wherein the nub was the preventing of an execution through testimony furnished by mental telegraph from the other side of the globe. I had a lot of people scattered about the globe who carried in their pockets something like the old mesmerizer-button, made of different metals, & when they wanted to call

up each other & have a talk, they "pressed the button" or did *some*thing, I don't remember what, & communication was at once, opened. I didn't finish the story, though I re-began it in several new ways, & spent altogether 70,000 words on it, then gave it up & threw it aside.[29]

Because there was a Simon Wheeler version in existence, at least in outline form prior to the play written in 1877, Twain may be correct in the details recalled from that earliest version, we have no way of knowing with any certainty, although it does seem doubtful that he wrote as many as 40,000 words on that first version. Even if one cannot prove the inaccuracy of Twain's memory on the details, the general tone of the entire comment is that of a recollection made from some distance. The comment suggests, that is, that Twain had not yet reviewed the manuscript after seeing Gillettte's play in 1896. The likelihood is that the recollection stirred Twain's interest in the story once again: some time after writing the letter to Howells, he resurrected the manuscript from his files, reviewed it, made some minor revisions in pencil, and jotted the note. Because he never acted on the suggestion in the note and never again referred to the story in the surviving letters and notebooks, he apparently once more concluded "it was dreadfully witless and flat" and beyond salvage.

I I

"I have very extravagantly burlesqued the detective business — if it is possible to burlesque that business extravagantly," Twain wrote to Howells in January 1879. The reservation expressed here is one which obviously did not occur to him in 1877–78. It results from a critical appraisal of his work, and during the initial period of composition he was in no mood for critical appraisals: he was having fun, riding high on a wave of delight and interest derived not from an artist's satisfaction with his work but from a satirist's gleeful previsions of his target's discomfiture. And Twain's glee was twofold, for he had two targets. One, Allan Pinkerton's detective stories, afforded an outlet for the exasperation aroused by perverted reason; the other, the Canadian publishers Belford Brothers (who had been pirating his works), afforded an outlet for a large accumulation of spleen.

In *Simon Wheeler* the satire of Allan Pinkerton's methods of detection and the burlesque of his stories are for the most part general rather than specific. Pinkerton himself is referred to as the celebrated "Flathead that writes the wonderful detective stories," and the repetition of the same initial letter in the names of the three detectives, Billings, Baxter, and Bullet, as well as the name Bullet itself, may represent a specific hit at George H. Bangs, Pinkerton's superintendent in New York City. Further the setting of *Simon Wheeler* seems to be indebted to Pinkerton's *The Somnambulist and the Detectives,* published by Keen, Cooke and Company in 1875. A moment's reflection will reveal to the reader of *Simon Wheeler* that its setting is somewhat unique. With the partial exception of *The Gilded Age,* the Simon Wheeler novel is the only one of Twain's novels dealing with the Mississippi River region which is not set in a river town; the Guilford of the novel is not another fictional version of Twain's own Hannibal, Missouri. It is set at some distance from the river in a region of hills and rocky gorges; only a small stream flows past the town and provides a scenic promenade for the townspeople. Such a setting rather closely approximates the surroundings of Atkinson, Mississippi, the locale of Pinkerton's narrative, and probably derives from it, for Atkinson boasted just such gorges, stream, and promenade.

The major satire is carried on, without reference to specific works, through the three detectives, who dramatically display the Pinkerton badge, a disc engraved with a staring human eye and bearing the legend "We Never Sleep," and through Simon Wheeler, an avid practitioner of the art of detection as he has learned it from the detective stories. With the detectives and Simon Wheeler, Twain manages to pour ridicule upon Pinkerton's three major devices in detection: the accumulation of exhaustive details both relevant and irrelevant, the constant surveillance of the suspect by detectives in disguise, and the securing of a confession by gaining the confidence of the suspect.

A Pinkerton investigation was an expensive procedure. At the outset of a case, Pinkerton's standard move was to dispatch one or more operatives to the scene of the crime. These men would go in disguise, and at least one would pose as a person wishing to establish himself in business in the vicinity. Their instructions were simple: to remit voluminous reports detailing the gossip about the crime, the movements of the various principals, family histories, and so forth, including sketches, tracings, and measurements. Nothing was too trival or too remote to be included. The various principals were indiscriminately "shadowed" wherever they went. If the case involved four or five people whose business required a fair amount of traveling, there was a great bustle and stir of extra operatives, summoned by telegraph, coming and going in various disguises, hot on the heels of the traveling businessmen. Even the modern reader frequently wonders why the station agent, at least, failed to notice the sudden increase in traffic. Finally from the welter of reports Pinkerton would extract enough to decide that the burden of suspicion rested on one particular person. Another operative, in disguise of course, would be assigned to "shadow" him (the others to remain at their posts and continue their daily reports of gossip, family histories, and so forth). At times this shadowing becomes as ridiculous as Simon Wheeler's efforts — more so, in fact, proving that Twain was right in wondering if the business could be burlesqued extravagantly. In *The Expressman and the Detectives,* the "shadow" is dressed as a German immigrant in his provincial clothes; under his peaked leather cap he sports a wig of long, unkempt yellow hair. Further equipped with a gaudy carpet-bag and long clay pipe, he pursues his quarry for weeks by rail and steamboat all over the South, sometimes sitting next to the suspect and once leaping onto a departing boat immediately behind his man. All one can say in retrospect is that, guilty or not, the suspect deserved to be hanged for not once noticing so ubiquitous a companion in so outrageous a costume. In another instance Pinkerton himself, in the get-up of an Irish hod-carrier complete with dinner-pail and a cement-encrusted shovel over his shoulder, trails his "watchful" and "wary" suspect through downtown Chicago, into the lobby of at least one fashionable hotel, to the railroad depot, and finally into a Pullman parlor car without once being noticed. This feat verges on the marvelous. In most of the cases which Pinkerton describes in his books, the final step depended upon Pinkerton's conviction that the guilty conscience must find an outlet in words either in nightmares or in conversation with a confidant. To act upon this theory it was necessary to assign another operative, in disguise, to the task of gaining the suspect's confidence and of becoming his closest companion, even living with him if possible (while the original group of operatives continue their reports and the "shadows" shadow). As his companion, the operative works upon the conscience of the suspect by making provocative remarks about the crime, at first quite oblique, later more and more clearly based upon the assumption of the suspect's guilt. Finally the suspect confesses — at least Pinkerton fails to record an instance when he did not confess. Arrested and brought to trial, he knows his doom is sealed when his bosom friend takes the witness stand, identifies himself as a detective, and, over the despairing shrieks of the criminal, relates the circumstances of the confession.

In *Simon Wheeler, Detective*, Twain furnishes the *reductio ad absurdum* of these methods. The Pinkerton men track their suspect, supposedly disguised as a cow, to his presumed hideout in the upper branches of a large tree. In true Pinkerton fashion there is much ado about staking out the various cow tracks, measuring each (to make certain it belongs to the same cow) and the distances between prints — all carefully recorded in the ever-ready notebooks. Simon is as adept in the art of disguise as Pinkerton himself apparently was and is motivated by the same theories. His questions are always oblique but "subtly" designed to force the suspect into incriminating revelations. And, of course, his hospitality to the "tramp" (Hugh Burnside) results from his assurance that familiar intercourse with the suspect will eventually bring a confession.

In all fairness to Pinkerton, one must admit that the staple and, in the great majority, the only technique of any investigation is the routine, painstaking gathering into one composite file of all available information concerning the crime and the various persons involved. But at the same time one must also allow that Pinkerton overdid the matter. He never seems to have considered the fact that an excess of irrelevant material could glut his files and thus endanger the success of the technique by obscuring the relevant facts. Even worse, the glut of essentially irrelevant materials could sometimes cast over the wrong suspect and his actions a sufficiently thick pall of suspicion as to bring a conviction of guilt without any real, direct evidence of complicity. Several times, as he reads through Pinkerton's various accounts, the modern reader is chilled by the realization that, so far as the tangible evidence goes, an innocent man has been punished. And the realization is not shaken even if the suspect confesses, for Pinkerton spared no effort, no matter how elaborate or long drawn-out, to force a confession. In several instances, he secured the imprisonment of his suspect for fairly long periods of time, once upwards of a year. During that time, the suspect was subjected to a constant barrage of disheartening news and accusing statements from a detective planted as a cell-mate, from especially printed newspapers, from falsified letters and documents. Knowing what we know about psychology, we must wonder how many innocent men gave up in despair and confessed to crimes they had not committed.

Twain does not comment directly on these more chilling aspects and consequences of a Pinkerton investigation. Although some reference to these is implied in his burlesque, his focus is primarily upon the absurd procedures. When he abandoned the Simon Wheeler novel, he still felt strongly enough on the subject to strike at least one blow in print. Using the general method and borrowing one Pinkerton character, Detective Bullet, who became Inspector Blunt, Twain wrote "The Stolen White Elephant," first intended as a chapter for *A Tramp Abroad,* but then withdrawn, expanded, and printed as a separate story.

Twain's amusement probably grew to almost boundless delight when he turned his attention to his other target, Belford Brothers, the Canadian publishers who had been pirating his books and articles. One can almost see Twain, hunched over his desk, his whole bearing expressive of intense glee as, in the pose of a Guilford newspaper editor, he pours out his invective upon the head of Alexander Belford in an editorial on Jack Belford, escaped desperado.

Twain's troubles with the Belfords began with the discovery in 1876 that the Canadian firm was circulating a pirated edition of *Tom Sawyer* in Canada and the United States. Because British law required first publication in England to secure copyright in England and its colonies, Twain had attempted to protect himself against piracy by publishing *Tom Sawyer* in England and entering it with the Stationers Company before publishing in the United States. He was both disconcerted and enraged when his brother, Orion, reported that a bookseller in Keokuk was distributing an edition circulated by Belford Brothers of Toronto. Orion, acting as agent for the American Publishing Company, the United States publisher of *Tom Sawyer,* stopped the Keokuk sales of the pirated edition by threatening legal action against the bookseller.[30] Meanwhile Twain, acting through Moncure D. Conway, in whose name he had secured the British copyright, sought to stop the circulation of *Tom Sawyer* by Belford Brothers or to secure royalties from them. From an exchange of letters with Conway and Andrew Chatto, his English publisher, he learned to his chagrin that Alexander Belford had found a legal way to circumvent his precautions. According to British law, publishers in three colonies, Canada, the Cape of Good Hope, and Natal, were privileged, not to reprint English copyright books, but to import foreign reprints and pay royalties only if the author had entered his copyright with the customs department of the colony. Because no American law prohibited the printing of English copyright books, Belford was printing copies of the English *Tom Sawyer* in the United States and importing these reprints into Canada both for local sale and for export to the United States.[31] Twain had neglected to enter his copyright with the Canadian customs; consequently he could do nothing but resolve in the future to see that his copyright was duly registered.

Meanwhile he was also contending with the Belford piracy of his magazine articles: Belford Brothers had brought out an edition of his "Old Times on the Mississippi" series published in the *Atlantic*. While still reeking with the odor of the crime, as Twain would no doubt have put it, the Canadians wrote to Howells on November 29 1876 seeking to make arrangements to publish Twain's future contributions to the *Atlantic* in *Belford's Monthly Magazine*. The firm expressed its willingness to pay "liberally" for the right, but it had the effrontery to add "although the law allows us *to pirate* them." Howells referred this proposal to Twain on December 4; on a postcard dated December 5, Twain replied, "The miserable thieves couldn't buy a sentence from me for any money." [32] To prevent further piracy by the Belfords, Twain made arrangements to send duplicate proofs of his *Atlantic* articles to the *Canadian Monthly*.[33]

The arrangements and resolutions furnished a means of forestalling the Belfords in the future, but Twain was left with no immediate means of reprisal for past wrongs, except his writing. Small wonder then that an innocuous beggar in the first draft of the Simon Wheeler play becomes in a revision an escaped criminal named Jake Belford, fleeing the gallows in the disguise of a tramp. Nor is it any wonder that Twain seized the opportunity in the novel to editorialize upon the character now renamed Jack Belford: "This inhuman miscreant who is to be hung next month and his crime-blackened soul sent to that place unmentionable to ears polite where it belongs . . ." (below, p 25). If Twain had been a devotee of the black arts, he probably would have constructed a wax image and thrust pins through it.

The editorial in the Guilford newspaper apparently only sharpened his appetite. Forced by his European trip to delay the presentation of this attack to the public, Twain planned a more immediate revenge in a projected episode for *A Tramp Abroad*. While en route to Europe and before beginning the book or making other plans for it, he wrote in his notebook, "Catch a Canadian Belford in a disgraceful matter on ship or in Europe." [34] The notation reveals how sharply Twain had felt the Belford sting.

III

"It was dreadfully witless & flat" — such was Twain's critical estimate of the Simon Wheeler story in 1879. Despite the subsequent efforts to do something further with the novel, he apparently continued to find it so; the delight and interest of 1877–78 never returned. Reading the novel as it stood when it was finally abandoned, one must admit that the judgment is substantially correct: the novel is for the most part flat if not witless. A necessary implication of this admission is that Twain was suffering from a massive case of critical blindness in 1877–78 when he wrote the play and plunged enthusiastically into the novel. But before one condemns Twain's critical abilities, several points must be considered. The enthusiasm and consequently the critical blindness resulted, as we have seen, from the satiric aim. Further, a detachment from his personal involvement in the satire resulted in a fairly correct estimate of the work, a search for remedies, and ultimately the abandonment of the whole project. Finally, before condemning him for wasting additional effort on a hopeless case, one must recall that Howells read or heard the play in October 1877, discussed with Twain its possibilities as a story or novel, and found it promising enough to demand it for the *Atlantic*. Howells was not, of course, an infallible critic, but neither was he a blind one, nor was he in the habit of adopting the role of sycophant either with Twain or with his other literary friends. One must assume that behind the witlessness and flatness he discerned the ingredients for a good story — and the ingredients are there. As it stands the uncompleted novel is the result of a morganatic marriage between a preposterous burlesque (the play itself is even more preposterous) and an impossibly melodramatic feud-love story peopled with stereotypes and narrated all too often with an imposing array of clichés. But bad as it is, one can discover in it instances of vivid characterization and genuine humor or comedy. One can also discern materials and motifs similar to those which contribute substantially to the worth of the later and much more important *Huckleberry Finn*.

The specific incidents and characters borrowed from *Simon Wheeler* and incorporated into *Huckleberry Finn* have already been cataloged elsewhere.[35] Of more significance is the fact that in the Simon Wheeler novel Twain first attempted to work out in fictional form the condemnation of the aristocratic code and of what in *Life on the Mississippi* he called "jejune romanticism" — a condemnation which lies at the imaginative center of his later work. In a notebook entry of 1895 he described *Huckleberry Finn* as "a book of mine where a sound heart & a deformed conscience come into collision & conscience suffers defeat." [36] Huck's sound heart, his innate goodness, that is, measures the extent of the deformity in the society which has formed his conscience. The same device, the opposition of innate goodness to social deformity, is used in *Simon Wheeler, Detective*.

I have already pointed out elsewhere that Judge Griswold is in physical appearance the model for Colonel Grangerford.[37] More important for the present discussion is the fact that he possesses the same "kind of image or shadow of sweetness," to use Matthew Arnold's phrase, as the Colonel. The "sweetness" was added when Twain began turning his play into a novel; in fact Griswold was totally transformed in the process. The difference between the Horace Griswold of the play and the Judge Griswold of the novel points the direction in which Twain was moving in constructing a theme for his novel.

A brief exchange (later revised to alter not the tone but one word) between Horace Griswold and his wife in the play clearly reveals the original conception of both characters. The two are discussing Horace's attempt to make Milly, the daughter, marry Charles Dexter, despite her love for Hugh Burnside, because Dexter will inherit a fortune. Matilda Griswold wins the argument with a bit of "feminine" logic. Horace exclaims, " 'Pah! You old fool!' "; Mrs Griswold retorts, " 'Pah, yourself, you old ass!' " (MTP). When one reads the play after reading the novel, such dialogue comes as a complete shock.

Unquestionably an aristocrat — "[the Judge] came of the oldest and best Kentucky Griswolds, and they from the oldest and proudest Griswolds of Virginia" (below, p 4) — he exhibits all the outward graces of birth and breeding: "Judge Griswold's manners and carriage were of the courtly old-fashioned sort" (p 4). Whenever and wherever we meet him in the novel, he never fails to act with flawless social grace. Unlike Colonel Grangerford, who, Huck Finn tells us, "was sunshine most always," Judge Griswold is "grave even to sternness," (p 5). But that this gravity is merely a matter of self-discipline which suppresses the outward manifestation of an intrinsically amiable nature is clear not only from his ill-concealed delight in and regard for his daughter, Milly, but also from his intuitive penetration of his wife's thoughts when they learn

of Milly's narrow escape and from his spontaneous resolution to save
Hugh Burnside's life if he can.

At the same time he exhibits the same pride verging on hauteur which
characterizes the later and better known aristocrats of *Huckleberry Finn*.
"He was a gentleman," Twain tells us:

> He so entered himself in the census list. To him that abused word
> still possessed what he called its only warrantable meaning. In
> his eyes, a man who came of gentle blood and fell to the ranks of
> scavengers and blacklegs, was still a gentleman and could not
> help it, since the word did not describe character but only birth;
> and a man who did not come of gentle blood might climb to the
> highest pinnacle of human grandeur but must still lack one thing
> — nothing could make him a gentleman; he might be called so
> by courtesy, but there an end. (below, p 4)

He carries on his feuding according to the same code which produces
his admirable manner. With obvious approbation he repeats Edward
Dexter's statement "'"Gentlemen do not war with children,"'" (p 8).
When Hale Dexter arrives, one of the Judge's first concerns is to assure
himself that the code will be adhered to, that Hale will identify himself
to his blood enemy and give him an equal chance on the field of honor.
Finally, unable himself to perform the duty of second to Dexter because
of his sister-in-law's illness which requires his presence in another town,
he arranges for a suitable substitute, his friend Major Barnes.

All this is quite honorable, but also quite empty. In the case of the
Judge, Twain uses the same device he later used in *Huckleberry Finn*
to expose the emptiness of the feud and consequently of the code. When
Mrs Griswold asks about the cause of the Griswold-Morgan feud (an
incident of which brought involvement in the Dexter-Burnside feud),
the Judge replies, "'I do not remember — that is, I never knew. I think
it never occurred to me to ask. But no matter; it is not likely that any of
my generation could have told me. Besides, the feud itself was the only
thing of consequence; how it originated was a circumstance of no interest.
I was only taught that when I should meet a Morgan there was a thing
to be done; it was very simple — kill him'" (p 9).

In the subsequent events of the novel Twain tests the code and reveals
its artificiality by affording the Judge the opportunity to choose between
gentleness and gentility. Required by a debt of honor to Edward Dexter
to aid Hale in the feud-killing of Hugh Burnside, indeed somewhat exas-

perated by Hale's unseemly delay in prosecuting the feud, the Judge suddenly finds himself faced with the fact that Hugh has saved his daughter Milly's life. Thus codified honor, the "deformed conscience," is opposed by feeling or heart. He is just as spontaneous in his choice as Huck Finn is later: with no perceptible hesitation, the heart overrules the code, and he is in the saddle, spurring toward Guilford, intending to halt the feud if he can, although, so far as he knows on the basis of what he had last heard Dexter say, to do so might well involve him directly in the feud, no longer as second, but as principal, this time as a Burnside supporter. The point implied in the handling of the Judge is that insofar as the gentlemanly code is a formalization of a desirable grace the code is good, even admirable. But in the very formalization lies the seed of deformity. Once it becomes inelastic, the code may actually come into opposition to the very grace it supposedly embodies and preserves. In its rigidity it becomes evil.

The same point is made in the handling of Hale Dexter, but in this instance Twain is quite explicit. When we first meet Hale in the encounter with Hugh and Clara Burnside, it soon becomes obvious that he will be the hero of the tale, the almost stereotyped hero of a love story; as such he is entitled to the fond indulgence from the reader usually reserved for such characters. That Twain intends us to admire him even more than one admires the young swain in love appears in the next encounter. Already a candidate for the title of "good stock" on the basis of Clara's speculations after the travelers separate, Dexter proves his gentlemanly nature (in the good sense) by his actions upon his arrival in Drytown. At the tavern where he intends to spend the night, he discovers a fight in progress, three stage-drivers against one, Simon Wheeler. The landlord and other spectators are grouped outside anxiously awaiting the outcome of the struggle within. Dexter is indignant and spontaneous in his choice: " 'Three on one, and you people allowing it? Is this Missouri style? Come in, and require fair play.' " No one accepts his invitation, but he enters, sides with the underdog, and helps rout the stage-drivers. Unquestionably he is a gentleman in the true sense of the word, a fact emphasized by Wheeler, who declares, " 'Give us your hand — you're true grit, stranger' " (p 21). The trueness of the grit is further emphasized in the next paragraph as Wheeler explains the origins of the fight. The stage-drivers had been bullying a " 'poor devil of a nigger hostler and that harmless old granny of a landlord' " (p 22). Wheeler entered the quarrel to even the odds, whereupon the hostler and the landlord fled, leaving him to face the three bullies alone. The credit which redounds to Wheeler for his interference doubly redounds to Dexter for his.

With such an introduction, the reader fully expects a refusal to participate in so senseless and essentially brutal an affair as a feud. He is disconcerted to find that the hero is flawed in the same manner as the Judge. When the Judge first states his assumption that Dexter has come to Guilford to carry on the feud according to his father's wishes, Dexter hesitates before replying in the affirmative. It is evident to the reader that there is no heart in the affirmation. The Judge fails to notice the hesitancy and pursues "the grisly theme of the ancient Dexter-Burnside feud, and as he pictured one after another its valorous encounters and their varying fortunes in all their chivalrous and bloody splendor, his fervor grew, the light of battle was in his eye, and it was as if the spirit of some old Gaelic bard had entered into him and he chanted the glories of a great past and of a mighty race that had departed and left not their like behind them" (p 30). The phrases Twain uses to describe the Judge's discourse, it should be noted, strongly suggest what he was later to call the "Walter Scott disease." That Dexter is infected with the same disease appears from his reactions to the "grisly theme": "Shade by shade, depression had passed from [his face], and ray by ray a proud enthusiasm had occupied its place with light and life. Now his eye hardened with an iron purpose." No longer hesitant, he asserts, " 'I will do my father's will.' " Because he is a gentleman (in the bad sense), he will kill Hugh Burnside according to the required ritual: " 'I wish to have him pointed out to me. Then I will name myself, and if he is not armed, wait till he arms himself' " (p 30).

In the treatment of Dexter's adherence as a gentleman to the burden of "honor" placed on him by the feud, Twain becomes quite explicit in his condemnation of the code. Alone in his room, the young man loses the enthusiasm engendered by the Judge's fervor as he contemplates the act he has pledged his word to perform:

> Presently a question that had been floating, vague and inarticulate, through his mind, condensed itself into words: "Why do I want to kill this man?" It may have seemed only a small matter at first, this little question, but the more he examined it, and reasoned around it, and assaulted it with answers in front and flank and rear, the more compact and impregnable it stood. At

the end of a long and harassing siege, he had to coldly confess that he was going to commit a crime of a dreadful nature partly in obedience to an authority which might possibly be questioned, partly because he must henceforth be despised by the Dexter clans if he refrained, and partly because there were witnesses that he had put his hand to the plow, wherefore he was ashamed to turn back now. So the thing was stripped of all its poor rags of justification, and stood naked before him: he did *not* want to kill this man; he had suffered no injury from this man — but, he would kill him. (p 33)

In short he faces the same dilemma which later would face Huck Finn; his is a conflict between a sound heart and a deformed conscience. Unlike Huck, he is quite capable of recognizing the deformity and verbalizing his thoughts about it. He himself strips the "poor rags of justification" from his conscience. Even so, such is the flaw in him, he chooses the gentleman's Valhalla; Huck finally declares, "All right, then, I'll *go* to hell!"

The point is reiterated on a much larger scale in the ironic reversal of the plot as far as Twain had developed it before he abandoned the novel. At the outset, both the Judge and Dexter are determined to kill Hugh to satisfy the demands of the code even though both of them must realize that to do so will plunge Mrs Burnside and Clara into grief. (Mrs Burnside makes the point explicit in her first conversation with Dexter, and Mrs Griswold previously has at least implied it in her conversation with the Judge.) Later, when so far as the Judge and Dexter know Hugh is accidentally killed by Dexter's hasty shot at a supposed wolf, both agree that humanity and honor demand a self-sacrificing attempt to assuage the grief of the mother and sister. One may argue that the difference lies in the fact that, at the time Dexter believes he has killed Hugh, he is engaged to Hugh's sister (he was not, before) and the Judge now knows that Milly is in love with Hugh. But the code makes no allowance for nearness of relationship: in pursuance of the code Edward Dexter had come to Guilford to kill his sister's husband and had bequeathed the legacy of blood to Hale. The proposition advanced by the gentlemanly code, so the irony of the plot declares, is that premeditated murder is honorable, the grief of the bereaved notwithstanding, but an accidental killing is dishonorable, and falsehood and dissembling are permissable to assuage the resultant grief. Beneath the melodrama and farce, one discerns a sardonic grin.

The Dexter-Burnside and Morgan-Griswold feuds are Twain's first attempts to use in fiction the Darnell-Watson feud which he describes in his 1882 notebook of the Mississippi River trip and in *Life on the Mississippi*. The details are not brought sharply into focus, probably because his memory was vague at the time he was writing the novel; but the general pattern of two feuding families, one from Kentucky, the other from Missouri, facing each other across the Mississippi is that of the Darnell-Watson feud. Furthermore the engagement in which Edward Dexter saves Judge Griswold's life is based on an incident in the actual feud. But there is a wide discrepancy between the character of the real and that of the fictional versions.

Outlining his Mississippi River trip in his notebook, Twain cautioned himself to stop at New Madrid and ask about the old feuds. The results of his inquiries appear in the stenographic notebook. The character of the actual feuds is clear in the following two entries:

> Darnell & Watson were the names of two men whose families had kept up a long quarrel. The old man Darnell & his 2 sons came to the conclusion to leave that part of the country. They started to take steamboat just above [Island] "No. 10." The Watsons got wind of it and as the young Darnells were walking up the companion way with their wives on their arms they shot them in the back.

> One of these families lived on the Kentucky side the other on Missouri side near New Madrid. Once a boy 12 years old connected with the Kentucky family was riding thro the woods on the Mo. side. He was overtaken by a full grown man and he shot that boy dead.[38]

Neither in the notebook entries nor in the further details of the Darnell-Watson feud given in chapter xxvi of *Life on the Mississippi* do we find a hint of a gentlemanly code. Brutal affairs, the feuds involved ambushes, shots in the back, and the slaughter of defenseless children. Furthermore, although Twain does not state the point, feuding was not the pastime solely of the southern gentleman; the Mink Snopeses of the region also participated. In *Simon Wheeler, Detective* the Judge makes but one statement about the feuding code which has the ring of truth: " 'I was only taught that when I should meet a Morgan there was a thing to be done; it was very simple — kill him' " (p 9). To the quite unadorned and straight-forward code of the vendetta, Twain added the more complex ritual of the code duello in order to focus his satire upon the southern aristocrat and to heighten the irony. Edward Dexter asserts, " ' "Gentlemen do not war on children." ' " Hale Dexter proposes to warn his blood enemy, permit him to arm, and then shoot it out face to face. When he first knowingly encounters Hugh Burnside, Hugh's back is turned: he approaches and says, " 'I will not take you at a disadvantage, sir . . .' " (p 34). In part, the first revision of the manuscript (probably, on the evidence of the ink, in 1878) was aimed at heightening the impression of ritual. The first version of Edward Dexter's resolve was in accordance with the simple vendetta code: " 'I will neither eat, drink nor sleep till I have killed my sister's husband' " (MS p 21). Revised, the resolve accords with the code duello: " ' "I will neither eat, drink nor sleep till I have warned my sister's husband and called him out and killed him" ' " (below, p 7). Later in the story, when Judge Griswold finds he cannot be present to aid Hale in killing Hugh, he first suggests Toby, the Negro slave, as a suitable substitute. In a feud all that counts is the killing and a successful escape from the vengeance of the surviving relatives of the victim. For this purpose, Toby would be just as acceptable as Judge Griswold. In revision, Twain changed the substitute from Toby to Major Barnes: the code duello demands an "honorable" second.

Certainly the ingredients for a good story are present in the welter of farce and melodrama, and a rather forceful satire was beginning to emerge. We have no way of knowing whether these were the ingredients which Howells discerned when he urged a continuation of the effort, but if they were he apparently failed to make the point clear to Twain. As we have seen, Twain abandoned his effort not because he could not shape the Griswold-Dexter-Burnside material but because he could not control the detective-story burlesque.

It was not until about a year and a half after he abandoned *Simon Wheeler* in 1878 that he found a way to make effective use of his feud plot and the attendant irony and satire. In late 1879 and in 1880 Twain returned to the *Huckleberry Finn* manuscript which he had abandoned in 1876. It was at this time that he transferred the emerging feud plot of *Simon Wheeler* to *Huckleberry Finn*: Judge Griswold was installed as Colonel Grangerford; Milly became Sophia Grangerford; and the Morgan-Griswold and Dexter-Burnside feuds were merged into the Grangerford-Shepherdson feud. More important the satire and irony of the uncom-

pleted novel, the attack upon the "deformed conscience," became a domi-
nant motif in *Huckleberry Finn*. Even after visiting the Mississippi in
1882 and refreshing his memory not only about the details of the actual
feuds but also about their brutality, he continued to build upon the
ritualistic code he had imposed upon the feuds in *Simon Wheeler*. The
major difference between the two fictional versions is the withdrawal, in
Huckleberry Finn, of any saving grace of innate goodness from the southern aristocrat and its transference to Huck. Twain permits only one admirable quality to show in his revised conception of the aristocrat: the courage which Colonel Sherburn exhibits when he faces the lynch mob. But
when the entire Colonel Sherburn episode is coupled with the Grangerford-Shepherdson sequence, the contrast with the earlier conception in
Simon Wheeler reveals the greater subtlety and deepened bitterness of
the later presentation.

In the overture to Sherburn's shooting of Boggs, Twain firmly estab-
lishes the cruelty and general degeneracy of the Bricksville loafers, who
will be the chorus, as it were, for the tragedy, and the harmlessness and
good nature of Boggs. The reader is induced to feel contempt for the
loafers and sympathy for Boggs. Having engendered these attitudes,
Twain introduces Colonel Sherburn and the one major deviation from
the actual shooting on which the incident is based,[39] Sherburn's warning
to Boggs: "'I'm tired of this; but I'll endure it till one o'clock. Till one
o'clock, mind — no longer. If you open your mouth against me only
once, after that time, you can't travel so far but I will find you'" (*HF*,
p 191). The Colonel's punctilio, which demands not only the warning
but a careful reiteration (a concession to Boggs' intoxication perhaps?)
of the time-limit carries with it a suggestion of the code duello which is
borne out in the description of the shooting itself: "[Sherburn] was standing perfectly still in the street, and had a pistol raised in his right hand —
not aiming it, but holding it out with the barrel tilted up toward the sky
[the duelist poised and waiting the signal of the seconds but honorably
refraining from taking aim]. . . . The pistol-barrel come down slow and
steady to a level. . . . Bang! goes the first shot, and [Boggs] staggers back,
clawing at the air — bang! goes the second one, and he tumbles back-
wards onto the ground, heavy and solid, with his arms spread out" (*HF*,
p 192). The careful enumeration of the two shots and the balanced coordi-
nate clauses suggest a ceremoniousness in the firing equal to that in the
warning and posture. The incident concludes with the culminating cere-

monial touch: "Colonel Sherburn he tossed his pistol on to the ground, and turned around on his heels and walked off," (*HF*, p 192). Clearly this was a ritualized murder (in which Boggs has been substituted for the armed and honorable antagonist) performed out of devotion to a code of personal honor, a code which appears as empty and vicious as the ceremonial during the killing.

Twain immediately shifts his focus to the loafers, who crowd around Boggs, later struggle with one another to peer through the window of the shop in which he expires, and finally find their supreme gratification in a callous burlesque pantomime of the shooting. The pantomime is one of the most subtle touches in the entire book. On the one hand it is the ultimate expression of the loafers' insensibility; on the other it initiates in the reader a relaxation of the previously induced antagonism toward the Colonel. The Sherburn-loafer contrast produced by the juxtaposition of the shooting and the pantomime suggests that Sherburn's devotion to his code may be a quality superior to the loafers' brutal self-gratification. The episode becomes, that is, a dramatic exploration of the meaning of the phrase "deformed conscience." If the code by which the Colonel governs himself is his "conscience," its deformity consists mainly in the rigidity, the inelasticity, which demands blood-satisfaction even for the supposed transgression of an innocuous old drunkard. Viewed in this manner the conscience is evil; but deformed though it may be, it is still a conscience, a self-discipline which is at least slightly superior to the thoroughly impulsive and gratuitous heartlessness of the pantomimist and those who salute his performance with upturned bottles. The implication of the shooting-pantomime juxtaposition becomes explicit when Colonel Sherburn faces the lynch mob. Sustained more by the courage both embodied in and fostered by the code than by the weapon he carries (against a concerted rush, he has but two shots), he subdues a mob which is sustained only by impulse. Paradoxically the code makes Sherburn a murderer, but the same code makes him the only courageous and respect-worthy man in the town.

But approaching the Sherburn episode after the Grangerford-Shepherdson feud, we find that whatever admiration we may feel for the Colonel's courage is tempered somewhat by our earlier exposure to the code and its workings. That the same code prevails here as in the Dexter-Burnside feud is clear from Colonel Grangerford's reaction to Buck's firing on Harney Shepherdson from ambush: " 'I don't like that shooting from behind a bush. Why didn't you step into the road, my boy?'" (*HF*, p 149). But in the subsequent encounters Twain introduces a variation upon the pattern established in *Simon Wheeler:* a deepening brutality and horror which derive from the omission of the punctilios. After an exchange between Huck and Buck about the origins of the feud, an exchange which, like that between Judge and Mrs Griswold, emphasizes the senselessness of the whole affair, Twain introduces the note of brutality with Buck's account of his cousin Bud, a fourteen-year-old who was riding unarmed through the woods on the other side of the river when he was seen by Baldy Shepherdson, an elder of the rival clan. Unable to escape, Bud "'stopped and faced around so as to have the bullet holes in front, you know, and the old man he rode up and shot him down'" (*HF*, p 151). Unarmed and trapped, Bud can find no refuge except in the code: unable to defend himself, he can at least die like a gentleman. His action ennobles him and by contrast brutalizes Baldy so much that Buck's hasty defense of Baldy against Huck's charge of cowardice finds little response in the reader. Buck's defense of Baldy is highly ironic because Buck himself is soon to fall in another ambush even more brutal than the one in which Bud dies, an ambush in which Buck is robbed even of the chance to die like a gentleman. Instead, wounded and helpless in the river, he and his cousin are slaughtered by a gang of Shepherdsons, as insensible to the demands of honor and feeling as the loafers of Bricksville, who "run along the bank shooting at them and singing out, 'Kill them, kill them!'" (*HF*, p 158).

It would be a mistake, I believe, to interpret the Shepherdsons' omission of the punctilios and Colonel Grangerford's insistence on them as a simple matter of black and white, to regard the Shepherdsons as villains and the Grangerfords as heroes. The two families together comprise the aristocracy of the region, and Huck tells us that the Shepherdsons "was as high-toned, and well born and rich and grand as the tribe of Grangerfords," (*HF*, p 148). We must assume that the Shepherdsons do nothing which the Grangerfords are not capable of. We must conclude that the code, which lends a certain grace to the Grangerford family life that Huck cherishes almost wistfully, can through the feud engender passions which its rituals cannot constrain. The code ennobles Sherburn before the lynch mob, but it also degrades the Shepherdsons to the level of Bricksville loafers — and the interval between Sherburn's courage and the Shepherdsons' brutality is a small one.

The contrast between the feud material in *Simon Wheeler* and *Huckleberry Finn* shows quite clearly that the difference in treatment is primarily one of quality. The emerging theme in *Simon Wheeler* is handled with none of the subtlety and restraint of the treatment in the later novel. Part of the trouble is that Twain was too explicit, as in the case of Dexter's dilemma, and he was trying too hard. A measure of just how hard he was trying appears in the encounter with Hugh when Dexter sallies forth to carry out his duty as a feuding Kentuckian. Hugh is bending over to pat a dog as Dexter approaches from behind. If one keeps Hugh's position in mind, Dexter's opening remark contains a double-entendre which sends a thrust through the heart (or seat?) of the code of honor: " 'I will not take you at a disadvantage, sir, but —' " (below, p 34). The word-play is reinforced in Hugh's reply: after straightening up and heartily welcoming Dexter, Hugh points to a chair and announces, " 'it's the seat of honor' " (p 35). The parody on "soul of honor" probably delighted Twain; but when one recalls what he did with the theme in *Huckleberry Finn* one can only shake one's head and say, "No, this won't do."

The exchange points toward another and greater source of the trouble in *Simon Wheeler, Detective*. The indictment of the code and the southern aristocrat is too closely surrounded by undisguised melodrama and broad farce. This is not to say that melodrama and broad farce are non-existent in *Huckleberry Finn*. The difference is primarily in the point of view. In *Simon Wheeler* they are Twain's own as author omniscient; in *Huckleberry Finn*, they are Huck's, whose naïveté makes them natural modes of expression.

Nevertheless, the essential worth is there. Transferred to the slowly growing *Huckleberry Finn*, given greater restraint and subtlety in the rewriting, gaining greater vividness and drama from recollections sharpened during the Mississippi River trip of 1882, the theme emerges at the heart of one of the most compelling books in literature. As far as it concerns the "deformed conscience" against which Huck struggles, *Simon Wheeler, Detective* may with some justification be considered a preliminary draft for *Huckleberry Finn*.

FRANKLIN R. ROGERS

Davis, California
November 15 1963

A Note on Editorial Practice

An effort has been made to present the text of *Simon Wheeler, Detective* as it appears in the manuscript housed in the Berg Collection of The New York Public Library. In general the spelling and punctuation of the manuscript have been preserved without editorial comment or alteration. Only two spelling errors, both obviously the result of haste, have been corrected without comment: the spelling "butt" for "but" and "horrrors" for "horrors." In a few instances where Twain's omissions in punctuation might result in momentary confusion the necessary marks have been supplied. In his manuscripts and letters Twain habitually used the ampersand; to achieve a more attractive appearance on the page all ampersands have been expanded to "and" except in the working notes. At some stage in the history of the manuscript, chapters 4 to 10 were lettered A^1 to G^1 in a hand other than Twain's although apparently with his knowledge and approval (see chapter 3, note 6); this lettering has been omitted.

The more extensive or significant revisions and deletions are given in the Notes to the text. The less extensive revisions are listed separately on pages 191–204.

PART I

SIMON WHEELER, DETECTIVE

The Text

Chapter 1

THE SCENE of this history is a sleepy little Missouri village
hidden away from the world in the heart of a cluster of
densely wooded hills, where railways and steamboats were not
known; where tourists and travelers never came; where the telegraph intruded not; where the only journals were a couple of [1]
chloroformed weeklies whose sole news was "local," whose
advertisers paid in trade, whose subscribers paid in cord-wood
and turnips, and whose editors discussed nothing but each other,
and not in Sunday-school terms either. In this drowsing hamlet
nothing changed during a generation; the weather and the crops
were the staple of conversation, as they had been always; Ossian
and Thaddeus of Warsaw were still read, fire and brimstone still
preached.

This village of Guilford ended suddenly at its northern extremity,
and one found himself at once upon the threshold of wild nature; a
charming expanse of woods and hills lay before him,[2] with green
meadow-glimpses here and there, two or three scattering cottages in
the distance, and a crooked and rugged gorge that reflected its
vines and crags in a tranquil little river.[3]

Leading northward from the village was a broad and well worn
footway, which faithfully followed the windings of this stream,[4]
threading its way among occasional great boulders, stealing through
the twilight mystery of brief forest patches, marching across open
grassy levels, and rustic bridges that spanned limpid, brawling, knee-
deep tributaries — and so, on and on, until, having traversed a mile
and a half of varied prettinesses and charming surprises, it entered
the gorge. Thence forward its surroundings were as rugged and picturesque as they had before been simple and pleasing. This river-path
was a favorite resort of the villagers on moonlit evenings in summer
or the earlier gloaming. It had several names. The practical called it

"Drytown Trail;" the romantic called it "Lover's Ramble;" a few super-artificials referred to it as "La Belle Promenade."

The two wealthiest families in Guilford were the Griswolds and the Burnsides. — "Judge" Burnside * had never been on the bench; but that was no matter; he was the first citizen of the place, he was a man of great personal dignity, therefore no power in this world could have saved him from a title. He had been dubbed Major, then Colonel, then Squire; but gradually the community settled upon "Judge," and Judge he remained, after that.

He was sixty years old; very tall, very spare, with a long, thin, smooth-shaven, intellectual face, and long black hair that lay close to his head, was kept to the rear by his ears as one keeps curtains back by brackets, and fell straight to his coat collar without a single tolerant kink or relenting curve. He had an eagle's beak and an eagle's eye. He was a Kentuckian by birth and rearing; he came of the oldest and best Kentucky Griswolds, and they from the oldest and proudest Griswolds of Virginia. Judge Griswold's manners and carriage were of the courtly old-fashioned sort; he had never worked; he was a gentleman. He so entered himself in the census list. To him that abused word still possessed what he called its only warrantable meaning. In his eyes, a man who came of gentle blood and fell to the ranks of scavengers and blacklegs was still a gentleman and could not help it, since the word did not describe character but only birth; and a man who did not come of gentle blood might climb to the highest pinnacle of human grandeur but must still lack one thing — nothing could make him a gentleman; he might be called so by courtesy, but there an end. In his younger days nobody had lightly used the word in the south; our modern fashion of speaking of everybody, indiscriminately, as ladies and gentlemen maddened him; and once when he read in a paper how that a hostler had clubbed "another gentleman" for talking disrespectfully of a tavern chambermaid and "another lady," he swore

* Note that in the next paragraph the name shifts to "Judge Griswold."

4

the first oath that had ever passed his lips, and followed it up with a lurid procession of profanity that was five-and-forty minutes passing a given point.

The Judge was punctiliously honorable, austerely upright. No man wanted his bond who had got his word. He was grave even to sternness; he seldom smiled. He loved strongly, but without demonstration; he hated implacably. He decorously attended church twice a month; but if he had a religion it was his own secret; religion was a subject he never mentioned.

His wife was about fifty; she was gentle, loving, patient, pious, and believed everything her husband believed about everybody and everything except the hereafter; no doubt she would have adopted his belief about that, too, if he had revealed one.

They had buried all their children but one: Milly, a simple little beauty of sixteen, with light hair hanging down her back in two long plaited tails tied at the ends with blue or pink ribbon according to the gown they were to "match." Her actions and her rounded form were full of girlish grace; she sang the ballads of the day, she read romantic little tales and cried over them, she still cherished cats; she was not even wholly estranged from her last doll, though nobody knew that but herself. She was a very sweet and dainty and artless little maid, the idol of her father, who sometimes manifested this by a look or a word, but never kissed and never petted her. One perceives that this girl was still a girl, nothing more, and yet she lived in a region where hers was a womanly age — at least a marrying age.[5]

Mrs. Burnside was a gracious and winning old lady, of fine family, whose life was wrapped up in her two remaining children, Hugh, aged twenty, and Clara, twenty-one. Clara had the delicacy and refinement of a woman, and the pluck, decision and spirit of a man. She was a beautiful creature, slender but shapely, a trifle above medium height, with brown eyes that were deep and tender when her soul was in repose, but burned with passion when it was stirred. Her usual humor

5

was happy and sparkling; and in this mood she had a bird-like fashion of setting her head aside and glancing up a trifle coquettishly, which was pretty to see; but there were other times and rarer when she was too severely in earnest for idle graces and nonsense.

Hugh was an innocent. He was giddy and thoughtless, when he was not sappy and sentimental. At twenty he was, during three-fourths of every day, still sixteen. He would hunt and fish all day, taking no heed of anything but his pleasure; and then, as likely as not, go off in a corner and pout over some imaginary slight inflicted by somebody who was entirely unconscious of having offered him one. The world was hollow to him, then, and he was more than likely to shut himself up in his room and write some stuff about "bruised hearts" or "the despised and friendless," and print it in one of the village journals under the impression that it was poetry. He was the butt of the town and the apple of his mother's eye.

One day, in the spring, Mrs. Griswold said to her husband —
"The Burnsides are to have a visitor."
"Well?"
Judge Griswold did not look up from the book he was reading.
"From Kentucky."
The Judge said nothing, and gave no sign. Plainly the matter did not interest him. Mrs. Griswold added —
"It is Mrs. Burnside's nephew — young Hale Dexter."
The Judge laid his book down and faced about. There was a strange light in his eye. Said he —
"It needed no prophet to say that this would happen some day."
Mrs. Griswold paled. She washed her hands helplessly together, and said in a voice so weak that it was hardly audible —
"I had hoped and believed that that was all ended long ago."
"Ended!" said the Judge — and the light of battle was in his eye — "a Kentucky feud never ends!"
Mrs. Griswold began an exclamation, but it perished in a gasp.

6

"It never ends! This stripling is coming here to kill his cousin Hugh. Now look you, my wife, we have a duty to perform. We must save him —"

"Hugh? — O yes, O surely!" eagerly interrupted Mrs. Griswold, white and trembling.

"*Hugh?* No! Dexter! We must be ready with horses and men and spirit him out of the country when the deed is done!"

Mrs. Griswold was past speaking. She dropped her countenance; she was not able to endure her husband's flaming eyes. He went on fervently, as one who recalls the blessed memories of a vanished time —

"The feud between the Burnsides and the Dexters has lasted longer than I can remember [6] — it cannot end till one house is extinct. When the sister of Hale Dexter's father married a Burnside, some weaklings imagined it was York and Lancaster wedded again, and the wars of the roses finished. Wiser heads took into account the fact that Edward Dexter was an invalid, a prisoner in his bed. He remained a prisoner ten years. What did he do then? The moment he was on his legs he took his gun and came to Missouri — to this village, Madam!"

Mrs. Griswold [7] looked up and gasped —

"Came here? I never knew it?"

"You were visiting at Hoxton.[8] I received him in this house. He was travel-worn, tired, hungry; but he would touch nothing. He said, 'I will neither eat, drink nor sleep till I have warned my sister's husband and called him out and killed him.' I beguiled him with questions and random talk — miserable expedients to delay the news I had not the heart to tell him at once. But when this would not answer longer, I blurted it out, and awkwardly enough — 'Burnside,' I said, 'is lying on his death-bed!' Poor fellow, he was unprepared for it. He sat where you are sitting now. He gave me such a look — so wounded, so stricken — his head fell listlessly against the wall, and he said, 'And I have waited ten years!'"

"God forgive him!" murmured Mrs. Griswold.

"Every day, and all day long, he watched the Burnside house from the attic window. He was too restless to talk; my presence only disturbed his thoughts. He cleaned his gun and reloaded it a dozen times a day. When he was not watching, he walked the floor and mumbled to himself. The servants thought he was crazy. I always carried him news of Burnside myself; but one day I had to send a servant — Mulatto Bob — with tidings that Burnside was better. Dexter embraced him furiously and gave him five dollars. Next day Bob begged to be messenger again, and I allowed him to go with the news that Burnside was worse. Dexter threw him down stairs and broke his leg."

Mrs. Burnside * had been in a recalling attitude for a minute. Now she said —

"They told me all about that, but *you* and *they* called that man Johnson."

"It was what he called himself, for better security.[9] It was a dismal day for me, the day I had to go up and tell him Burnside was dead. At first he raged about the room, cursing his ill luck. Then he quieted down and sat a long time thinking. By and by he asked about the Burnside family. I named the children and their ages. He brightened when I mentioned Hugh; saddened again when he remembered that Hugh could be only a little boy. He shook his head sorrowfully and said 'Gentlemen do not war with children.' Presently he said, 'I have nothing more to live for.' We sat silent, then, an age. Finally Dexter said, not as one who consciously speaks, but only thinks aloud, 'I, too, am leaving a boy behind me; he shall finish the work.' Then after a time he muttered in the same way, and with a smothered sigh, 'It is like all of life — a hope that buds in a promise, and blossoms in a disappointment; I shall be glad to go.' When he started home I did not ask him if he wished to leave any message for his sister, and I knew his delicacy would not allow him to afflict me with one without the asking. — He was going to leave his gun, but hesitated, muttered

---

* I e, Mrs Griswold.

8

something about his son and went into the house and got it again. Poor fellow, he dragged himself home and lay down and died."

There was a pensive silence for some seconds, and then Mrs. Griswold [10] absently murmured —

"Poor fellow!"

"Ah, then you pity him, too?" said the Judge with interest.

Mrs. Griswold was confused. She said —

"Why no! I hardly know what I *did* feel. For the moment I seemed to pity him, but why, Heaven only knows. I think I felt for the disappointment, forgetting for the instant what the nature of it was."

The Judge heard the beginning, but not the end. He had drifted back into his old memories again. Presently he said —

"He was a fine man, Dexter — good old Kentucky stock, with a good old Virginian root. Brave as Richard, chivalrous as Saladin. We were always friends. You know that when I was young the Griswolds and the Morgans had been at feud for three generations —"

"Yes, I know. What was it about?"

"I do not remember — that is, I never knew. I think it never occurred to me to ask. But no matter; it is not likely that any of my generation could have told me. Besides, the feud itself was the only thing of consequence; how it originated was a circumstance of no interest. I was only taught that when I should meet a Morgan there was a thing to be done; it was very simple — kill him."

"Or be killed yourself?" said Mrs. Griswold, with a falling inflection and a shudder.

"*That* is understood. As boys, I and my brothers built Morgans of snow, in winter, and of rubbish in summer, and killed them. Later on, came the killing in earnest. No matter about that — it is not what I wish to speak of. The point I am coming to is this: two Morgans and three of their friends met me unexpectedly on the road, once, when I was twenty-five. I drew — they did the same. Dexter came riding up, saw how the odds stood, and being my friend he reinforced me, of course, though he had nothing against the Morgans. Between us we killed three outright; the other two lingered a month. — I was not a well man for more than a year; Dexter was never a well man afterwards; at least he never was nearly so well as he had been before. — You perceive, I am under an obligation to him and his family. I am glad to keep it green in my memory. I shall be as a father to his son; I know you will be as a mother to him."

"You cannot doubt it — his father saved your life. His mother was my schoolmate and later friend. All that gratitude can prompt, and all that love can do, shall be done for him. This shall be his home; he shall be no guest, but one of us."

"You speak what I feel. I am glad, and thank you. Where is he?"

"Visiting that distant relative, old Humphrey, at Marley, for a few days."

"Is the old man any better?" [11]

"Worse, they say, but not really threatened with death."

"Still, he will not live long. His fortune will make Hale Dexter very rich."

"Yes, and all the villagers here very angry. They call him all sorts of hard names for leaving the money to a stranger whom they neither know nor care for, and who will carry it off to Kentucky. They say he might at least have divided the money, instead of giving it all to one cousin, to go to the other when the first recipient dies."

"Yes — both are so young that Hugh may likely find it weary waiting for Hale to die. Humphrey is a strange person and always was. When is Hale coming here?"

"His letter says day after tomorrow."

"We will make preparation." Then after a pause, "What name is he coming under?"

This gave Mrs. Griswold an electric shock — it brought the probable grim purpose of the visit back to her mind. But in another moment she said —

"His own."

Evidently the Judge was perplexed. He walked the floor a while, puzzling over the matter, then said —

"There is some mistake. Look at the letter again."

Mrs. Griswold did so.

"No," she said, "he does not mention any fictitious name. He encloses a brief note from his mother, recommending him to me — now that I observe it closer there are tear-stains on it — but she calls him by his own name, too. — There is no suggestion of mystery anywhere, except that Hale mentions, as in the most casual way, that he will time his journey so as to reach here at night."

"Ah," said the Judge. "His purpose is plain, though his method is puzzling."

"O, I pray God you are mistaken. It is awful to think of. That poor Hugh is as harmless as he can be, and at bottom is a good child. It would be *double* murder — it would kill his mother. I will not, can not, have it that you are right."

"But I am right. — I know the Dexter blood. It has a long memory and a deathless purpose. — This youth comes on the business his father left him. We must protect him till it is done, then get him away. My life shall be freely forfeited in his defence, if need be. Wife, keep his coming a secret until he is here. He will tell us how to proceed then."

At this point Milly entered, and all the grimness melted out of her father's eyes. The conversation ceased. Milly moved about the room from place to place, humming an air in happy contentment, and got a needle here, a strip of perforated cardboard there and some colored cruels out of a basket, her father's eyes following her lovingly the while, then she sat down and began to embroider one of the fearful and wonderful book-marks of the period. During half an hour the Judge walked the floor, planning the rescue to follow the coming tragedy. Mrs. Griswold sat thinking, and saying to herself, "He was near being slaughtered, Dexter saved him, we are married thirty years and then he casually mentions it for the first time; and as usual I find

11

I am only surprised that he ever mentioned it at all; he never explained 'Johnson' to me before; I can admire his reticence, and I do — to comprehend it is beyond a woman." Now and then she sighed and said to herself, "Poor Mary Burnside; poor Hugh — O my God!"

And all the while the young girl's soft music went on, and the bookmark grew. By and by she held it off, examined it with a critical eye, saw that her work was good, and blushed. Upon a neutral groundwork, within a half-completed, variegated border, it bore the word HUGH.

Chapter 2

HALE DEXTER had been something more than a day and a half in the saddle. It was becoming wearisome work, and tedious. He ceased to take interest in the scenery or anything else, and fell to drifting off into dreams and thinkings. About the middle of the afternoon he roused himself and looked about. He found himself in the midst of a maze of cattle paths — no road visible anywhere. He stopped his horse and considered. He could not remember when he had last observed the road; he did not know whether he had been out of it a long or a short time. He turned and looked back — nothing there but a web of paths that crossed and re-crossed each other in every direction. Here was a predicament. There was but one thing to do: try to return in his horse's hoof-tracks. He tried it, and failed early. — The horse had crossed grassy patches and broken the trail. It were as profitable to stand still as to move; but one can't stand still in such cases, therefore the young man moved — for a while in one direction, then in another, not making the matter worse, perhaps, but not bettering it any. At the end of an hour he was very tired of this, and very thoroughly vexed; and hungry and thirsty withal. One always gets hungry and thirsty as soon as he finds that food and water are far away.

Now he glanced rearward and saw two persons in the distance, — a welcome sight. He turned about and was soon with them. One of them was a stalwart young fellow with light hair and a good-humored face, the other a young lady. Young Dexter saluted; the young fellow bowed and said, "Good-day, sir," the young lady inclined her head slightly, but said nothing. Dexter's thought was, "It was worth getting lost, to see this girl's face;" the girl's thought was, "The stranger is handsome." Dexter spoke —

"I am sorry to trouble you, but I am a stranger and I am afraid I am lost."

The young girl thought, "He has a fine voice."

The young fellow delivered himself of the sort of bubbling laugh that goes with youth and a soul at peace, and said —

"I shouldn't be surprised if you could put it stronger and say you know you are. Which way did you come?"

"I — well, the truth is I don't know."

"I said it! A stranger can't be expected to find his way through this place — it pushes a native to do it. We saw you before you saw us; we noticed which way you were going — which was towards nowhere in particular. We said, there's somebody that's lost. So we whipped up to overtake you."

"It was very kind of you, indeed. I got out of the Drytown road without noticing it, and have been wandering about here a good while."

The young man and the young girl turned their horses about and struck into a trot, the former saying, with another comfortable laugh —

"It's not so bad as I thought; you weren't hunting for a short cut, but only nodding. There are plenty of short cuts here, but none to Drytown. The regular road's the directest."

"But you are turning back on your own journey. Do not do that; I can't allow you to take so much trouble."

"Why my dear sir, it's good three miles and a half back to the Drytown road." The speed was not slackened.

"Then I *can* not inconvenience you so much — and the young lady." Dexter reined in his horse. "If you will kindly point —" [1]

"Point the way? I will, of course; but I think it would be better if we went with you. And mind I tell you it's no easy thing to describe it so that a stranger —." He stopped, and searched the distance for a landmark. Shook his head. "It's a blind region. First you go —" He turned, with a perplexed look and found a smile on the young girl's face that suggested how considerably she was enjoying his difficulty. "Hang it, don't smile — that doesn't help any — give me an idea!"

The girl said —

"How can a body help but smile? Don't you know perfectly well that the route cannot be described so that one who has never traveled it can follow it? We are losing time."

She started her horse briskly forward; the gentlemen did likewise. Dexter said to himself, "More than half an hour to look at her in — it is worth being lost a week! I was in mortal fear they'd take me at my word and direct me instead of leading me." Then he made one more protest, aloud, about the trouble he was causing, but there was no heart in it. The girl's comrade said —

"O don't you bother about that. It's no inconvenience to me; and she — well, five or ten miles more or less is nothing to her; she don't mind it. Riding's no more to her than deciding; riding's nothing to me, but deciding's different — that is, when there's much of a puzzle about it."

The way was anything but straight. It wound hither and thither to avoid ridges, gullies and rocky outcrops, but the three were usually able to ride abreast. The broad young fellow had the middle place. While he discoursed cheerily about strangers who had come to grief in the mazes of this cattle-range, Dexter kept up an appearance of active interest by throwing in a "Yes?" or a "No?" or an "Indeed?" here and there in the wrong place, which encouraged the jovial story-teller to go on with his marvels, and left the stranger free to admire the young girl with charmed and furtive eye, and comment on her to himself. "How graceful she is — and beautiful! And her eye — ah, what an eye it is! So rich and deep and brown; so sweet — and some-times so mischievous! Such character in the face! Then the voice — I wish she would speak again. Only half an hour of her! Only that — but even that is worth being lost a month. I never can have any luck — another man would have been twice as badly lost. That would give him an hour of her. There — I caught her eye. I believe she blushed — I wish I had the pluck to look and see. I wonder what she is to this young fellow. Sweetheart? She smiled on him so archly; she

15

looked at him so affectionately; and he — he spoke of her so proudly. Ah, that's it, that's it — I wish I hadn't thought of it."

Then his face lost animation; took on a dejected cast. He forgot to throw in his "Yes's" and "No's;" but the historian's tongue wagged cheerfully on, dead to everything but the charm of its own music.

Meanwhile the young girl stole an occasional glance and communed with herself. "Yes, he is very handsome. Finely formed and manly. There is spirit in his face — and strength. Black hair, black eyes. Black hair and black eyes suit some faces; they suit his. He rides well. An odd place to go to — Drytown. I caught his eye, then — I believe I am blushing. — Vexation! — why should I be so confused? There's nothing to be confused about. If he should discover it! He cant, if he is minding his own affairs. It is impertinent in him to look at me. Why should he look at me? I wish we had left him where he was. Can he have noticed? B . . . . . . But it's nothing — nothing; I do not care a straw. Still, I wish I knew if he . . . . . . I *will* look again. Ah, now he is pouting; looks as injured and dejected as if somebody *else* had done something, when it's himself. Very well, let him pout; I'm sure *I* don't care. Hold up your head, won't you! and quit fretting at the bit! Take that! . . . . . . Now then . . . stay quiet, or you'll catch it again. — . . . . . . I wonder if he is pouting yet."

Dexter — to himself:

"There — she's vexed; she looks it. Acts it, too — I ought to have that cut, not the horse. 'Twas I that offended. But I didn't mean any harm, I was only worshipping. She is very much displeased. Well, well, it's a villain world; nothing ever goes right in it — for me, anyway. *Is* she his sweetheart?"

The historian cuts short his tale with a —

"Hold up, sister, here we are!"

Dexter, to himself —

"*Sister*! There's music in his voice! One last look!" —

The sister, to herself —

16

"I will just take one glance at this creature and see if he — why he's radiant!"

Dexter, to himself —

"Bless me, how she lights up!"

The brother —

"We'll leave you here, sir — here's the road. Keep straight ahead — you're all right, now."

"Why, we have come very quickly! I am very grateful to you, sir; and to the young lady your sister; and if I have not taxed your kindness too far —"

"O, that's no consequence — none in the world. If anybody's to be thanked, it's she, not me. I shouldn't have had any more wit than to direct you and confuse you, and leave you and lose you again. It's more my place to thank you. I haven't had such a good talk in a year. Generally people don't seem to care to listen to me; but with you it's different, and I like it."

"Well, I can say in all frankness that if you have enjoyed talking, I have not less enjoyed being near you while you did it." [2]

"Good! There — your throat-latch is unbuckled — keep your seat, I'll fix it. Now your hand — good-bye. Stick to the road and you're all right."

He shook hands heartily, turned his horse about, Dexter took off his hat and bowed to the girl, with some awkward half-audible thanks, which she received with a little inclination of the head and a not unpleased look, and the parties separated, the horses walking. After three or four steps, young Dexter ventured to steal a backward glance—and caught the girl in the same act. — She gave her horse a sharp cut with her whip, Dexter accommodated his animal with a spur-stab which expressed a trifle of vexation, and the distance widened rapidly between the new acquaintances. But presently Dexter got down to tighten his saddle-girth. He took hold of the strap, but paused to gaze; two figures were rising and falling to the undulating movement of a canter, and steadily receding. He watched them till they disappeared.

Then he mounted again, with a sigh and moved on his way. But he hadn't tightened his girth.

He was full of thinkings. By and by he started —

"What a blunder!" he said, "never to have thought of asking the young man his name! [3] A woman wouldn't have forgotten such a thing." Presently he said, "I like him. What a good-hearted, giddy chap he is! And she — what a numscull I have been!"

He drove the spurs home — though it was not really the horse's blunder.

The girl and her brother cantered on. The latter took up his history again with animation. The girl, listening without hearing, biting her lips, as one wrought upon by a secret vexation, by and by broke into the middle of a sentence, brightening hopefully as she spoke — [4]

"Now suppose Mr. . . . .er. . .er —"

"Who? That young fellow?"

"Yes! I was thinking, suppose Mr. . . . .er. . .er —"

"Well, suppose he *what*?"

"*Nothing!*" [5]

The historian proceeded. — After a little the girl severed the tale with another hopeful interruption —

"I suppose Mr. . . . er — . . . er — whatever his name is! — is just passing through the country — not going to stop."

"Yes — maybe so. *I* don't know. As I was saying, Jones finally got mixed up, and judged he was lost — knew he was, in fact. Well, the first thing he did was to —"

"Didn't he *say* anything about it?"

"Who? — Jones?"

"O, plague Jones!"

"O, you mean the other fellow. No — yes. Let me see. Once when you were ahead a little, he said — he said — well, I'll remember it presently. He looked around and said —"

"Said *what*?"

"He didn't say *any*thing. He was *going* to say, 'I'm up a stump,' but —"

"There, there — you were going to remember. Then why don't you leave off a minute and *try* to remember?"

"Well, I will. I only wanted to get through that, first. He said —"

"Well?"

"*I* can't remember what he said." A long pause. "No — I give it up. I thought I could remember, but I can't. But I like him — he's a good fellow."

Here he dropped into history again. His sister fretted a while, then put on an aspect of resignation. The history proceeded till it reached this point: "Jones took to a tree, the bull after him —" when the girl cut in with —

"I should say he was of good stock."

"Only so-so. Comes from the same old Warren county tribe. They all do."

"Did he say so?"

"Who? — Jones?"

"Burn Jones!"

"Burn him? He's a mighty good man, if he *is* short-stock. Why once when Hank Miller got the cramp in the river —"

The girl dropped into a reverie, and the history rolled over her, wave after wave, but disturbed her not. — Finally she walled the tide with —

"If *I* had been you, I would have taken the trouble to ask him —"

"Well — ask him what?"

"O, nothing."

"Well, I did. As I was saying, they pumped and pumped — well, they pumped about a barrel of water out of him, and by and by, sure enough, he came to. It was all owing to Jones. Everybody says that. By the way! I believe I'll write to him and tell him about that."

19

"Write to *whom*?"

"Why that young fellow. I forgot to tell it when I was talking. It's a prime story. I believe I'll do it — wouldn't you?"

The sister showed quick interest.

"Yes, I would," said she. "No — I wouldn't. He might not care for it, and then you are not well enough acquainted."

"Well, that's true. Yes, that's true. I won't write him. Jones told me once, that when he first came to this region —"

"But suppose you did know him well enough, and were going to write him —"

"Well?"

"How would you begin?"

"How would I begin?"

"Yes. Just begin, now, as if you were going to write him. You would be awkward enough about it, I fancy. Come — begin."

"It's perfectly easy. I should say, 'My Dear Sir: On the occasion that I had the honor to tell you some particulars about the region where you got lost, and where my sister and I had the good fortune and also the pleasure to —' "

"Why that is very good — very good indeed. I confess you could do it well. Next, how would you address the letter?"

"Address it?" The young fellow's face began to lose its animation and look blank. The young girl was watching it. When its change was complete, she lashed her horse suddenly and broke away, ejaculating, half audibly —

"I just knew it! He never asked him!" [6]

Hale Dexter arrived at the wretched little tavern at Drytown a trifle after dark and found the landlord, a couple of negro servants and a dozen villagers grouped about the front door, in listening attitude and looking very uncomfortable. There was a fine row going on within. Said the landlord —

"Gimme your hoss, stranger, and stay wher' you are. — Three stage-drivers are layin' into old Si Wheeler, in there, and it's warm times."

"Three on one, and you people allowing it? Is this Missouri style? Come in, and require fair play."

But nobody followed him in. The bar room was in an uproar; chairs and benches lay wrecked about it. A well built man of near fifty, with short, curly, yellow-reddish hair and a bloody but smiling face, stood in a corner, barricaded with a broad table which he had drawn in front of him, flourishing a heavy oaken cane, or rather club, and saying, "O come on, don't mind old Si, *he* don't 'mount to much!"

The three burly and gory stage-drivers had turned to see who had opened and closed the door. One of them squared himself before Hale and said —

"Stop wher' you are! Mix in, or leave! Who're you for, in this fight? State it quick, or vammus!"

"For the old man in the corner!" He had his hands full in a moment.

"Huray!" shouted the man in the corner, clearing his table at a bound and bringing down an enemy with his club, "it's an even thing, now — two *men* against three imitations!"

He threw away his club and went at his work as one who loves it. As fast as his two men could get up they went down again under his vigorous fist. They remained down presently, and both called for quarter. The victor turned.

"Well?" said he.

"My man is satisfied," said Dexter.

"He looks it. Give us your hand — you're true grit, stranger."

The landlord and the populace entered; a negro servant was ordered to show Dexter to his room, Si Wheeler followed, took a seat, and chatted freely and comfortably while Dexter removed his battle stains.

"What had you been doing to those roughs?" said the Kentuckian.

"Me? *I* didn't do anything to them. I'm only here for a few days on a matter in my little line of business, and I hadn't ever seen them before. One of them picked a quarrel with a poor devil of a nigger hostler and that harmless old granny of a landlord, and when I said I judged I'd take a hand myself to sort of even the thing up a little, the other two told me to mind my own business or they'd mix in, too. Says I, 'Mix! You've come to the right shop.' So in I went, — and out went the nigger and the landlord. I could 'a' cleaned them all, retail; but wholesale they ruther held over me. 'Twas lucky for me you chipped in. Say — you're good grit; and you've got a prime muscle. They *do* raise that sort down Ozark-way."

"I suppose so. But I'm not from there."

Wheeler — to himself —

"That didn't take. I'll try him on another lay." Then aloud: "I should 'a' thought you was from there. But a body's so apt to be mistaken. Laws, as like as not I missed it a hundred mile."

"About that — yes, more than that."

Wheeler — to himself —

"*That* didn't fetch him. Well, I'll try something else and come back to that." — Aloud: "You'd be surprised to see what curious names some people have around here. I know some named Waxy, and Abble, and Mucker, and Ding — O, all sorts of odd names. Then again there's a lot that ain't odd at all — like enough it's so down your way. My name ain't odd. My name 's Wheeler — Cap'n Si Wheeler."

Dexter — to himself —

"It's a queer old chap. If he wants to know my name and where I'm from, why doesn't he simply say so. Has an idea it wouldn't be polite, maybe." Then aloud: "Ah — Wheeler, is it? I'm glad to know it — and to know you. I ought to have mentioned mine, sooner, but I was absent-minded. My name is Dexter — Hale Dexter — from Kentucky. I am on my way to —"

A look of anguish spread itself over old Wheeler's face. "O, don't!" said he.

"What is the trouble, friend?"

"I wish you hadn't told me — it's such a pity — don't tell me any more."

"I am very sorry, Captain, but I had the idea that you wanted to know, and —"

"O, I *did* want to know, but not that way — not that way."

"Not that way? How, then?"

"O, there's better ways — more satisfactory. You see, I'm a bit of a detective; not a regular, you understand, not official, but just on my own hook — an *am*ature, so to speak. Well, a detective don't like to be told things — he likes to find them out. — You look at the detective books — you'll see."

"Ah — I see my mistake, now," said Dexter, a good deal amused.

"Yes. Well, a detective don't ever ask a question right out about what he wants to know. He asks questions away off yonder, round about, you know, that don't seem to bear on the matter at all, but bless you they're deep — deep as the sea. First thing a man knows, that detective has got all the information he wants, and that man don't ever suspect how he done it. See?"

"Yes. It must be a wonderful art?"

"Detecting? You bet it is. Why if you'd 'a' let me alone, I'd 'a' pumped you dry, and yet never asked you a thing that ever seemed to refer to anything in this world or the next."

"Well I won't interfere again, Captain — I only did it this time through ignorance and simplicity."

A negro appeared at the door and said "Supper's ready."

"Well, I'll go, now, Mr. Dexter. I'm going to be about here a day or two, working up a case, as we say, and if you're around day after to-morrow —"

"Tomorrow afternoon I go on to —"

"There — you're at it again! You leave it to me — I'll find it all out. All I want's a clew — the least little clew in the world — an old comb with a tooth gone's a plenty — and I'll find out anything I want to about the owner of it. Don't tell me anything — just leave me alone. Good-bye. Shake."

They shook hands and Wheeler went. But he put his head in again, and said —

"Here's the Guilford papers. You might like to run your eye over them. They're splendid papers. There ain't any better around this region. So-long." (Meaning Good-bye.) As he moved away, he observed to himself, "It's Hugh Burnside's cousin, that they say is going to have old [Humphrey]'s [7] pile of money when he dies. Old [Humphrey] is sick again, and like enough he sent for him. There's where he's bound for now; I could 'a' ciphered out the rest of it as easy as I've done this, if he'd 'a' let me alone."

"This *is* an odd fish," said Dexter to himself. He threw the newspapers on the bed and went down to supper.

By and by he returned to his room and sat down to smoke and think. Of what? Of that young girl. Her form floated before his imagination as in a tinted mist, the sound of her voice came and went, in his ear, fitfully and soft, like the distant murmur of music.

After a while his eye fell upon one of the newspapers, and he took it up. It was a wretchedly printed little sheet, being very vague and pale in spots, and in other spots so caked with ink as to be hardly decipherable. The first column was occupied by "Original Poetry" of the sappiest description. The next four were occupied by a selected story which was as sappy as the poetry. The remaining column of this first page was made up of short paragraphs of vapid, heart-breaking, infuriating rot entitled "Wit and Humor." The other outside page was built wholly of advertisements: three columns consisted mainly of glorified quack-poisons, stereotyped in various measures, headed with blurred portraits of the assassins who invented the nostrums, and tailed with lying testimonials from people who had never existed; the two remaining columns were thrown into one, which sang the praises of "Bagley's Celebrated One-Price Emporium" in riotous display-lines of forty-line pica shot full of shouting exclamation points. This whole page of advertisements was *repeated* on the inside without a blush or an apology. The editorial page was of double-leaded small-

24

pica, and the turned letters were so thick that it was nearly as easy to read it upside down as right side up. The other marvels of bad proof-reading covered all the vast possibilities, in that line, comprehensively, exhaustively, miraculously.

Dexter tried a specimen-editorial, to taste of its quality:

> (*Private* — Here let the compositor turn as many letters, mis-spell as many words, and scatter in as many wrong-font letters as shall be about right without exaggerating too much.)

THE DESPERADO JACK BELFORD.

> This inhuman miscreant who is to be hung next month and his crime-blackened soul sent to that place unmentionable to ears polite where it belongs, and who has twice before tried to break jail and would have succeeded but for the vigilance of the ever-efficient Sheriff of Boggsville,[8] the accomplished and gentlemanly Maj. Hoskins, who knows how to retain the guests of his hospitable little establishment when he once gets them into it, and who came near murdering head-keeper Hubbard the last time he tried to break out, made one more attempt last Thursday night, only the day before we went to press and so could not get it in type for last week's issue, tho' we issued an extra Friday noon with our accustomed enterprise and devotion to the interests of our patrons, but failed again, thanks to the Ever-efficient, who was on hand and up to snuff as usual in the discharge of his vigilant and onerous duties. We take this occasion to ask, What does the cowardly, lying, black-hearted, lily-livered filth-desseminator of the Guilford *Torch of Civilization* say to the purity and efficiency of Whig office-holders *now*? Will he defile the long-outraged public ear with another deluge of his peculiar language from his intellectual cess-pool, his hell-engendered brain, which no truly refined Christian man or woman dare read, and even blackguards blush at?

This being sufficient literary sustenance for his passing needs, and not feeling interest enough in the jail-breaking desperado to read further about him, Dexter returned to his musings about the afternoon's adventure and the girl.

Chapter 3

WHEN YOUNG DEXTER entered Judge Griswold's house in Guilford, the next evening, his head was still full of soft visions that refused to take their leave — and indeed they were not asked to. Mrs. Griswold received him with a warm welcome, though she paled a little and a momentary faintness passed over her as the thought of his possible mission recurred to her. But the thought and its signs went as quickly as they had come; admiration, beaming its expression from her eyes, took their place, and she said —

"What a fine manly creature you have grown to be, from the frail little lad you were seventeen years ago!"

"Yes, mother said she would have to certify me to you over her signature, to keep you from taking me for an impostor. She said you would be expecting a shadow."

"And no wonder, remembering how you began. People used to say they called you Hale because you weren't hale; since in this world the name never describes the man — the Cowards being always brave men, the Strongs always weak, and the Smalls overgrown."

The Judge said, courtly and stately, in a grave tone and without a smile —

"The son of my old friend is welcome. Consider yourself in your own house, sir, and at home."

This would have seemed a sort of funeral oration, but that the strong hand-grasp that accompanied it, translated it and gave it a very different and very agreeable meaning.

Young Dexter said —

"I thank you kindly, sir," and bowed.

A smiling, shrewd-faced young black, of eighteen or nineteen, was called in, and the Judge said to him —

"Toby, this is your young master Hale. You are his servant while he is here. — You will come and go at his beck and call;

you will obey no orders but his. Take his keys and arrange his things."

"Yes, Mars. Helm." *

"Your baggage arrived yesterday, Mr. Dexter. This is my daughter Milly — shake hands with Mr. Dexter, Milly."

Milly did so, with some diffidence and a blush.

Dexter thought, "What an earnest, gentle, pretty face it is!"

The girl's thought was, "If he is good to Toby, and can sing 'Roll on, Silver Moon,' I shall like him."

After some general talk, supper was announced. The Judge gave his arm to his wife, and the two young people dropped into their rear. Arrived at table, Mrs. Griswold bent her head, there was a moment or two of reverent silence, and then the meal began. As it progressed Dexter found himself growing more at home; Mrs. Griswold drew him on to talk, and his tongue presently got into smooth working order; Milly's shyness began to thaw and liberate a monosyllable here and there, then a brief sentence, then a clause, and finally her conversational ice-pack dissolved wholly and poured its shoal but fair and pleasant tributary to the general stream. The judge did not give forth wastefully, or even in a fluid state, so to speak, but set a stately berg afloat, at intervals, that made up in frozen grandeur what it lacked in glow and warmth. By and by Dexter touched upon the great Californian gold excitement and the marvelous things one was hearing daily from that far-off, mysterious land; [1] and from that he fell to describing his experiences of a fortnight before in a fantastic camp of hopeful and hilarious emigrants, westward bound; and warming to his theme he forgot everything else and did his work so well that when he came to himself and caught something in the nature of surprised admiration in two pairs of eyes and almost a compliment in the third pair, he was very much pleased with himself and knew these were fine people and that he should enjoy being with them.

* Presumably, first name of Judge Griswold.

When the party returned to the parlor the acquaintanceship was already ripe, already complete, all angles gone, all stiffness removed.

By half-past nine o'clock the newcomer had won Milly's deep regard; for without betraying the suffering it cost him, he had sung Roll On, Silver Moon, A Life on the Ocean Wave, and several other villanous ditties of a like sort.

At ten the Judge's hot whisky punch was brought, and Mrs. Griswold said to Dexter —

"Milly and I will say good-night, now. We are all satisfied with you — write your mother that; she will know it means a great deal when it comes from me. You are a member of this family, now, as long as you will stay with us; this is your home, and you are welcome. And always after this, I shall call you Hale, as I did when you were a little child. Good-night."

The young man was pleased and touched; the cordial clasp which the lady's hand delivered with her closing words touched him still more; so he found it easier to express his thanks in his return-pressure than to speak them. The Judge moved forward, held open the door, and tendered his wife a courtly bow as she passed out, and a grave "Good-night, my daughter," to Milly as she followed her. Then he sat down to his whisky punch again, and began to mix a tumbler for Dexter. Dexter sat down beaming with pleasure. He was happy and content to the core. There was a brief silence. Then the Judge's spoon stopped stirring; he looked up, and said with solemnity —

"Of course you have come to carry out your father's wishes. We all know that. Command me freely in any and all ways, for your father was my friend."

The words smote upon the young man's gladness like a tolling bell, and it vanished away. He could say nothing for a moment. He was dazed, confused — like a sleeper roused suddenly out of a gracious dream and confronted with some vague and formless horror. Then he gathered his disordered faculties together and said in a voice that had little of life in it —

29

"Yes — I come for that."

"Ah, good — you are your father's son. *I*, also, am satisfied with you."

It was the same testimony, in the same words, that had given so much pleasure five minutes before; how had those words lost their virtue?

The Judge took up the grisly theme of the ancient Dexter-Burnside feud, and as he pictured one after another its valorous encounters and their varying fortunes in all their chivalrous and bloody splendor, his fervor grew, the light of battle was in his eye,[2] and it was as if the spirit of some old Gaelic bard had entered into him and he chanted the glories of a great past and of a mighty race that had departed and left not their like behind them.

The old man finished. The younger man's face had been undergoing a change — not swift but gradual. Shade by shade, depression had passed from it, and ray by ray a proud enthusiasm had occupied its place with light and life. Now his eye hardened with an iron purpose. He said —

"I will do my father's will."

"He charged you with it, then? I knew he would. He said he would."

"Yes — on his death-bed."

"What is your plan?"[3]

"I have formed none — further than this.[4] I wish to have him pointed out to me. Then I will name myself, and if he is not armed, wait till he arms himself."

"That is right. Your father's gun came with your baggage; I recognized it. Is it in order?"

"It seems to be, but I do not know. I will examine it."

There was a considerable pause; both men sat thinking. Then the Judge said —

"In case of accident — have you made your will?"

"I have not a very great deal to leave, but —"

"You forget old Humphrey's fortune."

"If I fall, it goes to *him*."

"Ah — true."

"And if we both fall — what then?"

"That is easy — if one lives a distinguishable pulse-beat longer than the other. — If that should be you, your will would dispose of the property."

"Then I will draft a will."

"It is wisest."

There was a knock at the door, and a spare and severely neat lady of about forty-five entered, bonneted and shawled. There was a mingled kindliness and austerity in her face, but the austerity had a trifle the advantage, perhaps. The gentlemen rose, the Judge bowed, then waved his hand toward Dexter and said —

"Martha, this is the friend we were expecting — Mr. Dexter. My sister Miss Griswold, Mr. Dexter."

The lady bowed, then said —

"Brother, I stopped at the post office this morning, and got a letter for you, but I was on my way to the church to help arrange things for the fair, so I put it in my reticule, and have been so busy ever since that I never thought of it again until I left the church a quarter of an hour ago."

While she fumbled among the chaos of odds and ends in her reticule, the Judge said —

"Where is it from, Martha?"

"I didn't notice."

"Why it might be from Hoxton!"

"True as the world! — and I never once thought of it, I was so full of the festival plans. Ah, here it is. Open it and see what it says."

The Judge opened it, ran his eye down the page and looked very grave.

"The news is bad!" exclaimed the lady. "How can I be always so absorbed and heedless! What does it say?"

"She is very low."

31

"O, it is too bad! But I was expecting it."

"I was, too — but not so soon. Take it — but say nothing to Ruth about it to-night."

When the sister was gone, the Judge said —

"Her forgetfulness has saved my wife some hours of grief at any rate — so there was virtue in it. I sent to the post office just before noon; the idiot clerk said no letter had come. No news is good news, and my wife has been light of heart ever since. Now I am confronted with a difficulty. What shall I do? How can I surmount it? My wife's only sister lies very low, at Hoxton, three whole days' journey westward by stage, through a rough region.[5] My wife will go — that is of course, and as it should be." [6]

"And you will go with her. That also is a matter of course, and as it should be. You were thinking of me?"

"Yes. An affair like yours is one which is so important, and so requires —"

"Do not think of me for a moment. I shall not allow it — I will not hear of it!"

"But —"

"Not for a single moment! You will go with her — you must go with her. My affair is very simple."

The Judge gave himself up to thought during some moments, then he said —

"I see a way of arranging the matter.[7] I have a friend who would go through fire for me — Major Barnes, a distant relative of mine, and a thorough gentleman. No danger can shake his nerve, and no emergency find him wanting in expedients. He is younger and more vigorous than I, and therefore may be able to serve you even better than I could. Take him this note in the morning, and put yourself in his hands with entire confidence."

The Judge wrote the note and gave it to Dexter, with the remark —

"It is not a quarter of a mile; anybody can point you the way."

Chapter [4]

DEXTER sat late in his room that night; he drafted his will, he wrote his mother an affectionate letter which had no reference in it to the crime he was meditating; he cleaned and loaded his gun. With his murderous thoughts came the frequent suggestion, "My mother does not know; it will break her heart when she hears of it — there is the hardship of it all." Presently a question that had been floating, vague and inarticulate, through his mind, condensed itself into words: "Why do I want to kill this man?" It may have seemed only a small matter at first, this little question, but the more he examined it, and reasoned around it, and assaulted it with answers in front and flank and rear, the more compact and impregnable it stood. At the end of a long and harassing siege, he had to coldly confess that he was going to commit a crime of a dreadful nature partly in obedience to an authority which might possibly be questioned, partly because he must henceforth be despised by the Dexter clans if he refrained, and partly because there were witnesses that he had put his hand to the plow, wherefore he was ashamed to turn back now. So the thing was stripped of all its poor rags of justification, and stood naked before him: he did *not* want to kill this man; he had suffered no injury from this man — but, he would kill him.

The first gray of dawn had appeared before he finally dozed off into a dream-ridden, unrefreshing sleep. The last thing he was conscious of — and that but dimly — was the stage-horn and the sound of wheels. So he knew that the Griswolds were gone. He got up about the middle of the forenoon, ordered Toby to carry Judge Griswold's note to Major Barnes, then armed himself, and started down stairs; he heard a girlish voice below, singing some foolish ditty or other, and knew that Milly was coming along the hall. He stopped, like a guilty thing, and shrunk back out of possible sight. His cheeks burned when he recognized that his act had been involuntary, and that without reasoning he had been ashamed to meet innocence face to face. Milly sang herself away again and left the road clear; Dexter was quickly in the street. As he moved along, hardening himself to his purpose, he was presently hailed from behind by a voice which he recognized, and Captain Simon Wheeler rode up.

"Morning, Mr. Dexter — Glad to see you again. I was on the wrong scent, up yonder, so I didn't stay. Got a clew or two, though. How'd you find the Burnsides?"

"I — haven't seen them yet."

"No? Got in at night and roosted at the tavern, I reckon. Well, it's the best way. Don't ever take anybody by surprise, my old woman says; there's two kinds of surprises, and a body might strike the wrong kind."

The Captain rattled on. Dexter hardly heard him. He was busy thinking and planning. But this remark brought him suddenly to himself, with a cold shock —

"There's Hugh Burnside, now."

"Where!"

"In that door yonder. Good-bye — I turn off here."

Dexter moved diagonally across the street toward the man, and the thought shot through his brain, "It is no dream, then! and to think that this thing must be done, not tomorrow, next month, next year, but *now*! — it seems hideously sudden."

The man was stooping, patting a dog on the head. Dexter stood behind him a moment, waiting, then said in a voice that seemed not his own, so dreary and hollow it sounded —

"I will not take you at a disadvantage, sir, but —"

The man turned, and at sight of his face Dexter's speech died with a gasp. It was the jovial young historian of the cattle-maze. He siezed Dexter's hand with a cordial grasp and exclaimed —

"Hello! Why it's *you*! This is splendid! Come right in! — don't stand on ceremony; once met is an introduction in this region. Hi! mother! Clara! This way! — here's the gentleman that was lost in the cattle-

34

range! Here, take the rocking-chair — no, but you must — it's the seat of honor. Give me your hat. No, you needn't set your gun outside; I'll take care of her. Why look here! a minute ago you were as white as a sheet — now you're turning as red as the mischief. You ain't well — but never you mind, I've got some whisky that'll fix you."

The tremendous surprise of the situation had thrown Dexter's mind into a state of chaos. Only one thought took form and shape in this confusion. It was, "Thank God, the time has come and gone, and I shall never be a murderer, now." [1]

The women entered. The daughter bowed, smiled, and said —

"You are welcome, sir; [2] Mother, this is Mr. —"

"Hale Dexter, who is proud to be your relative."

Another surprise. The hand-shaking that immediately followed was hearty and general.

"By George!" said Hugh, "this is a wonderful state of things. So you are cousin Hale! Why look here! why the mischief didn't you say so, the other day?"

"Say what?" asked Clara.

"Why, that he was our cousin."

"How could he know it, then?"

"O, I didn't think of that. Come to think, I didn't even know enough to ask him his name. You said I was a —"

"When did you arrive, cousin Hale?" Clara broke in, while the color rose in her face.

"Last night."

"Then you stopped at the tavern," said the mother. "I hope you didn't rest well, for not coming straight to us. Come — tell me you had bad dreams and a troubled spirit."

Dexter felt the blood flowing into his own cheek, now, as he thought of his uneasy night and the reasons of it. He said —

"No, aunt, I did not stop at the tavern. I had bu-business — with Judge Griswold —"

35

"So you went there and cleared it off, and have come to us now, untrameled and ready for a good visit and with nothing to interfere? Well, it was not a bad idea. You finished the business, did you?"

"Ye-s — it is finished. O yes, it is entirely finished."

"Good. What was it?"

Poor Dexter was speechless. The question set his face on fire, but it seemed to freeze the rest of him. The innocent old lady and her son saw nothing; the young girl saw the young man's confusion, but pretended she did not, and quickly turned the talk to other matters. Presently Mrs. Burnside said —

"We must send for your baggage; for you must move here now."

Dexter said he would be more than glad to come after a few days. He explained the close friendship existing between his mother and Mrs. Griswold,[3] which made it his duty to remain where he was until the Griswolds should return from Hoxton, as protector of their household.

Conversation drifted into pleasant channels and flowed smoothly along. Dexter was charmed with his relatives, and they with him. Now and then the talk got upon uncomfortably shoal water or encountered a snag. For instance, after inquiring after her old Kentucky friends in detail, Mrs. Burnside said —

"Of course I never think of the friends there without thinking of the old dreadful feud days, and feeling grateful that they are gone forever. Sometimes I find myself looking upon them as nothing but an ugly dream, they have drifted so far from our later life. Just think of it for a moment and try to realize it. You come now with that innocent gun, and nothing is thought of it; but if it were in the old days I should drop lifeless, because I would know you had come to kill my Hugh!"

"You put it in a fearfully vivid way," gasped Dexter.[4]

"But *you* can't realize it, — now *can* you?"

"We-ll, ye-s — but perhaps not wholly."

"I should say not wholly, indeed! *I* can't, now; but once I could. Once I could imagine you coming to Hugh and saying, 'I am a Dexter

— go arm yourself.' And I could imagine the rest of it too: one or both of you stretched dead and bleeding on my threshold, and I standing there dumbly trying to realize the truth that my daughter's life and mine were blighted, wasted, ruined past help, by that wicked and useless act, when we had done no harm to any one — for in these hateful feuds a man's heart is cloven, but his wife's or mother's is broken — so the guilty is released with an instant's pang; and the long misery, the real suffering, falls upon the innocent."

Dexter thought, "If the subject could only be changed — to *anything*, no matter what, — I should be so humbly grateful."

When the noon meal was about ready Mrs. Burnside said —

"Maybe you would prefer to have it put off a little, Hale, if you had a late breakfast. Did you?"

He said, with inward embarrassment, that he had not breakfasted at all; then added that he had not thought of it or cared about it. The old lady patted him on the shoulder and said —

"It was so good of you to be so impatient to come and see us;" and she accompanied this with a smile of such sweet approval and endearment that it fairly blistered the young man's remorseful heart.

An hour later, Hugh took up Dexter's gun and fell to examining it. This disjointed the visitor's pleasant chat with Clara at once and made him nervously uncomfortable. Presently Hugh said —

"What sort of game did you start out after? Not small, I judge?"

"N-o. Large."

"Deer?"

"No — I hadn't thought of deer particularly."

"I reckon not — in the middle of the day. What then?"

"Well, I — I hadn't really made up my mind about the sort of game I wanted to hunt," said Dexter, nearly aground for a reply.

"Maybe hereditary instinct was stirring blindly within you and Hugh was the game you had in mind after all, without knowing it," said Clara gaily. But when she saw Dexter redden with confusion under her random remark, she hastened to add, "O I am so sorry! It

37

was only in jest, of course, but it was a cruel and foolish speech. Please don't be hurt; I am so ashamed of myself! You will not lay it up against me, will you?"

It was an easy promise to make; but it seemed to Dexter that he could almost bear another such shot for the pleasure of being so pleaded with again. By and by Hugh said —

"Sitting around here is dull. Let's go up into the woods and I'll show you where I'm on the watch for a wolf."

Dexter had been wishing that something might call Hugh away, in his individual capacity. This proposition banished that hope. For a moment he imagined he detected a look of disappointment in Clara's face, and this raised his spirits; but the next moment she said with a cheeriness that blighted his self-complacency —

"I'm glad you thought of that, Hugh, for I want some wild flowers. Please see that he gathers them, cousin Hale, won't you?"

When the young men were gone, she said to herself, with a sense of injury, "I think it might have occurred to them that if it is dull here with three or four people, it might be still duller when two of them go away."

Dexter wished to go by Judge Griswold's and make his excuses for his absence from breakfast. Hugh assented with alacrity. They found Milly in the parlor, at work at some trifle with her needle. She and Hugh did not seem to be aware of each other's presence after the first glance. Dexter said a word or two and then stepped out of the room to seek the aunt. Hugh now went to Milly and began to inquire into the nature of her work, evidently less to lay up information than to be near her. She explained that it was called hemistitching.

"Why no! is it?" — with surprised admiration.

"Certainly it is. There — don't you see?"

He drew his chair very close and bent over the work with intense interest.

"So *that* is hemistitching!" said he, after a speechless pause, much as another Missourian, standing upon Sandy Hook, might say, after impressive inspection, "So this is the Atlantic Ocean! — let me try to realize it."

Milly was as proud and pleased over this fraudful applause as if she had been the inventor of hemistitching and it was the one godlike art. Hugh took up an end of the work reverently and arranged it upon one of his broad palms for convenience of examination, and went on admiring and trying to think of another remark, while Milly experienced that exquisite and indescribable tingling of the scalp which has no name, but might fairly be called bliss, and which gives one the sense of being under a spell while it lasts — a spell which one longs to remain under, and dreads to see broken. Presently Hugh said——

"It's beautiful — beautiful. Very different from basting, I reckon."

"Basting! O, I should think so. Let me show you. Every one of these little three-cornered holes has to be made ever so carefully. O, ever so carefully!"

"No! is that so? I never should have thought it."

"But it's so — indeed it is. You have to pull out threads this way — and so — and so — and then you have to take your needle and —. Here, I'll make one, and you can see for yourself."

She began the marvel, and the two heads bent over it till they touched. Hugh watched every stitch with the profoundest interest, and when the miracle was finished he said —

"How *can* you do it!"

"O, it's easy after you know how. Why I do believe I could almost do it in the dark."

"No — but could you, though!" Then after a pause: "There was one part that I didn't exactly get the hang of. Won't you make another?"

She made another. Their hands touched occasionally, as well as their heads, now, and Hugh realized that there was a charm about hemistitching, under the right conditions, that amounted to fascination. The second lesson being finished, he sighed to think that he might not ask for another without risk of awaking suspicion. Presently

39

he fumbled in his pocket and drew out a folded paper which he gave to Milly and said —

"I wrote it for you. It's only a little thing."

It was some wretched drivel, in verse, entitled "The Wail of a Wounded Heart."

Milly read the first stanza, and said with rapture —

"It is so lovely! O, I *don't* see how you can do it!"

"O, it's nothing. I can do it any time. There's nothing about poetry that's difficult but the end-words. It crowds you to make them rhyme, sometimes. But put it away. — Don't read it now."

Milly, beaming with happiness and with pride in her poet, tucked the precious rubbish into her bosom to keep company with some spools, a thimble and an assorted cargo of other odds and ends.[5] Then she dexterously brought up from among these a something which she did not exhibit. Her heart increased its beat almost to a flutter, and she said, timidly, and watching Hugh's face wistfully —

"Do you like book-marks, Hugh?"

"O, what an idea!" laughed the burly youth. "A *man* don't care for such things. They're for girls and old women. A body might as well ask a man if he likes doll-babies. *Why?*"

The young girl's face was crimson, and her eyes were full of tears. Hugh exclaimed —

"Why Milly! What is the matter?"

She stepped quickly aside and turned away her head. — Hugh, filled with solicitude, stepped after her and siezed her hand; but she snatched it from him and ran out of the room, with her face still averted. She flew to her bed chamber, locked the door, put the book-mark and "The Wail of a Wounded Heart" together in a piece of paper which she laid away with mournful tenderness in a very private and sacred corner of one of her drawers, and said with a quivering voice —

"When I am gone they will find them, and then they will know." (The "they" referred to surviving friends and relatives.)

Then she flung herself on the bed and fell to sobbing bitterly.

Hugh, in the parlor, stood petrified. He wondered, and continued to wonder, what could have brought about this catastrophe, but no solution suggested itself. He was feeling very uncomfortable. He grew more and more so. He expected Milly to come back; but as minute after minute dragged by and still no footfall was heard, this expectation began to die a slow and miserable death. Presently his heart gave one jubilant bound, but straightway retired, weighted again with woe, for it was Dexter who entered.

"All right now — I'm ready!"

But Hugh was not ready. He wanted to examine the pictures on the walls — and it was time, for although he had seen them many a time before, he had never in the least examined them. He kept an expectant ear open, and started hopefully at every slight noise, but it was all vain — she never came. Finally Dexter was tired waiting, and said —

"Why, you must have seen these pictures a hundred times; do you always freeze to them like this?"

The Broken-hearted blushed, and sadly said he was ready to go. Milly heard the front door close behind the cousins. She got up and watched them move away, concealing herself with the window curtain. She said, deeply hurt, —

"Yes, there he goes, sure enough. One would think he would at least have wanted to ask what it all was. But no, it is nothing to him; that is plain."

She returned to the bed and cried harder than ever.

The young men strolled up the river road and into the forest, and Dexter had but a dreary time of it. He tried, for a while, to covertly lead up to some general talk about Clara, but all he got was absent-minded monosyllables punctuated with sighs — seven sighs to a monosyllable. So he gave it up, and was silent for some time. Finally he said —

"Are you often taken this way?"

"Taken how?" said Hugh, fiercely.

"O, no matter, if you don't observe any peculiarity," said Dexter, with a pretense of unsarcastic simplicity which was not wholly successful.

"If you don't like me the way you find me —"

"Now look here!" exclaimed Dexter, cutting him off abruptly, "let's not have any nonsense!"

"Well, then, don't peck at me. Can't you let a fellow alone when you see he's in trouble?"

The anger went out of Dexter's face, and he said —

"There — I was heedless, and I'm sorry. Shake hands, and I'll be more considerate."

Hugh received and returned the shake, then said with emotion —

"May you never suffer the agonies *I* suffer!"

Dexter was nearly surprised into laughing, but saved himself in time. — He was silent after this, out of respect for Hugh's woes. Hugh moved here and there in a corner of the wood trying to seek for wolf-signs, but his wits were on furlough and he discovered nothing. Finally Dexter said —

"Here — what is this?"

"Ah, those scoundrels have been at it again," said Hugh. "That's a piece of raw meat — but you see that yourself."

"Yes, and I understand it, too. I have heard of poisoning wolves before, to get the bounty."

"Yes, it's meaner than dirt. I wish I could catch them at it once. Old Si Wheeler's on the watch. He says he'll track out the villains that are spoiling all the sport this way. He has got clews, he says."

"This meat was put here last night, of course; so there was no wolf here this morning."

"No, they mighty seldom come. They're pretty scarce." He held up the meat and gazed at it absently for a while, then sighed deeply and said —

"It's full of strychnine. Ah, I wish it was cooked!"

He let it fall, with another sigh, and wiped away a tear. The more thoughtful Dexter turned a great stone over the meat, to save the wolf for the rifle. Then he reminded Hugh of the wild flowers, but the poor youth said, with a glassy eye —

"Flowers are a mockery. There is nothing real but the tomb."

He had the presence of mind to get out his note-book and set down this thought for future use in some peculiarly damnable poem.[6]

Dexter resolved to gather the flowers himself on the homeward stroll, and was not sorry to have the privilege. The moment the young men moved away from the tree they had been standing under, Captain Si Wheeler, thrust his head out from behind it and watched them until they disappeared. Then he began to talk to himself —

" 'Tain't any use to follow them any more; I haven't got enough out of this tramp to make it pay. When they do come to a halt they don't seem to talk much. — But *that's* a sign, itself! When people don't talk, it's because they're thinking. Now, the idea is, what are they thinking about?" He paused a good while, with contracted brow and his finger on the side of his nose, deep in rumination. Then he said: "I've found out Dexter hasn't been to see old Humphrey, after all. Well, that's because he knows he's going to get the property anyway. So I'll let that drop. Now what did Hugh wish that that poisoned meat was cooked, for? There's something in that — there's something mighty deep and dark about that!" After another long and thoughtful pause, he said: "Look here! the more I throw the detective eye on that thing, the blacker it looks. Let me just set down here and put this and that together and see what comes of it." He sat down on a log, took a red bandanna handkerchief out of his poor old battered plug hat, wiped his red brow, put back the handkerchief, put the hat on the ground in front of him and said, "You set there — I can follow my clews better with something to talk to." He addressed himself to the hat, and began to talk, accompanying himself with impressive gestures. "Now give me your attention for a minute. This young man comes here, all the way from Kentucky. Very good. Does a man come all the way from Kentucky for nothing? No, says you; and you're right. What does he come for? To get that money, you'll say.

Right again. He's got to wait a bit, for the old man to die. Very good; what's the natural thing for him to do while he's a-waiting? Stop with his aunt? Why, of course. What does his coming there remind his cousin Hugh of? O, you begin to see the point, do you? Well, to go on. Hugh gets to thinking, and don't talk. What's the natural thing for him to be thinking? This: if 'twarn't for Dexter, the money'd come to *me*. You're right again. What's his next thought? This: if Dexter was to die . . . . the money'd come to me! Right again — go it! What does such thoughts lead to? Sourness and brooding, says you. You never said a truer word. Is Hugh sour and brooding to-day? I don't say a word — I leave it to your own candor and honesty if he ain't. Now we come to the loudest and awfulest clew of all. You heard him say, with your own ears, that *he wished that poisoned meat was cooked!* What was the inside meaning of that remark? Can you put *two* meanings on it? *No,* sir! What does it mean in plain English? Just this: if that poisoned meat had been cooked, he would 'a' made him eat it! Now there you are! Is it neatly done? Have I followed the clews as straight as a bee-line and never missed a trick? O, *I* ain't no detective! of *course* not! I'm only a blundering old fool that don't know anything. *Any*body'll tell you that. But mind you — just keep quiet about this thing. Just wait — don't get impatient — just lay low and keep dark — *I'*ll show 'em, one of these days. You'll see. Now look here; do we stop where we are, or do we look ahead? Don't I *always* look ahead — I ask you that? Don't I? Well, what do I see ahead, now? *Only* this — he's a dead man if he eats beefsteak in the Burnside house! That's all. That's exactly the size of it. 'George, but this is a black affair! And to think that this whole community looks upon that young Burnside as a kind of a sweet, giddy, poetical muggins that wouldn't even hurt his grandmother in cold blood! And I ain't a-going to deny it — so did *I,* till I run my eye over these clews and found him out. But blame his murderous skin, he little thinks that there's a pair of eyes on him that's got for a motto, '*We never sleep.*'"

The old man put on his hat and moved slowly away, thinking. Soon he nodded his head with satisfaction and said: "Yes, that's the idea; it'll put him on his guard, and he'll never suspect who done it. And he won't mention it to anybody — he knows enough for that."

Half an hour later he was leaning lazily against the front of the post-office with his hand behind him. He was there some little time, apparently with no object but to yawn and enjoy his rest; but when he went away at last there was an envelop in the letter box addressed to "Mr. Hail Dexter;" with the addition, "*private and confidentiall.*"

"There," said he "that's the detective way of doing a little thing like that."

About this time Hugh and Dexter were drawing homeward. They met a gentleman whom Hugh bowed to and called "Major Barnes." Dexter thought, "Hang that note! I would give anything if I hadn't sent it. I've got to make this man's acquaintance pretty soon, and explain. And what shall I say? Tell him I was minded to kill —. Well, if I ever get out of this hobble I'll never get into another one like it."

He went on bothering over the matter and getting himself into a state of irritation of a larger size than the thing required or justified. However, he judged that when he came to show Clara what wonders he had done in the flower-gathering way, she would say something or look something that would improve the state of his mind. He hoped she would do something to stop Hugh's intolerable sighings, too.

But it was all a miscalculation. A dead and empty silence reigned in the Burnside house — a silence which the melancholy droning of a bee in the honeysuckles only intensified. A servant was called; she said Mrs. Burnside was gone to help at the church where the fair was to be, and that Miss Clara was not feeling well and had lain down. Dexter threw his flowers on the table with an air that said "The world is hollow and life is vain," and turned toward the door. Hugh said, in a sepulchral voice —

"Right. Leave me — this is no place for the gladsome and gay."

45

At supper that evening, Milly was subdued and silent, Dexter depressed and untalkative. Miss Martha Griswold could have talked about the church fair, but she preferred to think. The meal dragged solemnly to its close; then Miss Martha said —

"Ah, I forgot, Mr. Dexter — in truth I am always forgetting. Here is a letter for you which I got out of the office as I came along." —

Dexter carried the letter to his room. It read thus:

Dont eat Beefstake in the House wher you are stoping. Bewair.
"From a frend."

"Well, this *is* a cheerful addition!" said Dexter. "I get up in the morning to murder a man; I am in hot water, first here, then there, all day; and at night a maniac warns me against the Griswolds and their beefsteak."

He puzzled over the wretched writing a while, then threw it on the floor, and fell to wondering if Clara Burnside got sick intentionally or only by accident. The gloomiest mood must wear itself out eventually. Dexter's began to thin a little in the middle and fringe off into spitefulness at the edges; an unreasoning spitefulness, which should have chosen him as its target, to be just; but this mood is never just: witness how often it assaults innocent furniture or kicks a dog that is asleep. Still, this change was an improvement; for it was in the direction of good-humor, for the reason that when spitefulness follows heavy-heartedness, good-humor follows [spitefulness] [7] by a natural law. There was a knock at the door.

"Come in!" This with asperity.

Toby entered.

"Well, what do *you* want?"

Toby smiled widely and mollifyingly, bowed several times with embarrassed diffidence, and said —

"Mars. Hale, I come to ast if you wouldn't write a little letter for me, if it ain't too much trouble, sah."

46

"A letter! O, go along with you and don't bother me!"

Toby moved humbly toward the door, crushed, but still bowing, still smiling as well as he could. He said —

"Thank you, sah. I's very sorry, sah, but I didn't mean no harm."

Dexter felt a twinge of remorse. His mood being in a transition state, was like a ship's empty sails when the vessel is "going about" but has not quite swung to the point where she will fill away on the other tack — bellied, first this way and then that, by every passing puff of wind. He said —

"Hold on. What can you want to write a letter for? Who is it for?"

"My ole mother, sah — 'way down in Arkansas."

"O! That's a different matter. Of course I'll write it." Then with a burst of irritation—leveled at the wrong target, of course—"What the devil were you going away for? Did you suppose I wouldn't write it?"

"O, no, Mars. Hale. Please don't git mad, Mars. Hale, I know'd you'd write it if you said you'd do it."

"Well then, what the devil do you mean by — . Look here — can your mother read writing?"

"O, no, sah; but dey reads it to her — young Mars and Missis does — dey's good chillen. She very ole, now, an' I hain't seed her sence I was little. She like to git letters f'm me. Miss Milly she write 'em for me, every time I ast her; but she feelin' bad now, I reckon, so I wouldn't ast her."

This soft zephyr fanned the other side of the sail.

"Well, you come to me whenever you want to, Toby; I'll be your amanuensis."

"My . . . . . my which, Mars. Hale?"

"Amanuensis! Confound it, don't you know what an amanuensis is?"

"No, Mars. Hale, I's mighty ignorant, fo' my size, and I hain't never seed one — dat is, I don't 'member to."

"Well, *now* you see one. Now tell me what I'm to say, and....look here!" said Dexter, impetuously, rising and confronting Toby, "what ever possessed you to give that note to Major Barnes? — answer me that!"

47

"Please, Mars. Hale, don' look at me so turrible — I 'clah to goodness I didn't do it!"

"Say it again, and I'll hug you!"

"Please don't, Mars. Hale — I 'clah to goodness I didn't give it to him! I wisht I may never stir if I did!"

"Here — here's a quarter for the only speech I think I've heard to-day that didn't gall me. What did you do with the note?"

The negro hesitated, looked confused a moment, and then began to pour his words out in a zealous torrent —

"Well Mars Hale, I tell you jes' how it was. I was down dah in de parlor, and Miss Martha she was a-hurryin' me up, an' I says, s'I, 'I'm a-doin' my bes',' s'I, an' she say, 'Well, hurry up, hurry up, hurry up,' she say, — jes' so — an' s'I, 'Dey ain't no grass gwyne to grow under *my* hoof,' s'I, an' wid dat I heave' on a stick, an' it tore de letter out'n my han' an' 'fo' I could snatch it out she was burn't up. Dat's jes' de way it happen' Mars. Hale, I wisht I may die if — "

"O, rubbish! A fire in the parlor, in dead summer time?"

"What! did I say in de parlor, Mars. Hale? Well, if dat don' beat all! In de *parlor*! says I. Why 'twas in de kitchen, of course. Well, I 'clah to goodness if dis don' — "

"Well, never mind, it's all right, just so its burnt — I ain't particular where the fire was." Dexter sat down. His ship had made the turn, at last, and was filling away on the other tack with a wind that would stay. "Now I'm ready to begin, Toby. What shall I say to your mother?"

Toby swabbed the perspiration from his face with his sleeve, remarked to himself, " 'I jings, I never seed a nigger in no closter place 'n' what dat was! — I was mos' ketched, sure" — then produced a greasy little book. He wetted his thumb and began to flip the leaves over, pausing now and then to scan a page critically. At last he said in a gratified tone —

"Dah she is! 'I jings I 'gin to git afear'd she done gimme de slip. Dah, Mars. Hale, dat's de one."

48

"Do you mean to say you're not going to dictate the letter yourself, but are going to get it out of the book?"

"Dictate?" said Toby, scratching his head perplexedly; "Dic . . . . . Mars. Hale, please don' bust dem big words at me, I don't stan' no chance 'gin 'em. Yes, Mars. Hale, dat's a prime book; I gits de mos' o' my letters out'n dat book; dey ain't nuffin in de worl' but what dat book know 'bout it. I reckon Sol'mon writ dat book, but I don' know. But it *soun'* like Sol'mon, sometimes, — so de ole nigger preacher say, — and den it know so much, and say it so beautiful. — Mars. Hale, dah's *beautiful* words in dat book — great long beautiful words dat dey ain't *no* man kin understan'. My ole mother and my brother Jim is mons'us proud o' me on accounts o' dem letters dat I gits out'n dat book; dey ain't no mo' niggers roun' heah but me dat sends letters to anybody."

Dexter took the little open book, glanced at its back, and through the grime made out to decipher the title, "The People's Ready Letter-Writer." [8] Then he looked at the page indicated by Toby and burst into a laugh. Toby said —

"What is you laughin' 'bout, Mars. Hale?"

"Well — can you read, Toby?"

"Dat's a curus question to ast a po' nigger, Mars. Hale. 'Course I can't."

"That's the reason you've made a mistake. This is not the letter you were after, Toby."

"O yes 'tis, Mars. Hale; I knows it kase I marked it wid a piece o' fire-coal. You read it, Mars. Hale, you'll see."

Dexter read aloud, as follows:

From a Young Lady to a Suitor whom she greatly Esteems but feels obliged to reject because she cannot love him.

Esteemed Sir: I have perused your honored epistle with deep gratitude, but with flowing tears. For while my esteem for your lofty character and manifold virtues is boundless, I am admonished by my heart that I can never feel for you that affectionate

49

devotion of soul that the perfect marital relation requires. Therefore I am compelled to reject the noble offering which you have
laid at my feet, and to utter the edict that we can never be to
each other more than we are at present. Do not hope: for this
is final. Yet do not despair; but seek in fairer fields a companion
more worthy to adorn thy pure and beautiful life than she who
feels herself compelled to indite these lines. Farewell: and may
she whom thou shalt crown with the precious diadem of thy
love's rich gold, be to thee a double and treble recompense for
my poor loss; and as the river of Time glides to its unknown sea,
may thy bark float calm and peaceful upon its troubled waters,
unbuffeted by its storms, untossed by its tempests, and ride at last
secure in that haven where moths do not corrupt nor thieves
break through and steal. Farewell: and though we can be no
more, to each other, I beg that we may still be friends.

"Dat's de one, Mars. Hale, dat's de one! Don't dem words taste
good in you' mouf! don't dey 'mind you of suckin' a sugar-rag when
you was little? an' don't dey *soun'* softy and goody! Don' dey blobber-
blobber-blobber along like buttermilk googlin' out'n a jug! King Sol'-
mon he must 'a' writ dat, kase I reckon dey ain't nobody else dat kin
bounce words aroun' like dat. O yes, dat's de right letter, Mars. Hale.
I know'd dey warn't no mistake 'bout it."

"But here! Do you really want this letter sent to your *mother?* —
and as coming from *you?*"

"Yes, dat's it, dat's it, Mars. Hale. You see, fust I got Miss Milly to
write out dis letter and send it to my brother Jim, an' he — "

"To your brother Jim! This same letter?"

"Yes, Mars. Hale. You see Jim he's a fiel' han'; works in de cotton
fiel'; so de white chillen dey read de letter to Jim, an' lots o' other
niggers was dah, f'm de plantations aroun', kase it was a Sunday; an'
dey tole everybody 'bout it, an' so every Sunday sence den de niggers comes dah to hear dat letter; some of 'em walks fifteen mile; an'
dey all say *dey* ain't never hearn no sich letter as dat befo'. Dey keeps
a-comin' — de same niggers an' new ones — to hear dat letter — dey
don't ever seem to git enough of it. Well you see dat make Jim mighty

proud. He tote de letter 'roun' all de time, an' dad fetch him he mos' too good to speak to anybody now, less'n it's seven-hund'd-dollar niggers and sich-like high flyers. Well, you see, my ole mother she don' like to see Jim a-havin' it all to hisself so; so she ast one o' de little missises for to write and ast me to write *her* dat letter, too. An' you bet she'll be powerful glad when she git it, Mars. Hale. She's a good ole 'oman, too, dat she is!"

So Dexter copied the absurd thing, addressed it to "Old Mammy Betsy, Care of Col. Whiting, Bayou Noir Plantation, Arkansas," and signed it "Your Loving Son, Toby."

Toby's gratitude was outspoken, when Dexter handed him the letter complete and ready for the post-office.[9] But Toby had not been idle while the writing was going on. He had stolen an envelop, and also Capt. Wheeler's warning note, and concealed them about his person. On his way down stairs he got out the Wheeler note, also a soiled scrap of writing which he had found in the street, and lastly Judge Griswold's note to Major Barnes! — so this Phenix had thus early risen from its imaginary ashes. — He put his three treasures into his envelop and presently got Miss Martha to direct it to his brother Jim! — Apparently all was fish that came to Toby's correspondence-net.

Dexter was in quite a happy frame of mind, by this time. He no longer cared to moon in solitude. It was early yet, so he started down stairs with a definite purpose. As he was passing through the parlor, he noticed that Milly was sitting with her arms upon the piano and her face buried in them. She did not look up; was she feeling lonely? did she miss her parents? Dexter was ashamed of his selfishness in forgetting all sorrows but his own. He went to her and spoke her name softly. The little maid looked up wearily and made an effort to smile, but there was not much life in it. She had been thinking over her day, and now that the smart of the wound Hugh had given her had lost the most of its sharpness she was questioning if she had not been wrongfully abrupt with him. Dexter was gentle and persuasive, and presently beguiled her into talking; her depression began to yield. Now Dexter proposed a walk; she was undecided, nearly indifferent, but asked whither. He hesitated, as if considering, then said suddenly, as if the thought had just that moment occurred to him —

"Suppose we saunter over and see the Burnsides."

"Very well!" said Milly, and looked so pleased that Dexter remarked to himself, "I begin to think I suspect something!"

The Burnside supper that evening had been no more cheery than the Griswold supper. Hugh was morose, all through the meal, Clara thoughtful. Hugh's thinkings about Milly took this shape: "I hadn't done anything, yet she could treat me so! I will never look upon her more!" Clara's thoughts dwelt upon Dexter — to this effect: "It was not gracious, or even civil, in him to prefer the woods and Hugh, to me; but I wonder if it was altogether right or kind to let him come back to an empty, unwelcoming house? Will he come to-night? I hope he will, for my conscience is not entirely easy."

Supper was finished; then came two striplings, timid undeclared suitors: Tom Hooker, reporter and maid-of-all-work to the *Torch of [Civilization]*; [10] and Lem. Sackett, a clerk at Bagley's "Emporium." This invasion would have been tolerable to Clara at nearly any other time, but it irritated her now. The young chaps tried hard to be sprightly and agreeable, but Clara was gently sarcastic, and they began to grow uncomfortable. In time they very much wanted to go, but could find no way to launch themselves. Conversation ceased to pour, and began to drip, drearily. Clara sat near the window, and glanced nervously and anxiously out from time to time. Finally she said to herself, with a sigh, "No, he isn't coming." A moment or two later she said, with temper, "Very well, he needn't come if he doesn't want to." She left the window, took another seat, and shot poor

Hooker through the heart with a venomous sarcasm. Even the sullen, world-hating Hugh was moved to say to himself, "Poor devil, *he* wasn't doing anything." The next moment, Dexter and Milly entered, the one casting a beaming glance upon Clara, and the other its mate upon Hugh. The great pouting cub got up without a word and marched coldly, sternly, out of the room; the sister said, with a smile and an easy grace of manner that gave no sign of the vengeful spirit within —

"Why how pleasant!"

Introductions followed. "Good!" thought Dexter, "she's in an angelic mood; Toby has turned the luck."

Clara said —

"Why, my poor Milly, I thought you looked happy, a moment ago, but I see you are thinking of your father and mother. You shall be cheered up, you shall be comforted. Here is *my* mother, she will make you forget your loss. My cousin will help her."

She grouped the three together, began the comforting work herself, and when the conversation was well and happily under way, she rose and deserted, — to Dexter's crushing disappointment. She returned to her young fellows, and, to their grateful surprise, began to pour out upon them an animated badinage which was full of charm and free from sarcasm. By and by things stood thus: Milly and Mrs. Burnside were chirping along, softly and contentedly, the young chaps and Clara were blithely chatting and laughing, and Dexter sat empty-mouthed and with a sense of being a pretty conspicuous cipher. He had given up trying to talk to his aunt and Milly, since he could keep neither his eyes nor his jealous mind from the other group. If his eyes tried to wander elsewhere they never got further than the table, where the flowers still lay which he had gathered with such elaborate pains that day. — Their withered forms insulted his self-love sorely. After a while Clara stole a furtive, triumphant glance in Dexter's direction; he was idly inspecting his hands, with the air of one who was very much at a loss for some way to put in the time. The girl was stricken with a sudden shame, and resolved that she would put an end

53

at once to her inhospitable folly. She was about to rise, but young Hooker began a humorous anecdote and she halted, on nettles, for him to finish. A moment later she heard Dexter say — and the words filled her with a sort of vague dismay —

"No, the Judge's house is right on the way, and it will save steps if Hugh will come by for me, instead of my coming here. I will send Toby for my gun some time to-morrow, and be ready early next morning."

Clara sprang up, cutting short the Hooker anecdote, and was about to say something to Dexter, she hardly knew what, but he turned at that moment to answer some remark of his aunt's, and the opportunity passed. She stood where she was, undecided, and a moisture born of shame and of anger at herself came into her eyes. Dexter shook hands with his aunt, bowed pleasantly to Clara and the young men, and he and Milly went forth. For a moment or two Clara was half-conscious of wordy sounds at her ear, then wholly conscious of them — they formed the consumingly funny climax of the Hooker anecdote; then the jocund author paused, radiant, for the applause. The girl gazed into that shining face with vacant and mournful eyes; and in that moment the light of it was quenched, and the joke that had flamed out with such glorified promise lay a blasted and smouldering ruin there, with a blighted spirit and a blistered heart behind it.

In a little while the joker and his friend, blue and forlorn, were wending homeward,[11] and Clara sat alone in the parlor seeking in her heart for some excuse, some crumb of palliation of her evening's behavior, and finding none.

Hugh entered, solemnly, and began to ransack the table for a pen. The flowers were in his way. He threw them petulantly into the empty fire-place.

"I loathe flowers!" said he.

"Then you needn't have gathered them."

"I didn't."

"You didn't?" said Clara with a quick interest; "who did, then?"

"*He* did."

54

Clara felt another remorseful pang, but there was a pleasureable something about it at the same time.

"Did he gather them for . . . . . for me?" she asked, with a hesitating diffidence.

"Of course. Who else? The cat?"

The dismal poet found pen and paper; sat down and wrote a line, then remained still, during fifteen minutes, gazing overhead, with the feather-end of his quill thrust into his nostril, trying to think of a rhyme for it.

Clara sat silent, thinking; at intervals breathing long sighs. She said to herself, "I am bad — bad all through — bone and fibre and tissue — bad at heart. It must be so." Presently she said, "The next time, I will not wound or . . . . . Folly! there will never be any next time!" [12]

During two sweltering hours the poet travailed, and then the birth-pains were over. The result was a ten-line deformity, christened "The Crushed Heart's Farewell," and leading off with this couplet, — by way of head and shoulders:

55

The poet read his ten lines over and found them faultless, since they moved him to tears. They might have had the same effect upon Milly if he had carried them himself instead of entrusting them to Toby: as it was, they were greatly admired on the Arkansas plantation a week or ten days later.

Hugh turned, and looked surprised and touched —

"Clara! you here yet! Ah, I do not deserve such devotion!" — He came and kissed her tenderly, heaved a sigh, and said in a dead voice —

"There — remember that I loved you, when I am gone. Something tells me I am not long for this vale."

He dragged his sorrows wearily up stairs, and when Clara heard his door shut she took the forlorn flowers from the fire-place and carried them to her chamber. In a little while all the household were asleep but Hugh. He was abed, building a waking-dream wherein he saved Milly from a burning house, but at the cost of his own woe-worn young life; and when at last he dozed off to sleep, he left her weeping over the corpse.

Milly and Dexter were full of thought when they started homeward. So they walked slowly along without speaking. Dexter, thinking of Clara, said to himself, "She has a strong aversion for me — that is plain. I am a scorched moth, now; I must keep away from her, else I shall be a consumed one." Presently Milly sighed. Dexter smiled, and said this knowing thing to himself: "There — it is a hundred to one that this inexperienced little creature is taking the most glaring and palpable signs of Hugh's love for her to mean just the opposite. How blind a person can be at her age!"

As they passed a narrow alleyway, a bent and coarsely-clad old woman, with her jaws muffled in a red handkerchief, stepped out and hobbled along in their wake supporting herself with a cane. Shortly she muttered —

"Yes, they don't talk — they're in love. Sure sign. Well, good match; good stock, and both'll be rich."

She overtook the young people, bent her breast down upon her cane, held out her hand, and said in a reedy falsetto —

"A dime for the old gipsy and she'll read your palms and tell your fortune. A dime for the old woman, please."

Dexter paid, and said —

"Here is our opportunity, Milly; stretch out your palm."

She did so, and the old woman examined it attentively, then said —

"There's much trouble in store for you, and much joy. You will be very rich, by and by. You will marry a dark, handsome gentleman from another State, and be very happy — provided he keeps a sharp look-out on his enemies and gets the better of designs which they are hatching up now against his life. Your great grandchildren will come to great distinction, though you may not live to see it."

Milly was deeply impressed by these prophecies, and wondered how a mere human being could map out and foretell the future with such accuracy. The gipsy examined Dexter's hand and said with solemnity —

"You love a blonde lady that's only two-thirds your own age, and your love is returned. You are a-going to be rich and happy if you overcome the designs of your enemies. But don't be afeard — you have powerful friends about you: among them there's one that's a-watching always." Then in a whisper, at Dexter's ear, "Young man, beware of beefsteak! You turned a rock over one to-day to save the wolves — do the same for your *own* sake!"

The gipsy hobbled briskly around a corner and disappeared, muttering, "I've saved him from poison, anyway; and I'm the man that can save him from any job Hugh can put up on him. I bet I ain't going to let a man be murdered that chipped in and took a hand when I was

57

in a close place — and played it like a major, too! If anybody thinks different, they don't know Si Wheeler the detective!"

Dexter went to bed much perplexed, that night. Said he —

"So there are *two* lunatics at large! One a man — by the handwriting — the other a woman. How in the world did this witch know I turned a rock over that beefsteak? I think I do need a sane guardian angel, but I am not going to discomfort myself over the absurdities of these mad ones."

He dismissed the subject from his mind. Straightway Clara Burnside took its place. He dismissed her, too — reluctantly, but promptly. "There is no safety but in keeping her entirely out of my thoughts," said he.

As Dexter stepped out of the front door, the next morning he was troubled to perceive that his resolution to keep away from temptation had so weakened already that his steps were turning in her direction unconsciously — and not only that, but gladly. He put a stop to all that, at once. Now came Hugh briskly along, in high spirits, and hailed him with a proposition to go boating, riding, fishing, or roaming the woods and hills — anything that might be agreeable. So they struck for the woods.

Hugh's wind-mill was in fine working order to-day, its clack was incessant; one could hardly believe it was the same that so lagged and creaked and groaned the day before. Dexter found the simple and hearty fellow good company and his liking for him grew steadily. When at last the top of the highest bluff was reached and the two sat down to rest, Dexter said —

"Now tell me something. I'm a little puzzled. Have you seen Milly this morning?"

"No."

"Did you see her last night after she went home?"

"No."

"Then what has put you in such spirits to-day?"

"Why, what has she got to do with it?"

"Everything!"

"Well, that's an idea!"

"It's a sound idea.—You know very well you love her. Wait—don't deny it. You were just going to. Don't do it—because I know better."

"Well, then . . . . . but look here, who could have told you that?"

"Nobody told me. I saw it myself. But never mind about that. That isn't the puzzle. The puzzle is your cheeriness to-day. I can't account for it."

"All right; if that's all, I'll account for it for you."

"Good — go on."

"I don't love her any more!"

"O, nonsense!"

"It isn't nonsense. I'm going to make a clean breast of it Hale. — I did love her, and I thought she loved me — though I never told her so and she never told me so. Well, yesterday morning she treated me shabbily, and I thought it all over, all day, and I saw she didn't love me. I was so miserable! I was miserable all the evening. I couldn't go to bed till I'd written a poem to show how I felt. Then I went to sleep, but I woke up by and by, my sufferings and the mosquitoes distressed me so. I got up and dressed, and took that poem and hung around her house, perfectly miserable. — Finally I shoved the poetry under the kitchen door, because there was a light in the front of the house,* and then I said, 'What's the use? let her go; she don't care for me; I will tear her out of my heart though it kills me.' So I tore her out and it did nearly kill me, for a while; but I'm over it now, and I'll never go near her again. There, that's the whole thing, clean and straight. So I'm feeling good, to-day, you see."

* Twain seems to have forgotten that a few pages earlier Hugh entrusted the poem to Toby, who dispatched it to Arkansas.

59

Dexter was thoughtful a while; then he said —

"Just by signs I found out you loved her, didn't I?"

"Yes."

"Well, I know by signs that she loves you, Hugh."

"No. She don't."

"But she does."

Dexter tried hard to convince him, but Hugh's romantic mind was full of the charm that goes with blighted hopes and severed ties, and he was not to be persuaded. Dexter felt nearer to Hugh than ever, now that both their hearts were in a state of blight and both their minds bent upon a like resolve. He determined upon a confidence. He said —

"Hugh, I'll make a confession. I've been disappointed too. I've been singed, and have retired from the candle, so to speak, just as you have done."

"No! Is that so? Give me your hand! Let's be brothers in misfortune. Now I like this. I didn't suppose I should, but I do. I like it better than the other way. Don't you?"

"Ye-s, I think so. O, yes."

"But you're in better luck than me, Hale. You're a way off here in Missouri where you *can't* see your girl; but look at me — I'm likely to run across mine any time. But I'm firm. You'll see."

As the friends wandered homeward late in the afternoon, still chatting, Hugh gathered a fine bouquet of wild flowers for his sister, but Dexter felt no disposition to help, after his late experience in that line. When they arrived in sight of the Burnside home, Dexter said —

"I'll turn off here. I'll expect you early in the morning."

"But ain't you coming home with me? They'll be expecting you."

But Dexter made his excuses and they parted. Hugh found his sister looking rather low-spirited, but when he gave her the flowers she brightened up and seemed about to ask a question, but she ended by keeping it to herself. — Hugh said —

"I noticed you had the others in water, this morning, so that reminded me not to forget, this time."

60

"That was good of you. They are very beautiful."

"Yes, I took a good deal of pains in selecting them."

Hugh went off about his affairs, and Clara laid the flowers down, absently, and took up her cheerless reflections again.

At the earliest dawn, next morning, the young men were in the woods with their guns, but they found no wolf. They found tracks, but not the animal. They practiced long at a mark and Hugh discovered that Dexter was an incurably bad marksman, with a rifle. He explained that he was only used to shot guns and feathered game, but believed he could hit a wolf if he should see one, because living game would bring up his powers more effectually than an inanimate target. Hugh differed with him there.

The friends were gay during the first half of the day, but their spirits calmed, after that, and they presently lost interest in everything but silence and thought. They were soon exquisitely unhappy.[13]

Now followed two or three days of black solemnity. They were moping in the twilight on the river road about seven o'clock one evening. There had been a long silence. — Suddenly Hugh broke it. He said there must be a change; he could not live under this state of things. Said he —

"You're as dismal as I am, and I don't find anything better at home; Clara's as dreary as both of us put together. I can't understand it; it's not her way. I think she's in love."

Dexter winced, and said, with pretended indifference —

"Who is it?"

"O, I don't know. This morning she said that since you had come I was never around any more; said she was lonesome and wished Hooker or somebody would come."

Dexter said to himself, hotly: "I will end this boyish foolishness and be a man again. If being in love makes such a baby of me, I want no more experience of it. Since the spell has been on me I am so pitiful and silly that I am ashamed to be in my own company. I will go straight to her this very evening and tell her I have been absurd but am cured. I'll say, 'Now let us be plain sensible acquaintances, you to curb your prejudice against me as much as you can, I to make myself as endurable as possible — and go ahead on this basis; for while I am in the town we *must* be together more or less, we being cousins.' There — I feel healthier already!" Then aloud —

"Hugh, we are a couple of fools!"

Instantly the sunshine burst through the black misery of Hugh's face and he siezed Dexter's hand with enthusiasm. Said he —

"Shake hands on it! They're the noblest words that were ever spoken! You're going to stop all this foolishness — I see it in your face."

"That is precisely what I'm going to do!"

"Me, too. Shake again! It's been in my mind two days; I hadn't the pluck to out with it. Hale, I feel a hundred years younger and a hundred tons lighter! Now — when to begin?"

"The quicker the better."

"That's the right word again! You'll go by our house and say a word to the folks; I take the shortest cut from here to the Judge's. Good-bye."

"Good-bye."

As Dexter approached the Burnside house he saw young Hooker leave it with a springy gait and a happy air. This spectacle smote him sharply, and he wished he had been spared it; for now he should have a chilly and awkward interview and make a failure. The door was open. He stepped within without knocking, and stood a moment undecided; for Clara sat before him, bent over some work and did not raise her head. He could not believe she did not know he was there, so she must be maliciously enjoying his embarrassment. He was sinking into a mire of humiliation; he wished he was out again, yet was ashamed to retreat. He hesitated a fraction of an instant, then stepped fearfully forward and stumbled against a footstool. The girl looked up, in a startled way, then she sprang to her feet with a face alive with pleasure, and siezed both of the unfortunate's hands, exclaiming —

"I am so glad to see you!"

This sort of a reception was so entirely unlooked-for that Dexter's defeat was complete; he forgot his mission, he forgot his speech, his brain offered no suggestion, his mind was a blank. He could only hold the girl's hands and look stupidly and blissfully into her eloquent eyes and worship the enchanting beauty of her face.

Let us condense. At the end of a half hour there had been a good deal of conversation between these, and of a most agreeable and cheery kind. Then there was a knock at the door, — which had meantime been closed, — and young Hooker entered. What he saw seemed to disconcert him for a moment; then he said —

"I hope you have made up your mind favorably, Miss Clara; it is a lovely evening."

She said —

"I was very favorably inclined, but I am going to ask you to excuse me this time, Mr. Hooker."

"You said you thought you'd go," said Hooker, a little ruefully.

"Yes, that is true, but upon second thought I decided differently. — I hope you will not mind it."

When young Hooker was gone, Dexter said —

"What was it? — a ramble up the river road?"

"Yes."

"You changed your mind?"

"Yes."

"Why?"

A faint tinge of red showed in the girl's cheeks, and she said —

"Well, I — I don't care for walking — that is, not much — not generally, I mean. Walking is a dull matter."

The subject was changed, and the conversation wandered pleasantly afar in other channels. By and by Dexter said —

"Clara, shan't we go walking? It is a perfect night?"

The girl's face gave a quick consent; then she looked up, hesitating, and said, as one who has been confronted with a doubt —

"Would it be right, after refusing him? What do you think?"

"Well, I don't know, exactly. Will you go tomorrow night?"

The girl answered, with simplicity untrameled with doubt —

"O, yes — if you wish it."

By nine o'clock they were playing chess together — and both sitting on the same side of the table, which was too wide for any other arrangement — a thing which both spoke of with regret, but did not dwell upon. Occasionally the young girl heedlessly moved a knight into a wrong square. Instead of telling her so, the young man gently closed his hand over the hand that held the piece and lifted both to the proper square; and while she protested that she was right and he protested the contrary, her hand remained a prisoner, neither party seeming to think of that. These disputes grew more and more frequent and charming; the hand became so used to captivity, by custom, that it came to have a discontented look during its intervals of liberty, and presently got to drifting into imprisonment of its own accord, apparently. Things were progressing.

At eleven o'clock all was quiet everywhere — outside in the street, and in the house as well. The young man was sitting on the sofa with the young girl's head upon his breast and his arm around her waist. Conversation had ceased; words were not equal to the occasion.

Hugh burst suddenly into the room, with a jubilant "It's all right with *me!*" He paused, transfixed, while the couple before him unclasped themselves in confusion; then he added — to Dexter: "And it looks as if it is all right with you, too!"

"Indeed it is," said Dexter, smiling, and putting his arm, unforbidden, where it was before.

Hugh struggled with the situation, but could not seem to comprehend it entirely. Said he —

"Yes, it's all well enough, but look here! What you going to do about the Kentucky girl?"

"What Kentucky girl?" asked Dexter, amused at Hugh's perplexity.

Hugh leaned a hand upon the table, for bodily and mental support, stroked his troubled forehead with the other, and said —

"Maybe joy has joggled my mind off its balance a little, but as I understand it *I* was to make a final settlement one way or the other with my Milly to-night, who is the very perfection of her sex! and you were to clear out for Kentucky and make short work with *your* girl!"

"Well, I *have* made short work with 'my girl,' as you call her, as you can see for yourself — but I didn't say she was in Kentucky. That was your own deduction — but I thought I wouldn't meddle with it."

"Well, I'll be hanged if . . . . . so you ain't going to Kentucky at all, then?"

"I can't say that, exactly — that is, I can't state the time. It will depend mainly upon this young lady," said Dexter, glancing at Clara.

Hugh said —

"Are you two engaged?"

"I hope to be able to tell you before long that that mere formality has been arrived at," said Dexter. "Indeed, if you hadn't interrupted, there's a possibility that —"

"Now you have asked questions enough, Hugh," said Clara, bridling a little and covered with blushes, "go along with you and harass yourself with some other matter."

"So you are not engaged! Good — I'm ahead at last!" shouted Hugh, "for I *am!*" He paused a moment, and said, "Honest, now, Hale, wasn't there any Kentucky girl at all?"

"No."

"Was it my sister all the time?"

"Yes, all the time."

"Then it's all right, and I'm glad, and we'll shake hands all around — for I *like* you, and when I say a thing like that, I mean it!"

After the nightmare the happy dream, the semi-lethargy of rapture. The days no longer went on crutches, now; they were winged, and flew. It was curious to see how naturally and with what easy facility the lovers cast off their accustomed reserves and took to themselves the ways that belonged to their new relationship. The matter was as speedy and simple as is the putting off one familiar garment and putting on another that is equally familiar, and even fits a trifle better. The very first morning after that most memorable evening of her life, Clara Burnside found herself making her toilet under wholly new conditions: without perceiving anything odd or strange about it, she was not concerning herself as to whether her adornments might please herself or her mother or the world, but whether "he" would like them. She would cast aside a well-beloved ribbon, without a pang, saying simply, "No, he would not prefer that." She sang low to herself all through the mystery of the toilet service, but was hardly aware of it, since it was her heart that sang, her mind being busy with dreams, pictures, that followed one upon the other with augmenting splendors, like the gaudy surprises of the kaleidoscope.

When she came down stairs she saw that her mother knew everything, and also that she was profoundly happy and content in the knowledge. Dexter came early: the day slipped by, in a lingering ecstasy; the four lovers rambled the river road in the evening; then the elder couple had the Burnside parlor to themselves till a late hour. Everything was changed; everything was new, but nothing strange. When the two first entered and the girl laid aside her hat, it seemed a natural thing for the young man to smoothe her deranged hair with his awkward but caressing hands, and equally natural for her to bend her head with naive docility and endure and enjoy it. When she observed that his cravat was out of line with the horizon, it seemed a

natural procedure for her to tip-toe and re-tie it with her dainty fingers — and also natural for her to pull it out and tie and re-tie and tie
it again, although both knew that the first effort was successful and
that the later ones were nothing more; and it seemed equally natural
for him to steady her with his broad hands upon her shoulders while
she did her work, steal a kiss when she looked up for her thanks at its
conclusion, and take her requiting love-box as a grace, although it
was plainly intended as a punishment. When she threw off her shawl,
he, with the manner of one having authority, commanded her to put
it on again and not catch her death of cold; and she answered, with
the manner of one who is under authority —

"Let me keep it off only a minute — I'm so warm."

"No, not a minute; it is the most imprudent thing you can do; put it
on at once."

She, pleadingly —

"Do let me — only just the least little while."

He simply replied by taking the shawl and enveloping her in it
with his own hands and hooping it to her form with his arm around
her shoulders. She being obliged to endure these close quarters,
did so, only saying, in the meek voice of the oppressed and helpless —

"Well, have it your own way — I can't prevent it."

All the history of the acquaintanceship was gone over that evening,
and each precious detail of it lovingly dwelt upon. She charmed him
by confessing that she had loved him at first sight, and he enchanted
her with a confession that was the fellow to it. More than once, as the
talk went on, he mentioned that it was late and perhaps he had better
go, but she said it *could* not be as late as the clock pretended, and so
detained him, he being very willing. Late passers in the street judged
that there was sickness in the Burnside house, and they were not
strictly wrong; but there was nothing dangerous about it.

Other intoxicating days followed. Once Clara said —

"Did you ever imagine what it was like, before?"

"No, not even dimly, vaguely, faintly! My conception of what true happiness must be, was crude to grotesqueness; it was a pauper's idea of wealth, a blind man's notion of the sun."

That suggests the state they were in. They could talk of nothing but their marvelous happiness; they did nothing but contemplate it, wonder at it, inspect it from different standpoints, — walk around it, (so to speak,) trying to get a realizing sense of its mighty proportions and its bewildering altitude; and they always ended with honestly believing that the loves which the world had seen before were but Brooklyn Heights and Ben Lomonds to their Chimborazo.

As for Hugh the romantic, there was one little lack, his bliss could not be absolutely perfect until that lack should be supplied. The time quickly came for the eradication of this single defect.[14] Upon the highest summit north of the village was a small cottage which Judge Griswold had built as a pleasure resort for his wife. She had long been in the habit of driving to this place in warm weather and spending a part of the day there. She took a few friends with her and a servant or two; a dinner cooked on the spot, the bracing air, the wide prospect, and the luxurious rest after the fatigues of the steep and toilsome drive, made up a sufficient bill of compensations for the trouble taken.

One day Miss Martha drove up to Mrs. Burnside's door in the family carriage, followed by a buggy and a light open wagon; the buggy contained Milly and Toby; the wagon was freighted with colored servants and provisions. Mrs. Burnside, Clara, and Dexter were taken into the carriage, and the procession moved on. Hugh's chance to drive Milly to the Hill Cottage was lost, for he was absent — so Toby retained his place. However, word was left for Hugh to follow, when he should come home.[15]

The cavalcade prosecuted its slow and wearisome journey up the long hill, along a narrow, winding road bordered by a steep bank on one side and a precipice, "guarded" by a rotten fence, on the other, and finally halted on a sharp turn, five hundred yards below the Cottage, to give the horses a last rest. The view from this point was very fine, but Mrs. Burnside could not confine her thoughts to this feature. She said —

"Has there ever been a runaway here, Miss Martha?"

"No — God forbid!"

"We will suppose one, then. What would be the result?"

"A runaway horse might come from the Cottage down to this turn, alive, because the road is straight, and only tolerably steep; but neither horse, carriage nor driver could ever pass this turn and live."

"I should think that, myself."

"Think it! I *know* it! Destruction would be inevitable. If the horse kept straight on, there's the precipice. If he made this turn at full speed, the vehicle wouldn't make it, but would whirl instantly upside down and go crashing over the verge. Whoever tried to stop a running horse at this place would simply lose his own life and save nobody else's. There — you see, yourself, that a runaway here means death — nothing less."

Mrs. Burnside realized that all this was true. She shuddered, and proposed a change of subject.

The five hundred yards of straight road were soon traversed, and the fun began. Dexter and Clara wandered off together, the elderly ladies took post upon the front porch to talk and enjoy the superb view, and Milly found an isolated outlook and sat down in the shade of a tree, ostensibly to read, but her mind was elsewhere.[16] Dinner was served in due time and the horn called the loiterers home. Two or three pleasant hours followed, and then, late in the afternoon, the horses were brought, for the return journey. Milly went outside the fence and got into her buggy, to wait for Toby, who had gone to the barn for something. The other white people were grouped upon the front porch, ready to step into the carriage, and three or four colored servants were gathered together on the lawn before the house observing the proceedings and waiting for their wagon. Clara said —

"Milly's impatient; she is starting without Toby."

Miss Martha glanced toward the road and said —

"That is very imprudent. The horse is young and not to be depended on."

Clara looked again, and said —

"Look at her — she doesn't know that she is driving too fast for a down grade."

At that moment Milly turned her head and cast toward the group an appealing glance for help that turned every heart to stone with dismay. The horse was breaking into a run! Dexter started down through the grounds, with the servants shrieking in his wake. The three ladies stood white and motionless upon the porch gazing down the road after the flying vehicle. At every second it struck an obstruction and bounded high in the air. It traversed three hundred yards of the straight road in this frightful way, then flashed past a grove of trees and vanished like a thought. All along the path of its flight rose a thick cloud of dust.

The coachman had started down the hill, now, with the empty family carriage. All the servants had gone, before. The three women still stood looking in the one direction, speechless, almost breathless. After all the noise and turmoil and movement, had succeeded a stillness and absence of life and motion that was like death. The same thought was in each mind: "How many seconds will it take to reach the turn?" When they knew that the necessary time had elapsed, they glanced at each other's faces — a look which said "All is over." They shuddered, but no one spoke, no one shed a tear. They began to softly and unconsciously wash their hands together — that dumb expression of a suffering that is beyond conveying in words.

The family carriage came into view, returning. It climbed the hill tediously and slow, the servants following after it. Dexter was riding with the driver. Twice he shouted, as he approached. His voice brought a sharp shock to the three women, though they only divined the meaning — they could not understand the words. The carriage drove in, with its curtains all closed, and stopped before the three women; and while they hesitated as to who should first uncover its awful secret, Milly stepped out, alive and unhurt!

What fright had failed to do, the sudden and supreme joy of this moment accomplished: it swept away the strength of the three watchers, and they sunk into their chairs helpless and drowned in tears. — Then followed a season of devouring the young girl with kisses and caresses, and Mrs. Burnside said —

"We were not prepared for this, and not expecting it. The revulsion from despair to joy was overwhelming."

Dexter said —

"I shouted to you that all was safe and nobody hurt."

Mrs. Burnside said —

"It is very strange. — I heard the words, but they made no impression. I could not realize that the child *could* be saved; I heard the words distinctly, and yet I no more grasped their true meaning than if they had been said in an unknown tongue."

This was found to have been the case with her companions, also. Miss Martha gathered Milly to her arms for the third time, and said —

"You are alive, child, but it will take days to realize it; one can only believe it, now, nothing more. If you had been lost it would have killed your father. But how were you saved? What miracle did it? — and who was the instrument?"

"Hugh!"

The history followed, as Dexter had received it from the hero's lips. Hugh was on his way to the Cottage, on foot. He stopped at the sharp turn to rest. A farmer's heavy two-horse wagon, upward bound, stood upon the turn. Suddenly the farmer sprung from his seat and sought a safe place, shouting, "Out of the road, young man!"

Hugh glanced up and saw a horse coming furiously down toward him, throwing his forefeet high in the air with every plunge, a buggy bounding aloft behind him, and a cloud of dust following after. His first impulse was to save himself, but just then he recognized Milly. He siezed the farmer's horses and turned them across the roadway, so that the wagon formed a V-shaped angle with the fence; into this opening the runaway must come, there being no where else for him to go. Then he sprang into the opening himself, braced his big frame firmly, and as the horse plunged by, siezed the bit and surged back upon him.

That was the whole story. On the face of it it was impossible, and yet it was done. Hugh was not conscious of having really taken thought — he had only acted; there was not time for thought. Dexter concluded with —

"I have told it to you just as it happened. — You may go there and look at the ground, and you will say just what I say, 'It was absolutely impossible to do it, and yet it was done.' "

Hugh had remained behind, while a farmer's wife bandaged his cuts and bruises, but came in sight, now, driving Milly's horse. Very few heroes have ever received a more rapturous welcome than fell to his lot.

His bliss was perfect now. The one lack which he had felt before was supplied. That is to say, he had been conscious that his happiness could never be rounded and complete until he should save Milly's life in some splendid and blood-curdling way.

The adventure was a marvelous thing in the eyes of the servants. They discussed it, gilded it, and amplified it, with measureless satisfaction. Two of the elder ones were rabid and implacable religious disputatants, and were always engaged in a holy war. "Aunt Hanner" was orthodox, "Uncle Jim" was a sort of free-thinker. The former was overheard to say, in a burst of triumph —

"Dah, now, Jim, I reckon dis settles it! I reckon dis'll shet you mouf fo' you! Don't tell *me* no mo' dat dey ain't no special prov'dences! Dey ain't no use tryin' to git aroun' it *dis* time: de Lord sent Mars. Hugh dah for to stop dat hoss — you kin see it you own self!"

"Den who sent de hoss dah in sich a shape? — dat's what *I* wants to know!"

The next day found Hugh a hero to the whole village. Many people climbed the hill to look at the spot where the impossible feat had been performed. The two village papers published accounts of the affair three days later. The accounts differed in several respects; the facts suffered in both; neither account was a photograph of the matter, yet both bore a resemblance to it — that sort of remote likeness which protects the horses of amateur painters from being mistaken for alligators, or their storm pieces from being regarded as prairies on fire. — One of these accounts said —

> *To Compositor* — Please mis-spell a little, turn some letters and get in some wrong fonts. S.L.C.
>
> (Put this ¶ in small type.)

HEROIC ACHIEVEMENT. — On the 26th inst., as the family of Judge Griswold were descending the long hill from the Hill Cottage, in the family carriage, consisting of Miss Martha Griswold and Miss Milly, the other occupants being Mrs. and Miss Burnside and Mr. Hale Dexter, lately arrived from Kentucky, and two negro servants in front with the driver, the others following in another two-horse wagon and a buggy, they ran off and came plunging down the hill with frightful rapidity and constantly accelerating speed, and had just burst past the dangerous turn and were in the act of plunging into space over the precipice into instant and inevitable death, all the occupants shrieking and giving themselves up for lost, when our valued townsman and contributor to the Poet's Column of this journal over the signature "H" and the nom de plume "Alphonso," Mr. Hugh Burnside, and which has been copied extensively and greatly admired in this region, especially his shorter pieces and emanations of sentiment, sprang forward, he being fortunately on his way to the Hill Cottage at that moment, riding on the manure wagon of one of our oldest and most esteemed subscribers, Mr. Buck Farley, who had been to town and was on his way home again this early in the day with his manure on account of his wife being sick, and siezed the off horse by the throat latch, with herculean strength and threw him upon his haunches as he would a child, and held him there, which checked the other's onward flight and saved the entire family including servants and coachman from a sickening and horrible death too dreadful to contemplate even in imagination, though he sustained some severe but not serious injuries himself, through his noble self-sacrificing act, mainly in his legs and adjacent portions of his head and body, though no bones broken, thanks be to Him who suffereth not even a sparrow to fall to the ground unnoted, let alone people like the Griswolds,

73

whose position in this community is too well known by all to require endorsement from us, and is now about the village again the recipient of praises and congratulations from high and low, and the cynosure of all eyes, the observed of all observers, may his glory diminish not and his shadow never be less! Will the lying slave of the *Torch of [Civilization]* [17] attempt to pervert the facts in *this* noble episode as in all others where he drags his slimy length athwart the fair fields of truth, leaving it blistered and smouldering behind him with the corruption of his fetid utterance and the venomous blight of his crime-festered soul?

The history of the adventure, as given in the other paper, was as near the truth as this, and closed with a vigorous reflection upon the editor whom I have been quoting, the cracker on the end of it being a suggestion that his family of beggars had improved in raiment since he had been appointed to hand around the contribution-box in church, and yet were manifestly giving the neighboring clotheslines a rest.

Milly wrote a glowing and grateful account of her peril and preservation to her parents, and gave it into the hands of Toby, who sent it to his mother in Arkansas. Miss Martha's account, with interesting additions about our four lovers, traveled the same road.

Dexter and Hugh had become pretty constant companions — at least during the earliest part of the mornings, before their dearer friends were up. Hugh had bagged one wolf with his gun, one had been poisoned by some bounty-seeking pelt-hunter, and Dexter had had one chance — but missed. Dexter was sorer about his marksmanship than he allowed to appear on the surface; for, to be a Kentuckian and a bad shot was to be unpleasantly conspicuous. It was a new thing in nature. The honor of his State was at stake in his person; so he resolved to achieve a triumph if perserverance could compass it. Every morning found him haunting the wolves' lurking place.

Three weeks after the date of the beginning of this story, there came an unlucky day for Hugh Burnside. Everything went wrong with him. By nightfall he had reached a very advanced stage of irritation. Now appeared Clara with a copy of the [*Torch of Civilization*] [18] damp from the press, and assailed her brother in caustic terms about a poem in the paper entitled "Hail, Cupid's Holy Darlings!" and signed "Alphonzo." The verses were so frankly descriptive and significant, that there was no need to name names; it was plain to all that our four lovers were the darlings whom the poet exalted with his laudations and bedewed with his sentimental sap. — Hugh was astonished to find that Clara was not charmed and grateful. He said as much. Clara burst into tears of mortification, then flew into a rage and delivered herself of such a volley of sharp and lacerating words that the poor poet was hurt beyond help. A great and portentous calm settled down upon the soul which the day's ill luck had so tortured and bedeviled, and he rose up as one who is wounded in the house of his friends, and said in a voice choked with emotion —

"My mother has chidden me for another's fault, I have tried to do honor to my sister in my poor way and she tramples ruthless upon my heart for reward. I have tried to do right, but the unfortunate are ever at odds with fate. I have often felt that I was not wanted here, yet strove to blind myself to the bitter truth. But have your will. I go forth to wander friendless in the cold world — perhaps to die. So be it. And if you shall sometime chance to hear that the poor outcast is no more, say of him, 'His merit was small, his virtues few, but his true heart ceased not to beat for his own while life remained, even though they despised him all his days, and in the frail blossom of his helpless youth spurned him from the home of his fathers with loathing.'"

He stood upon the threshold, cast one agonized look around the house of his fathers, then solemnly departed.

Clara said —

"O, the huge intolerable baby! Now he will come back at midnight with the appetite of a menagerie, and then sit up till morning churning his clabber brains for buttery rhymes of woe and suffering — a pest take all poets, amen!" Then after a pause: "In his right mind he is so good and dear — it is only when he is inspired that one wants to kill him."

In due time the sufferer, staggering under the burden of his woe, entered the Griswold parlor, with tragic mien. — Milly was there alone, crying over his odious poem. She raised her wet face and exclaimed with anguish —

"O, go away, go away! I don't see how you can look anybody in the face!"

Hugh straightened himself up, folded his arms, then dropped his chin upon his breast. He said, with dismal resignation —

"This, then, is the fiat! Very well. So be it. Spurned with contumely by those allied to me by ties of blood, driven forth from the home of my fathers almost with blows, it is fitting that I be banished with ignominy, forever and without a hearing, by one whose slave I was and am and ever shall be, yet to whom I am nothing — nothing but despised dust, a hated viper! It is well. I go — and may heaven forgive you for what you have done, as I do. All is over. Here — take your book-mark, — imperishable symbol of a perishable love —"

"O, Hugh!"

"Take it. Return to me the tributes of affection which I have given you in happier hours, that no memento of my wronged heart's beguilement shall remain to mock my few remaining moments of existence in this troubled world."

"O, Hugh, what can you mean? Why do you —"

"Hear me, woman! When I am no more, say of me, 'He' " —

The frightened girl waited to hear no more, but flew from the room calling hysterically for her aunt, and the next moment Dexter entered from another door. Said he, furiously —

"You incredible ass! You deserve a hiding! What the mischief could have possessed you to — to —"

76

"Spare your reproaches, sir," said Hugh, with lofty dignity. "You have insulted me. Yesterday I would have taken your life for it. To-day I am a crushed and broken being, whose pride is gone, whose self-love is dead, who desires only to lay his ruined life in the grave and be at peace. That life will I sacrifice with my own hand. Seek me on the morrow and you shall find not me, but only my poor corse. Spend your fury upon that; dishonor my remains — what else shall they be good for?"

"Your remains will be good to feed worms with. That is what I will do with them."

Judge Griswold, dusty with travel, thrust his head in at the door just in time to hear this last remark, smiled grimly at Dexter, then drew back and closed the door softly. Dexter continued —

"Look here, Hugh, drop this calf-talk, and do drop writing poetry, too. If you must write it, write it about yourself, and leave other people alone."

"My end is near — I shall never write more."

"O, rubbish! There is no danger of your committing suicide, but there *is* danger of your wailing around and threatening it until you make yourself the laughing-stock of the village."

Hugh said with gloomy impressiveness —

"Rail on, if it pleases you — I am dead to affront. By this hand I die before the morrow's sun shall gild the eastern hills."

"What an idiot! Go home and take a pill!"

Hugh said, mournfully —

"You little imagine with what fatal fidelity I shall follow your mocking counsel." He put out his hand. "Farewell — do you forgive me?"

"For your infernal poem? Yes — and it's a good deal to do, too. Now take a dose of paregoric and go to bed."

They shook hands, and Hugh said, tearfully —

"When I am gone, —"

"O go and be hanged!" cried Dexter, cheerfully, and the stricken one moved solemnly away.

Dexter watched him a moment or two, musingly, then said —

"I shall have to go after the wolves betimes, in the morning, if I want to be ahead of him, for this mood will keep him grinding doggerel all night and give him an early start."

There was a knock at the door, and a servant ushered in four men, Captain Simon Wheeler at the head. He said a word was desired with Mr. Dexter. He introduced them as Mr. Baxter, Mr. Billings, and Mr. Bullet, and added —

"The most celebrated detectives in America — all belong to Inspector Flathead's celebrated St. Louis Detective Agency — Flathead that writes the wonderful detective tales, you know."

There was something contagious about the Captain's adoring admiration of the great personages. It infected Dexter somewhat.

"Sir," said the little red-headed, quick-motioned person, named as Baxter, speaking rapidly, "please to allow us to put a few questions to you in a professional way. You are aware that the desperado Jack Belford has broke jail again?"

"Yes — I saw the notice three days ago." *

"Just so. Here it is — five hundred dollars reward, dead or alive. A great pity, very great pity — he was to be hung tomorrow. Large build — Had on when he escaped, prison uniform, and so-f'rth and so-f'rth and so-f'rth — no use to go into particulars if you've read it. You hunt in a certain part of the woods every morning, I understand."

"Yes."

"Seen any suspicious characters around?"

"No."

---

* Dexter has reference here to a reward poster, not to the newspaper account which he read in chapter 2. Even so there seems to be some discrepancy in time resulting from Twain's extensive revision and expansion of the story. On MS p 243, Twain asserts that the day of Hugh's dismissal and Dexter's meeting with the detectives is "Three weeks after the date of the beginning of this story." One has to assume, then, that the sheriff of Boggsville took four weeks (the escape occurred the week before Dexter read about it) to get the reward posters printed and circulated.

The short, slow, dull-looking man called Billings, lifted a fat finger, paused a moment, then said with weighty deliberation —

"That is, in prison uniform?"

"No."

Billings nodded his head slowly three times, and muttered "Um" each time.

Nobody spoke for a moment or two. Then the long lean man called Bullet, who had been sitting pondering, with the end of one of his talons pressed against his forehead, looked up, fixed his eyes upon Dexter and said —

"Tracks?"

"Do you mean have I seen any?"

"Yes."

"What sort?"

"Human."

"I remember none."

"Think."

Dexter thought — then said —

"No — I call to mind none but wolf tracks."

A look of intelligence passed between the several detectives. Bullet murmured —

"So? — in disguise!"

Billings murmured —

"Aha — just so — in disguise."

Baxter murmured —

"As one might expect — in disguise."

Capt. Wheeler slapped his thigh and murmured, admiringly —

"O, don't they know how to go about it, though! You bet your life!"

A considerable silence ensued. Then Billings raised his fat finger, paused a moment, and said —

"Were the tracks bare, or shod?"

Dexter looked a trifle surprised, then said —

"I would not know a wolf's track if the beast were shod."

Billings nodded his head slowly three times, and gravely muttered "Um" each time.

Baxter rattled off a sharp fire of questions about matters that seemed foreign to the subject, and appeared to value the enlightenment he got out of the answers. By and by the lean Bullet removed his reflective finger from his forehead and broke the silence —

"No other tracks?"

"Well — if it is worth mentioning — I've seen a cow's tracks there."

Another look of intelligence was exchanged between the detectives. — Bullet murmured —

"So? — another disguise!"

Billings murmured —

"Another disguise!"

Baxter muttered irritably —

"Confound it, this complicates it!"

Captain Wheeler muttered under his breath, and suffocating with admiration — [19]

"Dad blame 'em, nothing can't escape 'em — they're inspired!"

There was deep pondering, now, and a long silence. Then the fat finger came up impressively, there was a pause, and Billings said —

"Was the cow shod?"

Dexter stared a moment, then said —

"They don't shoe cows here."

Billings nodded and "Um'd" as gravely as before.

At the end of two hours the interview came to an end, and detective Baxter said —

"We are much obliged to you sir. You must excuse our intruding here the moment we reached the village, for ours is a profession that cannot wait and never rests. You perceive our motto."

The three men threw open their coats, and displayed, pinned to each vest, a big silver disk with a staring human eye engraved upon it, surrounded by the modest legend, "WE NEVER SLEEP."

They took their leave, and as Capt. Wheeler passed out he whispered in Dexter's ear —

"You see what they are, hey? By George if he was disguised in a chipmunk's hide, let alone a cow's, they'd find him."

Dexter found that supper had been waiting some time; but the family were not visible. — Toby answered his call, and said —

"Ole missis sick. She didn't git no furder dan Drytown. I reckon she considable sick, too, kase ole Mars. he come an' make Miss Martha pack right up an' tuck her away a-boomin'." [20]

"That is bad news. Did he leave any word for me?"

"Yes sah. He gimme dis little note, an' he say he gwyne to bust my head if I fo'git to gim it to you."

The note read thus:

> "I had but a moment to stay. I had often wondered what could be delaying your mission, but I heard a sentence from your lips that showed me that its consummation is now close at hand; therefore I would not interrupt your conversation. I shall return with all possible speed to compass your escape, and shall be here as early as I can in the morning. If you should need assistance before, apply promptly to Major Barnes, who will furnish fleet horses and everything necessary."

Dexter said to himself —

"This is odd. Either nobody has written him or else the letters have miscarried. He is not a brute, but a gentleman. If he knew that Hugh saved Milly's life, he would stand between Hugh and any man's bullet, instead of making himself an accessory to his murder. Very well; he will hear all about it before he gets to Drytown; and then in place of despising me for not killing Hugh he will be pretty sincerely grateful. It's a comical thing that he should have overheard about the only sentence in my whole talk with Hugh that *could* be misunderstood!"

Toby wanted a letter written to his old mother, after supper. He showed the one he preferred, in the Ready Letter-Writer, and Dexter sat down and copied it — to-wit:

Form for a Letter of a Young Gentleman of Fortune to the Father of a Young Lady, requesting permission to pay his addresses to her.

HONORED SIR: I am a young gentleman of position, education and independent means, of which matters you can satisfy yourself by applying to[*here insert name or names.*] I have observed with deep interest, the varied excellencies of your angel daughter, in whom I find rare and exquisite beauty, combined with the nobler charms of purity, truthfulness, a sensitive and poetical nature, a fine mind, equipped with elegant accomplishments, and that sweetest of feminine functions, the gift of song. Such a life-companion, to cast the oil of peace upon the troubled waters of the arid desert of my lonely life and bid its flowers spring anew adown its blighted, joy-tombed vistas, my heart has longed to call its own, all unworthy as I am, of such a Boon. With your permission, kind sir, I desire to lay the poor offering of self and fortune at the feet of Miss [*here insert name of party,*] with a view to ultimate matrimony, if my suit shall prosper and this the faint dim ray of my early hope expand into the rich and clustered fruit of perfected fruition.

With sentiments of Exalted esteem, I beg to sign myself,

[*Name.*] [21]

It was duly signed "Your loving Son, TOBY," and forwarded to "Old Mammy Betsy" in Arkansas.

Chapter [5]

DURING the tedious journey to Drytown, Judge Griswold sat absorbed in thought. He could not understand Dexter's long delay in so important a matter as the destruction of a fellow being for duty's sake. However, those words about feeding Hugh to the worms, meant that the delay was to cease now. That, at any rate, was satisfactory. Miss Martha's several efforts to start a conversation got small attention; so she finally gave up and went to sleep. Drytown was reached about midnight.

Mrs. Griswold said she was feeling better, and believed she should be able to go home in a day or two. Miss Martha said —

"I judged by brother's letter that you were only worn out with watching, and with grief for your great loss, and that a good rest would make you well again."

"Yes, watching and grief — and another matter that lay heavy upon my mind." Here she looked wistfully at her husband, but he gave no sign. He knew what she referred to. He found himself in an uneasy position; for he wanted to be hurrying toward Guilford, to be ready for the coming tragedy, yet did not know what excuse to make for going, since he did not wish to make any distressful revelations to his wife in her present circumstances. Mrs. Griswold boded no good from the Judge's silence. She was troubled and thoughtful a moment; then she said to Miss Martha —

"I was expecting mournful news from home. I still am."

"Then you may set your mind at rest, for there's none of that sort for you — very far from it."

Mrs. Griswold's face lighted with a surprised gladness, and she said —

"You have no bad news to tell? I can hardly credit it. Then what news have you?"

"Well, no news is good news, isn't it? There's nothing new since that which we told you in our letters, and surely that was good news."

"Your letters! — Whose letters?"

"Mine and Milly's."

"We have not had a line from either of you."

"Not a line from either of us? That is astonishing. Then you don't know that Milly escaped horrible mutilation and death by what was simply a miracle and nothing less?"

Mrs. Griswold's face blanched, and the sudden dismay paralyzed her tongue. The iron Judge, too, was stricken for once, and he betrayed that he was human. He showed strong excitement — an unusual thing for him; he even trembled like a girl. Evidently the hidden great deeps of his nature had been touched at last.

"Tell it!" he said; "tell the whole matter! We know nothing of it. — Go on, go on — why do you hesitate!"

His eye flamed upon his sister as if it would consume her. She began her story, with loving attention to detail and dramatic circumstance; and as she proceeded the fire in the Judge's eyes burned more and more eloquently, and few had seen him so stirred in all his long life. When the story was finished, he exclaimed —

"And we came so near losing her! — It was superbly done! Strength, courage, generalship — there are not two men in the State who could have done it. Now, no more dramatic concealments — who is this marvelous man?"

"You would not guess in an hour, brother."

"I do not wish to guess. I want to go and tell him he has saved our all and he can command our all!"

"He can command your all?"

"Yes — I have said it. Why?"

"He is young; he is a gentleman; he loves Milly, she loves him. *She* is the reward he will demand."

"Then he shall have her! Tell me his name."

"Hugh Burnside!"

84

The Judge was standing. This shot almost brought him to the ground, so great was the unexpectedness of it. Mrs. Griswold sprang partly up in bed, turned an imploring look upon her husband, and fell back again, exhausted with terror, without speaking the words that were in her mind. The Judge strode swiftly to her side and bent down and whispered in her ear —

"Tell Martha nothing. I will be in the saddle in five minutes. I will save him. Never fear; I shall be in time. No harm shall come to him."

Mrs. Griswold looked her gratitude, and the next moment the Judge was gone. A few minutes later he was spurring toward Guilford with a long journey before him but a fleet horse under him.

Mrs. Griswold said to Miss Martha —

"There, now you may go to your bed, and tell me the rest of the news in the morning. I could bear no more to-night, good or bad. You little imagine the full importance of the tidings you have given us, nor how thankful we shall be, all our lives, that they came so timely."

Chapter [6]

TOWARD THE MIDDLE of the same night of which we have just been speaking, two young druggist clerks, of Guilford, were on their way home. — They were laughing over something that had just happened. One said —

"O, there's no danger of its hurting him. It will only make him sleep like a brazen image for a few hours and then he'll come out of it all right. *He* commit suicide, indeed! It will be the best joke on him we've ever had in the village. We'll never let him hear the last of it!"

"Good — so we will. But look here: suppose he just takes enough to make him stupid, and goes mooning around and tumbles into the river?"

The other thought a moment, then said —

"There's something in that. Somebody might have seen him buy the stuff, without our knowing it; or he might tell somebody he bought it."

"Yes; then we'd be in a pretty fix. If the bottle was never found, we couldn't prove it wasn't poison we sold him."

"It begins to look less and less funny to me, Jimmy."

"Dog'd if it don't to me, too, Bob. Now I'll tell you what we've got to do. We've got to keep perfectly mum about this business if anything happens to that fool — don't you know that?"

"You bet you I know it! Mum's the word. I ain't in as much of a hurry to run and tell about this thing as I was."

About this time Hugh Burnside was passing Mrs. Higgins's, the last house at the north end of the village. He moved on, with groping, uncertain steps, up the river road, some fifty-yards to a grassy open in the hazels. He said plaintively, and with a thick utterance —

"It has begun its fatal work! How drowsy I am! The sleep of death — the welcome sleep that the sore-hearted and the banished long for — is coming. Here, in this public spot, where the first passers will see my lonely form, I will lay me down and forget my trials forever.

87

At last the hard hearts will soften, perchance. At last there will be some to pity the poor outcast who never did any harm and yet was ever repulsed and despised."

He sat down on a huge log, a favorite resting place for village promenaders, leaned his head upon his hand and began to breathe heavily. Gradually the drowsiness stole over him and he muttered as one does in sleep —

"Will she, the stony-hearted, recognize her cruel work and be smitten with remorse at last? Will she — will she — shed one little tear of pity over — over —"

He was nearly asleep. He was silent a little while, then muttered —

"This — then — is — is Death! . . . . Awful thought! . . . . . . I — I — took more — th — than I — intended to."

His voice sunk to incoherent mutterings, and he presently fell and lay stretched upon his face in front of the great log, torpid and motionless. The sympathetic moon, hidden until now, put her face to first one and then another ragged window in the drifting cloud-rack and peeped pathetically down upon her sorrow-worn calf.

Now came Captain Wheeler picking his stealthy way on tip-toe along the river path, stopping occasionally to listen. When he reached the grassy open, he halted, some six feet from where Hugh lay, and began to talk to himself —

"I wonder wher' he could 'a' went to." He scratched his head in a puzzled way, and continued. "I knew by the way he hung around in the shadows by the drug store that he was up to some murderous villainy or other — got the cold eye of a pirate, that poet. I see him slink away with that bottle. He thought he was playing his game pretty sharp, but he had the old detective's eye on him — unerring as fate. But rot him, I've lost track of him! Can't seem to start sight of him anywhers. Well, I'll take a minute's rest here and think it over. This moonlight ain't bright enough for detective work, hardly — that is, when a body hasn't got his clews arranged and decided on."

He sat down on Hugh's big frame, and leaned his back comfortably against the log. He put his hat on the ground in front of him and proceeded to talk to it —

"Now gimme your attention a minute. I've lost him, but my! it's only for a minute or so — when I get on a man's track, you understand, he might as well throw up the sponge. *You* know me well enough to know that, don't you? Very well; then you just bet all you're worth that he's my meat, sooner or later. There ain't no escaping me — I'm as bound to trace him out and get him as if he was a spectator at a riot and I was a random bullet. Ain't that so? Don't you forget it! There's something awful about being a detective. If you're a true detective, night's just the same as daylight to you — a whisper's just the same as a yell — nobody can't hide a secret from you *no* way. — Just give you a clew and that's all you want. Just an old glove's enough — or a foot-print from a ragged boot — or an old cigar-stub with the defendant's particular chew-mark on the end of it. If a detective's got three or four little clews like that, they just lead him as dead straight to his man as a train of powder would show fire the way to the magazine. Why, when that great mysterious murder was done yonder in Chicago, what sort of clews did the detectives have? Nothing in the world but a sledge-hammer, and one of the criminal's boots, and his handkercher with his name on it, and his ambrotype, and some other little traps of his'n. That's all the clews they had. They've got 'm yet. Do you reckon that that assassin 'll escape? Never! Not if he lives long enough. You bet your life, they'll get him . . . . This log's mighty warm; mighty soft, too: rotten, I reckon. Sort of uncomfortable."

He got up, took his hat, and moved off a step or two, buried in reflection. — He stood musing awhile, then said —

"Now lemme see — how'll I go to work to track out this chap and find him? . . . . . . Good! I've got it — got it sure! In five minutes I'll lay my hand on him! I'm as dead sure of him now as if I had him in my grip. In just five minutes by the clock, if I don't take him into camp, call me no detective!"

Then he hurried away toward the village.

The Captain was hardly gone before Tom Hooker, the reporter, came strolling along. He was talking to himself, after the manner of persons in a certain condition — no, uncertain condition is the better phrase. But for one thing, this trim and tidy youth would have looked as he always looked. — That one thing was, that he had his cap on wrong side before. Trivial as this variation was, it transformed the young fellow. It changed him from himself into an ingenious and artistic caricature of himself. It was as significant, too, as Ophelia's straws. Tom Hooker had been drinking. He had not drank enough to make him stagger, but enough to make him just a shade uncertain on his legs. A random hiccup afflicted him at intervals. He halted in Hugh's neighborhood and began to fumble in a thick-fingered way about his forehead. Presently he stopped, and looked puzzled. He thought awhile, shook his head, then fumbled again. Again he desisted, and said —

"Tha('k!) that's curious. Brim's gone. I thought I brought it with me."

He fumbled about his forehead again, without result, then took off the cap and examined it, following its circle around until he found the missing brim. He was greatly pleased. He said —

"Here 'tis! I must 'a' o('hk!) overlooked it before."

He put it on again — wrong side first, as formerly — then felt, to make sure all was right.

"Brim gone again! Something's matter wi'this cap; I ca('k!) can't unstan' it."

He took it off, searched and found the brim once more, and was greatly surprised and puzzled. He stood thinking it over and inspecting the cap in silence. Finally he said —

"I see how 'tis. Somebody's played a j('k!) a j('k!) a j('k!)oke on me. They've turned the cap around and sewed the brim on the back side. Fix that easy enough, — get tailor to s('ic!) sew it on front side where it belongs."

90

He ripped the brim off, put it in his pocket, and put the rest of the cap on his head again, with a satisfied heart and a mind at peace.[1]

He took a couple of steps, stopped, and said —

"There — my legs are so weak. It is on account of love. That is, d(*uck!*)isappointed love. I wish Dexter hadn't come. I wish I'd never seen *her*. None know her but to see her, none lose her but to praise, — p('ic!) poet says." (Here he observed Hugh, and his spirits lifted at once.) "Hey? *Dead* man? — Noble item! O, *this* ain't any good find, I reckon! There hasn't been an item in six months that could begin with it. Suicide, I wonder? . . . . . . 'S('k!) 'Sass*ination*, I hope! A suicide's a prime thing in its way, but it don't begin with 'n' assassination. You've got to be mighty reserved and respectful about a suicide, or you'll have the surviving relatives in your hair. You can't spread, you know — family won't stand it. You've got to cramp your item down to a short quarter of a column — and you've always got to say it's t('k!)emporary aber*ration*. Temporary abberation! — and half these suicides haven't got anything to aberrate!"

Still rattling cheerfully along, as if he were entertaining a company instead of himself, he sat comfortably down on Hugh's sturdy bulk, got out a pipe, cleaned it, knocked it on his palm, blew through it, then proceeded to load it.

"But you let a man be assassinated once, and you can string him out to five columns. More you say, more the family like it." (Scrapes a match on the "corpse;" forgets it, talks on; it burns out, scorching his fingers with it[s] last gasp.) "Yes, a suicide's a kind of lean stuff for literature, but" (giving the "corpse" an approving slap,) "y(ic!) *you're* the right sort, m' fren'! I wish they'd gashed you up a little. You'd show up a nation sight gaudier in print. I wonder if it wouldn't be all fair in the way of business to gash him up a little myself . . . . . . No, 'twouldn't be pleasant. I couldn't do it. But I regret exceedingly that it was o('k!) overlooked. Now half the time" (scraping another match on the "corpse" — without result, since he scraped the wrong end of the match — though he enclosed it carefully in the hollow of his hand and went on talking while he waited for it to burn,) "half the time, what you take for a suicide's only a drunk — that's all — only a drunk — and all of a sudden he comes alive on the inquest, and where's your item? — That's it — where's your item. G('k!) gone where the woodbine twineth! A bogus suicide's a painful object. It's discouraging to journalism. But" (slapping the "corpse" affectionately), "*you're* all right, you know. I'm proud of you; and you're worthy to be proud of, too. . . . . . . I've got him all to myself, too! Won't the other paper feel sore when I fetch him out with thunder-and-lightning display-lines in the morning!"

Here a disturbing thought struck him, and he got up and stood pondering a while. Presently he said —

"No, there's no getting around it. It's after midnight; our paper's gone to press. Too late to get him into this week's issue! O, this is too bad. If he stays here, the other paper will get him too. Come, that won't do. I found him — he belongs to me. . . . . . . Can't I hide him somewhere till next week, and then realize on him? . . . . . . It's a g('k!) good idea. I'll take him home. If my room-mate objects I'll flog him . . . . . . Yes, I'll take him home and hide him under the bed till I want him. It's pretty warm weather but I reckon he'll . . . ." [2]

The rest of the sentence died out in mutterings as he walked away. He traversed the fifty-yards between Hugh's grassy retreat and the widow Higgins's boarding house and presently returned with a wheelbarrow. With infinite trouble he finally managed to get his limp treasure across the barrow, and then proceeded toward Mrs. Higgins's, remarking —

"Noblest item of the age! Perfect m(ic!) mine of literature!"

His room was a back one on the ground floor. His room mate, Lem Sackett, had found his bed unendurable because of the heat, and was stretched upon the carpet, sound asleep. Hooker trundled his barrow softly in there, stumbled over something in the dark, and his freight slid ponderously out and rested, limp and massive, across Sackett's face. Sackett struggled from under it, half smothered, sprang up and came in contact with Hooker, whom he floored with a random blow, then lost his balance, and went down with him. But he immediately mounted his adversary's breast and began to pound him well. As soon as Hooker could get his breath, he exclaimed, in a guarded voice —

"Hold up, you fool! — it's nobody but me."

Sackett desisted, and said —

"You, is it? Well, what do you come sprawling over me for?"

"I didn't sprawl over you."

"You did. Somebody did."

"It wasn't me — it was the dead man."

"The what!"

"Dead man."

"What dead man?" asked Lem, with a shudder.

"The one I fetched here."

"Gracious! where is he?"

"He's around here somewhere. Feel for him."

"Feel for him yourself if you want him. — I don't. . . . . . Ugh! here he is!"

Sackett recoiled from the touch, then shrunk away, out of reach of the object. Said he —

"Did you kill him?"

"Me? No!"

"Who did?"

"I don't know."

"Well then, how does he come to be with you?"

"I found him."

"You found him, you idiot! You talk as if he was a valuable property."

"That's what I take him to be."

"Tom Hooker, have you lost your mind?"

"Why?"

93

"You find a dead man lying around, and you lug him home with you, as if it never occurred to you that he would be tracked here, and you and me be —"

"Good land, I never thought of that! I've been drinking, but I'm sober enough now to begin to feel sick about this business. What shall we do?"

"Do? Why we've got to get him out of this, in less than two minutes. Not a second to lose. Pretty soon it will be dawn."

"I tell you, Lem, I begin to feel scared. Where 'll we take him to?"

"Put him where you got him. Is it far?"

"No. Right up yonder at the Lover's Roost."

"Well, come! — don't fool away any time. I'm getting in an awful state."

They freighted the wheelbarrow with Hugh and trundled him softly away, with many a frightened glance over their shoulders. They deposited him where Tom had originally found him, and then retired to a safe distance and sat down on the river bank, tired, puffing and perspiring, to steal a moment's rest. The moon was hidden, there were no sounds, all nature lay in a boding gloom. Presently Lem said, in a low, dismal voice —

"It's a nice piece of business — that's what it is. We'll swing for this."

"Well, it's your own fault, Lem — to hop up and smash a friend's nose for nothing, that way. I never saw such a peppery devil."

"For nothing! Slam a clammy corpse across a man when he's sound asleep! — Call that nothing?"

"It was dark as pitch, — how could I help it?"

"Confound it, what did you want to bring the grisly thing there, for, anyhow?"

"Where else could I put him? — in the buttery?"

"No — leave him where you found him."

"Yes, it's all well enough to say that, *now* — anybody can tell what ought to have been done, *now*. But I was trying to save him for an item." Then he added, regretfully, "and he would have made the very

94

sublimest item this poor little one-horse town ever saw, too! I had a monopoly; but now he's got to be divided with the other paper, of course. I can't ever seem to have any luck."

Lem said, gloomily —

"There's another item that's got to be divided, too — that's our hand in this business."

Tom said, with a shiver —

"Yes, that's so. And Lem, who knows but we've had more hand in the business than we think for?"

Lem started, with a vague apprehension —

"What do you mean, Tom?"

"I mean, suppose he wasn't dead, in the first place, but only stunned?"

"O, Tom, it's been in my mind a dozen times!"

"He was very limp, Lem. Maybe he wasn't dead — at first."

"It's awful, Tom! He tumbled out on me —"

"And when I fell, I fell on him — heavy, too! I thought I heard him groan! I *did* hear him! Seems to me I did, anyway."

"Tom, he was only stunned at first, sure as you live. *We* finished him, O my goodness!"

"No, *I* did, Lem. I tumbled him out — I fell on him. I wish I was dead!"

"No, it ain't any use mincing it — it was *us*. If I hadn't hit you, you wouldn't have fallen on him. — It was falling on him that finished him. No, we are brother murderers, Tom. And doomed!"

"Lemmy, I feel worse about it now, than I did before — ever so much."

"So do I, Tom — because before I didn't seem to be to blame. But now! — it don't make any difference if it *was* an accident, the very idea of killing a human being, even accidently, is horrible. O, I kept thinking maybe he would come to."

"So did I, Lem. But he was good and dead when we got done with him."

"So he was, so he was, poor devil. Tom, shall you ever be able to sleep again? I know I shan't."

"Nor I. I'll always see him, night and day, as long as I live."

Now that fear had set their imaginations at work, there was no end to the horrors that were conjured up. They succeeded in convincing themselves, by the absurdest reasoning, that they had killed that man and could never hope for peace of mind again.

The young fellows went home and finished their conversation in their room, in the dark. Tom said —

"We must save our lives as long as we can. As soon as it is light we must straighten things up, here, and then go to bed and stay there all day. We must pretend to be sick, and say we were not out of the house in the night.'"

"What is the use, Tom?" said Lem, despondently, "didn't your nose bleed all over the body? and didn't it bleed all along the road? Its a track that a detective —"

"Don't you worry about detectives. The average detective couldn't see it, if it was pointed out to him; and he couldn't follow it if it was eleven foot wide. But other people will find us out. Maybe the other boarders —"

"No, it won't be them, I reckon, because they never hear anything and never see anything. But it's all one — somebody will find us out."

"Lem, let us be brothers from this out, and stand by each other, through thick and thin, till we go to the gallows."

"There is my hand on it, Tom — but don't speak that awful word any more. It kills me to hear it. Tom, we must never divulge."

"Never! Not even on the rack."

"The dawn is breaking — there will not be many more for us to see. Tom, we are so young to die!"

"I know it — and yet I feel old — so old and miserable!"

Chapter [7]

A S LEM HAD SAID, the dawn was breaking.[1] The grey twilight stole gradually upon the still world, and the features of the soft summer landscape began to reveal themselves. Hugh Burnside stirred uneasily in his torpor; turned over; turned again, and presently sat up and looked about him wonderingly. He reflected awhile, then said to himself —

"No, it is not the other world. I am very glad of that. Plainly I didn't take enough. I am very glad of that, too. I have been a fool. Well, it is the last time I'll be one. I'll go home and be sensible."

He got up and stretched his stiff limbs and was about to start, when another thought struck him, and with violence, too —

"No! I should be a greater fool than ever to do that. Those drug clerks will make me the laughing-stock of the whole town. That won't answer. Now what shall I do? I think my cue is to mysteriously disappear for a while. That is the very thing to do. The drug clerks will keep still — no question about that. Mother will grieve over her injustice to me; Clara will grieve for having ordered me to never cross the threshold of my childhood's home again; and *she*, even she whose unexacting slave I was, may peradventure feel some touch of remorse for banishing me her father's house with threats and execrations when she comes to know the full extent of her awful work. The cruel public will pity me and will cease at last, when too late, to make jibes about me. Then be it so. I will mysteriously disappear from the haunts and the eyes of men. There is nothing in literature more romantic than such a fate. None is so mourned as such a victim, if he be young and persecuted by those who should have befriended him."

While he was still reveling in the bliss of limitless castle-building, an odd sound broke upon his ear. He listened; evidently it was approaching. He detected the long-drawn, wheezy agony of "The

Last Rose of Summer;" somebody was grinding it out of a peculiarly execrable hand-organ — a reluctant hand organ — a hand organ that valued it, and wanted to keep it, and hated to give it up, and ought to have been humored in its whim. The musician presently arrived. He was a great, broad-shouldered tramp, arrayed in a fluttering chaos of rags, and otherwise adorned with blue goggles and false whiskers. He saluted Hugh, and asked an alms. Hugh said —

"I am not in a giving humor, but I am ready for a trade."

"Trade what?"

"Outfits."

"Well that's a rum go! Clothes, you mean?"

"Yes — everything. I want to have a bit of a lark."

The tramp hesitated. He thought, "Have I struck luck at last? This is the most dangerous disguise I could have." He said, aloud —

"I'm very poor, and I hope you ain't saying it just to make fun of me."

"No, I'm in earnest — I want to disguise myself and have some fun."

"All right, then, I'm ready to trade."

"Come into the woods, and we'll exchange; and mind, don't you go into the village — you might get into trouble on account of my clothes."

"Very well, I'll go some other direction — it's all one to me." He added to himself, "Belford, you are in luck, sure."

The exchange was soon made. The tramp, in Hugh's clothes, struck deeper into the woods, and Hugh, in the tramp's fantastic array, slung the hand-organ about his neck and returned to the "Lover's Roost" and sat down to lay out a plan for his future course.

The tramp had moved stealthily through the thick wood for a long distance, picking his way carefully, for there was a plentiful lack of light there, when a gunshot suddenly startled him and a bullet whizzed past his head. He dropped instantly on his face, muttering, "If it is an officer, I'm out of luck again; if it is a hunter, I'll play dead till he goes for assistance."

In another moment Hale Dexter was bending over him, exclaiming—

"Hugh! Hugh! Speak! answer me! O, he is dead, and I have killed him. What shall I do! what shall I do! To think that the one true-aimed shot of my life should have a result like this! Fool, fool, I might have known he would be here before me. Fool, to think every shadowy form that stirs in this place must needs be a wolf! . . . . . . Not a sound, not a motion — poor boy, there is no hope; he is dead. . . . . . Ah, there was no crime in the intent, but my heedlessness was a crime — in my own eyes I shall be a murderer, always. . . . . . Sh! was that a noise?" [2]

He broke away and fled through the wood. He ran some distance, then stopped in a thicket and listened, with a beating heart. He heard nothing. He began to commune with himself. He tried to map out a course of action, but his mind was a chaos of conflicting thoughts. At times he had the impulse to go and tell what he had done. But before he could take a step this thought always followed: "How can I ever bear to let his mother and his sister know it was I that did it!"

Presently he plunged away at random through the wood, not heeding the direction, his brain feverishly creating plan after plan, and adhering to none, and at last, to his great surprise, for he could hardly believe he had come so far, he found himself emerging upon the Drytown road. In the same moment Judge Griswold came flying by on a horse that was white with foam. The old gentleman came to an instant halt, threw himself from the saddle, and exclaimed —

"In time, thank God! Don't touch a hair of his head, for my sake!"

He came eagerly toward Dexter, holding out his hand. The young man stood silent, with his head down. Judge Griswold stopped and the gladness began to fade out of his face. There was a moment of painful suspense, then Dexter said, scarcely audibly —

"It is too late."

Neither spoke, for some seconds, then Judge Griswold said, mournfully — [3]

"I had rather it had been me. I was hoping I should be in time. But for the miscarrying mails . . . . . . but no matter. We were fated not to know. I do not blame you — You only did your duty. But we must not be loitering here. Hide yourself till I bring horses."

"No, I am not going to fly the country."

"What do you mean?" — said the Judge, surprised.

"I was innocent of any intent to take his life. I did it by accident."

In view of the portentous remark which the Judge had heard Dexter make to Hugh, this assertion had a suspicious sound, but when he had listened to the young man's account of the tragedy, and learned of the new relation in which he stood toward Hugh's sister, there seemed to be no ground for doubting. At length the old gentleman said —

"You are right. There is no need to fly the country. There were no witnesses; you will never be suspected. You would be safe in giving yourself up, in the circumstances — that is, safe from any hurt at the hands of the law; but you would find that where one man believed your story, two would find more pleasure in doubting it, — these are about the proportions of generosity and malice in the world.[4] It would be hard enough for Mrs. Burnside and her daughter to know that you killed poor Hugh, although by accident; it would be hard for them to be haunted night and day with the thought that if you had not come here he would be alive yet; to add to these burdens the consciousness that more than half of the community held you under grave suspicion, would be to banish sunshine from their lives utterly, and make the misery complete. The day would soon come when you would have to part; you would only suffer in each other's presence."

"I know it," said Dexter, with dull despair in his voice; "the sight of me would become unendurable to them." Presently he added: "See how I am placed! [5] I was to have removed to their house as soon as you and Mrs. Griswold came home. It is impossible — impossible! To look into their stricken faces hourly, see their tears flow, hear them lament, with that secret shut up in my breast — I could not endure it. I should lose my reason. What shall I say? How can I explain?"

Judge Griswold saw all the perplexity of the situation, but could offer no suggestion at the moment. He proposed that they go to his house and consider further. They forded the river and took the nearest way.

Meantime something had been happening in the forest where we left the escaped desperado, Jack Belford, personating the corpse of Hugh Burnside. The three St Louis detectives arrived in that vicinity. Mr. Baxter said —

"According to the discription, this must be about the spot."

He bent down and began to search the ground critically. Billings and Bullet did likewise. Baxter picked up a stick, with which he flirted the fallen leaves aside as he proceeded, as boys do when they hunt chestnuts. Billings and Bullet got sticks and followed suit. Thus the three stooping men wandered about in procession, saying nothing. The only sound heard was that which the sticks and the leaves made. — At the end of ten minutes Baxter stopped and bent lower. His comrades ranged up to him, bent low and clustered their heads with his, all gazing intently at the ground, nobody saying anything. Baxter pointed to the ground with his finger, then looked into his friends' faces. Said he —

"Is it a cow track?"

The two nodded a gratified assent. Baxter stuck a stick in the ground to mark the place, and the procession moved on. Presently another cow-track was found, and then another. These also were duly staked. Baxter got out a tape-line and measured the three tracks elaborately. His friends got out tape-lines, and each in his turn measured the tracks and set down the dimensions in their note-books. Baxter said —

"You see, they are the same."

"Exactly the same," said Billings, nodding his slow head two or three times, with gravity.

"The same man made all three," said Bullet, after a thoughtful pause.

"We will proceed to shadow him," said Baxter.

The procession formed again, and traced the cow-tracks here and there, some twenty yards; then the trail was lost at the foot of a tree. Baxter glanced significantly at his comrades and lifted his hand to impose silence. The other detectives nodded acquiescence. At this moment Jack Belford came stealing rapidly through the bushes, and his quick eye detected the detectives just in time to prevent his own discovery. He halted, under cover, within five steps of them and began to watch them anxiously.

The detectives went tip-toeing around the tree, gazing up into the thick foliage. Presently they grouped themselves together for counsel, almost at Belford's elbow. Baxter said, in a low voice —

"Well, to sum up: What do the cow-tracks mean?"

"They mean Jack Belford — in disguise," said the others, with muffled voice. The hidden scoundrel was within an ace of ruining himself with an explosion of laughter.

"The cow-tracks stop at the tree," said Baxter. "What does that mean, gentlemen?" said Baxter.

"It means that he's up the tree," said the others.

"Right," said Baxter. "Follow me — and be wary."

Baxter started to climb the tree; he was followed silently by the rest of the procession. They presently disappeared among the boughs and foliage.

The concealed malefactor remarked to himself —

"These are detectives. I am in luck again. It's a true saying that it's always darkest just before the dawn. Every time I get into a very close place Providence sends me a detective to get me out of it. Young hands buy them — but I am an old hand."

He crept away and took up a position twenty or thirty steps from the tree, and waited until he saw the detectives descend; then he approached and gave them good morning, and added —

"Gentlemen, have you seen any suspicious characters around here this morning?"

"No," said Baxter. "Why?"

"O, nothing, only I reckon I'm putting the thing up about right. He has slid for Illinois."

"Who has?"

"Well, a man I'm after. It wouldn't interest you — but it interests a detective."

The friends pricked up their ears.

"Are you a detective?" asked Baxter.

"Well, that's what they call me, up around Boggsville, there," said Belford, with an air of self-complacency. "I'm only a country detective, as you may say, — O, yes, only a mere *country* detective, that's all — but if you live in these parts I reckon maybe you've heard of Bob Tufts once or twice, or maybe even as much as three times. I see you know the name!"

The veterans smiled inwardly; then with a great show of having heard the name before, they exclaimed in one voice —

"No! Are you the famous Tufts?"

"Well that's about the size of it; and if I had authority to go to Illinois I'd make it lively for one Jack Belford pretty soon, and don't you make any mistake about it! And I'm not going to fool around these woods more than a day or two more, I can tell you. I mean to get that authority, somehow. Good-day, gentlemen."

"Good day, Mr. Tufts," replied the detectives.

"Tufts" started away, and the detectives had just begun to laugh privately over the country detective, and congratulate themselves

103

upon their easy riddance of his competition, when he turned, with a hail, and came toward them again. Said he —

"Do I look like a maniac?"

"Certainly not," said the veterans.

"Look at me good. *Do* I look like a maniac?"

"Very far from it," said Baxter.

"Well you'll think very differently in about a half a second. Do you see that tree yonder? Well, I've seen a cow climb that tree!"

"What!" cried the detectives with one voice; and at the same time a lightning-glance of pride and triumph passed between them.

"There, I said so," said Tufts. "Call me a maniac. It's all right. I don't ask you to believe it, but if I didn't see a cow climb that tree I wish I may never die. Good day again, gentlemen — and just chew that over at your leisure."

"Hold on, please," said Baxter, quietly. "This is a very strange thing. We should very much like if you would tell us more about it."

"There's nothing to it but this. I was watching here for my man yesterday evening, and just about dark I saw a cow climb that very tree there. First I thought it was strange; and the more I thought about it the stranger it seemed. So I hid in the bushes this morning, and while it was still dark I saw her come down and go away. Now you needn't believe that, but the proof of the thing is in the seeing. It's my opinion that that cow lives up in that tree. I haven't any doubt but it's a new kind of a cow.[6] Now I'll tell you what I'm going to do. I'm going to be here tonight with a double-barreled shot gun loaded with slugs — and you listen to what I say: that cow'll never climb another tree. I don't ask you to believe my racket, but I wish you'd make it a point to be here and see for yourselves, gentlemen."

Baxter the nervous, could hardly keep his happy excitement from showing in his face. He said —

"The thing you have told us is marvelous. It is a great pity that our business is so urgent that we cannot be here this evening. Couldn't you put it off three or four days? If those are the cow's habits it will be safe, you know?"

"Certainly I'll do it, if it is any favor. Meantime I'll run over to Illinois."

The veterans exchanged gratified glances. But "Tufts" added —

"No, come to think, I can't run over to Illinois — that authority is wanting. I'll watch her a day or two, and put some corn at the foot of the tree to encourage her in her habits and let her know she's got friends, and when you are ready you come and I'll finish her."

The wary Baxter did not care to see his game scared away with corn; so he said as quietly as he could —

"I'll offer a better plan if I can. What sort of authority is it you refer to?"

"Authority to arrest that fellow in Illinois. It has to come from the governor, you know."

"Yes — or from detective head-quarters in St Louis — of course you have heard of the new law?"

"O yes; O certainly; I had forgotten about the new law," said "Tufts" with the air of a man who is not in the habit of confessing ignorance on any point.

At a sign from Baxter, the three detectives opened their coats and displayed their staring silver badges with the diffident motto. The "country detective" was apparently overwhelmed with pride and gratification to find himself in such distinguished company. Introductions followed, and he exclaimed over each illustrious name as it fell upon his ear. He was soon furnished with a page torn from a note-book whereon was inscribed a writing vesting in him full authority from the St Louis detective head-quarters to "prosecute official business in the State of Illinois," and recommending "detective Robert Tufts" to the "confidence and assistance of all officers of the law in the States of Missouri and Illinois."

The desperado took his leave, then, saying to himself, "No more night travel for Yours Truly; no more starvation, no more hunting beds under haystacks. I will eat with sheriffs, drink with constables, sleep with detectives, and borrow money from them all. I bid a long adieu to these regions. My hardships are over — I've got a soft thing."

The three city detectives had a consuming laugh over the simplicity of the "country detective," and then started townward, after planning to return at nightfall with lariats and lasso the eccentric cow.[7]

While the events which we have been describing were taking place, Capt. Wheeler was on his way to the Burnside home, accompanied by his wife, a simple-hearted creature who loved him for his native goodness and admired him for his detective talent. The Captain said —

"You see, Jenny, this is the way I put it up. If he committed suicide at home, he's here yet. — If he committed suicide away from home, he ain't here. Now how would you go about finding out which it is?"

"Well, I would ask his mother where he committed suicide, Simon."

"Now that is the difference between the ordinary run of people and a detective, Jenny. A detective wouldn't say a word about suicide at all. He always keeps the main business in the dark."

"Then what would you ask, Simon?"

"*I* wouldn't ask anything, Jenny. Because if he has done it away from home, *my* asking them a question would scare them to death, I being a detective. *You* are to ask the questions while I keep out of the way. Then they won't be scared."

"I wouldn't have thought of that."

"Of course you wouldn't, Jenny, because you haven't been trained, and so you don't know the importance of these things."

The Captain then furnished his wife with half a dozen mysterious questions, and stood aside in the dim gray twilight while she roused up the household and delivered herself of her mission. She found that

Hugh had not been home, and that Clara and her mother were not alarmed about it; but by the time those ingenious questions were ended the very effect had been produced which the Captain had framed them to prevent; that is to say, the mother and daughter were frightened out of their wits.

The detective and his wife moved on, and Clara and her mother dressed themselves hastily and were soon on their way to Judge Griswold's to make inquiries.

As the Captain approached Mrs. Higgins's house, by and by, he said in a low voice —

"It was right along here that I lost him, Jenny. It is getting light enough for me to strike his track, now. I'll run him down before long."

Twenty or thirty steps beyond the house the captain was expatiating with effusion upon a "theory," about the suicide, which he was forming in his mind, when he fell over the wheelbarrow, which the youths had forgotten and left beside the path, at the spot where they had sat down to rest and talk. He got up rubbing his shin and said —

"There — anybody but a detective would 'a' gone by it without noticing it; but nothing escapes a detective's eye. Wait, Jenny — I'll examine it. It might be a clew. Just wait a minute — I'll shadow this wheelbarrow."

He examined it carefully, and then began to search the ground in its vicinity. Once or twice he picked up something. Then he stood under a tree and peered up through its foliage; plucked off a leaf and compared it with one which he had found half way between the tree and the wheelbarrow; broke off a twig and compared it with a twig which he had found near the leaf. Now he dropped his head on his breast in profound study, and remained so for perhaps a minute. Then he began to walk to and fro, telling off his cogitations on his fingers, nodding his head when they pleased him, shaking it when they perplexed him. Presently his face assumed a look of calm satisfaction and he came up to his wife and said —

"Jenny, prepare yourself for the worst."

"O, Simon!"

"He didn't commit suicide!"

"O, I am so glad, on his poor mother's account!"

"So am I, Jenny. He was murdered!"

"Gracious me! O, don't say that, Simon. — Ain't there some hope? — Some hope that there's a mistake?"

"There's some little, maybe, but not much. — I'm afraid not much, Jenny. The clews are too awfully straightfor'ard and outspoken."

"O, his poor mother! — and that sweet sister of his! They'll never, never get over it, Simon. And he was such a good young man. What a pity — and he so young. Tell me about it, Simon."

"Well, it was a dreadful thing. This is the way it happened. You see, he started out to commit suicide. That was his idea at first; because I saw him get that stuff at the drug store — poison, of course. But he changed his mind — I don't know why, because there's a clew missing, there; but it ain't important, anyway. Do you see these leaves?"

"Yes. Are they a clew?"

"That's what *I* call 'm. Same as the leaves on that tree there. Jenny, he clumb that tree."

"Laws, I never would have thought of that."

"Because you ain't a detective — that's the reason."

"What did he climb the tree for, Simon?"

"Well, there's a clew missing as to that; but my theory about it is this. He had concluded he wouldn't commit suicide, and here was his poison left on his hands. Would he throw it away? Of course he wouldn't. Could he sell it? There ain't any market for it. He clumb that tree to have a quiet place to study out what to do with that truck so as to get his money's worth out of it. What does he conclude to do? What's the most unnatural thing for him to conclude to do with it?"

"I don't know; but I should think the most *natural* thing would be to —"

"Hold up!" said the Captain, interrupting. "There's the difference between the common herd and the trained detective again. The common herd always goes hunting after the *natural* thing for a man to do. The trained detective knows better; he always hunts after *un-naturalest* thing a man would do — and just there is the little point that makes him superior to the common herd. — Very well; what we want to know, now, is, what was the most unnatural thing for this poet to do to get his money back?"

"What should you say, Simon?"

"It's as plain as your nose on your face: — kill somebody else with it!"

"O!"

"That's it. Now what we want to think out, next, is, who was it most unnatural for him to conclude to kill with that stuff?"

Jenny thought deeply, a moment, while the Captain contemplated her uneducated gropings with smiling complacently; then she looked up, hesitating, and timidly asked —

"Might it be the cat?"

"The cat! What an idea!" Then with deep impressiveness: "Prepare yourself Jenny."

"O, Simon, you make me shudder. Who was it he concluded to kill?"

"The author of his being — his mother!"

"O, the horrid creature! It takes my breath away!"

"But there's a Providence over us all. A higher power interposed to beat that villain. Let us proceed. What we come to now, is, what was the most unnatural thing for him to do while he was contriving to kill his own mother?"

"My poor head is all upside down with these awful things. I couldn't ever guess. You tell me, Simon."

"Very well. The most unnatural thing for him to do when he was contriving to kill his mother, was to go to sleep."

"Simon, it's perfectly wonderful! I never would have thought of that, but now as soon as you mentioned it, I can see myself that

that *was* the most unnatural thing for him to do. Simon Wheeler, I do think you get to be more gifted every day you live."

"It's practice, Jenny, only practice. Practice can do anything. Very well, he went to sleep. Pretty soon a man came along here — a kind of a loafer — a thief — and he —"

"What makes you think he was that sort of a person, Simon?"

"Because he stole this wheelbarrow, which is Mrs. Higgins's, aint it?"

"Yes, it is."

"She don't leave her wheelbarrow out nights, does she, this way?"

"No."

"Then it's as I say. That loafer stole it."

"Well why didn't he take it away?"

"You'll see, in a minute. He was a very powerful man — most unusually powerful man."

"Simon, it's wonderful! How *can* you tell?"

"You wait. He was a-sneaking along here, with the wheelbarrow, and just as he was passing under the tree, this inhuman poet went to turn over in his sleep, and of course down he comes! See this twig, broken off — that's how I know he fell down 'stead of climbing down. He takes this loafer exactly on top of the head and drives him partway into the ground like he was a nail. Here's where he was, then — do you see this deep foot-track?"

"Yes. How marvelously you do trace things out. But there's only one deep foot-print, Simon. Was he a one-legged man?"

"My dear, does a man walk with both feet on the ground at the same time?"

"Of course not! How little I do know about detecting! Go on, Simon — it is as exciting as a tale."

"This loafer was in a perfect fury, of course. What does he do? — See this dent in the edge of the wheelbarrow? See this leaf? I found it by the barrow. What do these two clews say? Why, that loafing thief ups with the wheelbarrow and smashes Hugh in the head with it."

"O, my, does it say that, Simon?"

"Say it? It don't simply *say* it, it *yells* it! I've never run across louder clews in all my days. For dead moral certainty, a clew like that is better than to see the thing done. I said this fellow was powerful. Am I right? You try to lift that wheelbarrow once. There ain't a man in this camp can swing it round his head. Hugh Burnside himself couldn't do it, and he's a shade stronger than I am. That is, he *was*, poor devil, before this loafer laid him out."

"Poor boy! Simon, where do you reckon the body is?"

"Well, my theory is, that this vagabond wheeled it away off into the woods and robbed it and buried it, and got this far on his way to town, when he heard something or saw somebody, and dropped it and skipped into the woods again. Let others find poor Hugh; my business, from this out, is to hunt down this sin-seared, bloody-minded, left-handed loafer that murdered him! It's the biggest case I've ever had, Jenny — a heap the biggest. If I work it up right and make a strike on it, I wouldn't wonder if it was worth three or four hundred dollars to me."

"Simon, it would make us easy for life! [8] I do hope you'll get it, or even the half of it. But what makes you think he is left-handed?"

"Why Jenny, if you had read as many detective tales as I have, you would know that pretty much all the murders are done by left-handed people. In the stories, the detectives most always notice that the wound is made in a way that couldn't be made only by a left-handed man. Now keep quiet a minute — let me think . . . . . . The parson — no, he's right-handed . . . . . . The magistrate — no, he's right-handed, too . . . . . . The butcher — right-handed . . . . . . Hello, yonder goes a man! — and he — yes, — no, — yes, it's so, thank heaven! — he's scratching his head with his left hand! Travel, Jenny! — home with you! I'll run this villain down!"

He flew through the brush and disappeared in the wood. His wife took her way homeward. Presently the Captain returned, panting, and growling to himself —

"Hang him, he was right-handed, after all. Blast a right-handed man, you can't make no use of them in our business. 'Twasn't anybody but Crazy Hackett. It was well for him he wasn't left handed — prowling around here this way when there's been a murder done."

The Captain walked along the river road, cogitating. He approached Hugh's retreat. Hugh had been thinking diligently,[9] but had found it impossible to contrive any satisfactory way of disposing of himself and his time during the week or two which he wished to devote to a mysterious disappearance. So he concluded to leave planning alone and trust to luck. Wherefore he rose up, in his fearful and wonderful disguise, with his hand-organ swung about his neck, and stood a moment pondering whether to go toward the town or toward the gorge. He had in his left hand the stick which was to support the organ whenever he should stop to entertain the public. At this moment Capt. Wheeler reached the grassy nook he stood in. Hugh was not aware of it. The detective eye was upon him; it glared with delight, too. The Captain said to himself —

"There's the murderer, for a million! That's the assassin of the inhuman poet, the bloody-minded Burnside! Left-handed, too, by the holy poker! — Now would a true detective go and grab him and put him on his guard? No, sir, he'd worm his crime out of him with the innocentest-looking questions in the world — questions that an angel might ask." — He cleared his throat, to attract Hugh's attention, and said—

"Good morning, friend."

"Good morning sir," answered Hugh, who added, to himself, "I shall have to play deaf and dumb to everybody else, but old Wheeler will never recognize my voice, if I disguise it ever so little."

The Captain bent a wary eye upon the dilapidated tramp and said—

"Have you seen anything of an old yellow tom-cat going along here with a blue velvet collar on?"

Hugh paused, wondering, and said to himself, "Nobody nor nothing is safe from this busy detective's suspicions: now what can he

suspect that poor cat of?" The Captain marked the hesitation —
"guilty hesitation," he termed it in his own mind. Hugh spoke up
and said —

"I believe I don't remember seeing the animal."

"Ah. I hoped you might have seen him — that is, if you'd been
over yonder way." He indicated the direction with a nod.

"I *have* been over there — that is, around about there in a sort of a
general way, but —"

"But what?"

"Nothing. I was only going to say that that was earlier. I have been
in the *woods*, since then."

The Captain almost betrayed his joy. He said to himself, "A hundred to one he was there burying the body! What an evil eye he's
got!" Then, although he was raging with interest, he asked with
counterfeited indifference —

"Been in the woods long?"

"No, only long enough to attend to a little matter that fell in my
way."

The Captain shuddered. He said to himself, "He calls it a little
matter; a body would suppose it was a dog he'd been burying, 'stead
of a widow's only son, and him a poet made partially in the image of
his maker." Then he asked, aloud?

"Been there alone?"

"Well-a — not entirely." Hugh added, to himself, "What can he
be up to? Does he suspect me of being an accomplice of the cat?"

The Captain's thought was, "Well I never saw simplicity and black
heartedness mixed up the way they are in this hellion, before. He's
walking right into the trap!" Then he said aloud, carelessly —

"*Friend* with you, perhaps?"

"Well, not exactly what you might call a bosom *friend*. We didn't
shed any tears at parting."

The Captain gazed with horror upon this abandoned villain who
could come with light speech upon his lips from such hideous work.

He considered a moment, then said — with trembling misgivings that the question might be too pointed —

"You-a — you left him there?"

Hugh answered cheerfully —

"O yes, I was done with him, and he won't have any more use for me."

The Captain started, in spite of himself, and almost said aloud, "The heartless butcher!"

Hugh said to himself, "What ails the man? He started as if he had been shot. There is no question about it, now — I am implicated with the cat."

The Captain was charmed with the progress he was making, and the neatness and ingenuity with which he was weaving the fatal toils about his victim. He summoned all his artfulness to the task of throwing the utmost indifference of manner and voice into his next question —

"You left him *comfortable*, I suppose?"

"Well, he didn't *say* he wasn't."

The Captain said to himself, "Poor devil, I judge he didn't! O, this is a grisly scoundrel! This is the very worst face I've ever seen in all my detective experience. Now for a finisher! now for an entire broadside! If I don't make him jump clean out of his skin, call me no detective!" Then he fixed his eyes steadily upon Hugh's, wagged a punctuating finger before his face, and said in an impressive stage-whisper —

"My friend — there's been — a poet . . . . . . MURDERED here, last night!" Then to himself, "Why, damn him, he looks pleased!"

For Hugh's instant thought was, "So they think I've been murdered! This is superb! It will be talked about, both papers will be full of it, I shall be a hero! My plan is fixed — I'll not turn up for a year! What a tremendous sensation it will make when I come back!"

The Captain, utterly stupefied, stood watching the jubilant play of expression in Hugh Burnside's face, and muttering to himself, "Well, this stumps *me*!" It occurred to him, now, that if he could secure a monopoly of this tramp for a few weeks, and keep him always under his eye, he could so ply him with ingenious questions as to trap him into a confession at last. Therefore he presently said —

"Trampy, are you going to lay around this village long?"

Hugh said to himself, "Why I *am* a tramp! — I had almost forgotten it. Very well, I will play the character; and I will try to exaggerate it enough to get some private fun out of it." In answer to the Captain's question he said, aloud, indolently —

"Maybe — if it pays."

"Well, you'll saw stove-wood stuff for grub, I reckon?"

"Yes. That's my line. Hot grub required."

"All right — I want to get you to saw a stick for me. Come along."

But Hugh did not move. He absorbed himself in making an imaginary calculation on his fingers, while saying to himself, "This is luck; his house is a safe out-of-the-way place; I must billet myself on him. He will stand it, for he has a deep purpose of some kind in view. Now I must keep up my tramp-character — and the more extravagantly the better." Meanwhile the Captain was waiting and wondering. Hugh ceased from his arithmetical labors and calmly asked —

"How many times do you want that stick sawed in two?"

The Captain exclaimed to himself, "*That* stick! Well that's good! But no matter." Then he said aloud —

"Three times."

Hugh said, reluctantly —

"It is a longer stick than I am accustomed to. How much of it shall you want done per day?"

"Whew! Why how much time would you like to have on such a job?"

"Well, more or less, according to size and hardness of the stick."

"All right, you fix it to suit yourself. There ain't no occasion to rush the job."

"What kind of timber is it?"

"There's several kinds. There's oak, there's hickory, there's —"

Hugh interrupted him with a protesting wave of the hand, and said with wounded dignity —

115

"Sir, I have done nothing to deserve this affront."

"Affront?"

"Sir, there are *grades* in tramps. I am not a hard-wood tramp."

"Good land! what *is* your line?"

"I do the delicate kindlings for the parlor stove."

The Captain made a profound bow of mock humility, and said —

"I *beg* your pardon, sire. Parlor kindlings is your line —"

"That is, when I am in adversity."

"O, I see! What is your line when you're in prosperity?"

"I uncurl shavings for the drawing-room stoves of the opulent."

The Captain contemplated him a moment with stupefaction, then asked —

"At how much?"

Hugh, yawning —

"A shaving a meal."

Capt. Wheeler looked puzzled, and said to himself, "He's pretty high-priced — but I've got to have him, anyway." Then aloud — with deference, fearing to offend again —

"Are — are you in adversity *now*?"

"Alas, yes."

"Well," said the Captain, charmed, "Would you be willing to tackle a *pine* stick —"

Hugh interrupting —

"*Kind* of pine, please?"

The Captain, eagerly —

"White — thoroughly seasoned — soft as butter —"

Hugh interrupting —

"Thickness, please?"

"Just the thickness of a yard-stick — if anything, not so thick."

Hugh, pondering —

"To be sawed in two three times . . . . . . To do it right, and make a tasteful and elegant job of it, I shall require a little time to make estimates, lay out the work properly, consult authorities —"

The Captain, interrupting, "and select an overseer, appoint subordinates, get up working models, take out a license, bid good-bye to
your family, make your will — O, take all the time you want. Time
ain't any object, just so this job's done right. I don't want it for utility,
I want to send it to the British Museum! . . . . . . Well, ain't it all settled? Come along. What are you waiting for, *now*?"

Hugh yawned again, and asked —

"Is it far?"

"Far? No! 'Tain't over a mile, or a mile and a half."

Hugh — after pondering a while —

"Could you get a hack?"

The Captain was obliged to support himself to keep from fainting.
Then he said, pleadingly —

"O *don't* require that, Trampy. I'm poor — *I* can't afford such
things, you know."

Hugh, mournfully, and shaking his head —

"I have conceived a great liking for you, sir; I would do much to
accommodate you, but I must take care of my strength."

The Captain started away, slowly, with his despondent head down,
and breaking his heart over this great loss, this noble chance to
achieve fortune and reputation when they seemed verily in his grasp.
But suddenly a saving idea struck him, and he darted away and disappeared — just in time to prevent Hugh from yielding his point,
for he perceived that for the sake of the fun he was carrying his fantastic requirements too far. In a twinkling Capt. Wheeler re-
appeared, beaming with delight, and exclaimed —

"Here you are, my boy! On with you!"

It was the Higgins wheelbarrow. In another moment Hugh had
become for a second time its passenger; and as the Captain went
wheeling him off, up the lovely river road, now lighted by the earliest
beams of the sun, the tourist awoke his lyre, so to speak, and added
the wheezy anguish of The Last Rose of Summer to the ravishing
music of the birds.

Chapter [8]

JUDGE GRISWOLD AND DEXTER had but a brief conference at home.[1] Before any conclusion was reached, Mrs. and Miss Burnside arrived. They swept past the sleepy and marveling servant who admitted them and burst in upon the two gentlemen, unannounced. Dexter almost dropped from his chair; even the Judge was disconcerted; but both rose and advanced. There was a trying time, for a while, for both women had allowed Mrs. Wheeler's strange and dark questionings to work upon their imaginations until they were now thoroughly frightened. They had met one of the young drug clerks, on the way, and he had acted so strangely and looked so scared when Mrs. Burnside poured out her fears and inquiries upon him, that the poor lady exclaimed, "O dear! You look as if you know something has happened to him!" Whereupon the young fellow stammered out something about a frightful dream he had had concerning Hugh, and then got himself away as quickly as he could.

Clara was full of self-upbraidings for her conduct of the day before toward her brother, and eloquent with resolves to be kinder to him in future if she should ever see him again. Her mother sat rocking herself to and fro in anguish, sobbing, and voicing her distress in moans and broken exclamations freighted with despair, with pathetic repetitions of Hugh's name, and supplications for divine help. This spectacle of suffering wrung the heart-strings of the men, and yet they were obliged to witness it almost in silence, since their tongues were tied by the secret that was hidden in their breasts. The few words of hope and comfort which they forced themselves to utter, grated upon their own ears, they were so false, so artificial, and seemed so like wanton trifling with the misery they were meant to assuage.

But at length the storm of grief and apprehension spent its force and the women began to dry their tears and take hope from the calm-

119

ness of the gentlemen — for they could not know that it was a frozen and compulsory calm that came of the impossibility of saying any honest thing of a cheering nature. A revulsion followed the tempest, and Clara was the first to see how femininely "absurd" she and her mother had been. She said a stranger would suppose her brother was a child and had never been from home by night before, instead of a great stalwart creature able to protect himself from all harms. The more she examined the matter the more unwarrantable her late fears appeared and the more comical they became in their new and more rational aspect. She recounted the hour's events in this vein, exaggerated its mock terrors and laughed at them, and kept up her raillery until even her mother began to feel rather ashamed of her fright and her lavish exhibition of feeling.

The grief of the mother and daughter had been so hard for Dexter to bear, that he was grateful when it began to subside; but this gay and cheery badinage that had taken its place was a hundred times harder to bear. It made him shudder, it made his blood run cold; for the laughing girl's form was no plainer to his vision than was that other form which he still saw, in his mind's eye, lying out yonder in the wood. He thought of a time when Clara would know all and would recall this moment and this light talk and break her heart over the remembrance.

The topic changed, but it brought no comfort, for every unwitting sentence had some remote reference to Hugh as a person alive and well, and so brought its pang. Once Clara turned suddenly and said:

"Hale, do you know we are going to do you a great honor?"

"Me? When?"

"When you come to stay at our house."

"How?"

"You are to have Hugh's room, and we will make him sleep in narrower quarters." [2]

That simple phrase almost wrung a groan from Dexter. He said to himself, "She little knows that half of her blank cartridges turn to bullets before they reach me." Another time she said —

"I am glad it all happened, although I suffered so; because I know, now, how much I love Hugh, and I didn't know before. It would kill me to lose him: now I could not have believed that, yesterday. We have always been lovers [sic], but I supposed the feeling had limits. I am impatient to see him and tell him my discovery. If you should see him first, Hale, you are to say nothing — I want all the pleasure of telling him myself. He has become your rival, now, in my affections — think of that!"

Dexter was suffering. The thought crossed his mind, "I can hardly bear it *now* — it will break my heart to hear her when she knows the ghastly truth — I must fly the country!"

In the same moment Clara said, playfully —

"Do you know how to break the rivalry and make me value you above him? *You* must disappear, too! Loss so increases love. — You must disappear, in the most mysterious way — but only for a day; that will be long enough. There! that is Hugh's step, now! an hour ago I thought I should never hear it again! I'll go and tell him."

She ran into the hall, but came back in a moment and said it was only a servant.[3]

After a little more conversation, in which the gentlemen did not shine very brightly, the ladies took their leave, fully restored in mind and heart. Clara's good-bye to Dexter was in a whisper — to this effect —

"There — do you see what you are to me? I come, harassed with bodings and terrors, and the mere sight of your face, with hardly a word spoken, banishes them and gives me peace. The mere sense of being near you is succor from all threatenings and impending harms. You are my refuge!"

The two men found themselves alone. Neither spoke for some moments. Then Dexter said in a voice which manifested a firm purpose —[4]

"My course is plain."

"I think so."

"My mind is made up."

"Tell me your plan."

"Before their visit, all was confusion in my mind; now all is clear. I had thought of flight, confession, suicide — a hundred selfish, treacherous things. But all that is at an end.[5] I realize, now, how they are going to suffer. It would be cowardly to desert."

"Their visit clarified my mind, also. I had been thinking far more of how to diminish your share of the siege of horrors that is to begin to-day than anything else; I perceive, now, that the higher and worthier consideration will be, how to diminish these bereaved women's share of it. You have chosen rightly, I feel sure.[6] — But let us look the ground over and be perfectly certain."

"Very well. To begin: One's first thought is to confess publicly — but that door is barred."

"Yes. There would be a trial, acquittal, and lasting suspicion. It would end relations between you and the Burnsides — without prejudice or hard feeling, but still it would end them, eventually. That door is barred."

"One's next thought is private confession to the bereaved ones. But that door, also, is barred."

"Yes. You could never be happy in each other's society, for your presence would keep the memory of the fatal accident always alive — it would be a cloud that nothing could ever dissipate. That door is barred."

"One thinks next of flight. That door, likewise, is barred."

"Beyond all question. It would be confession, with disgrace added. Those women's lives would not be worth the living, afterward."

"And last, suicide suggests itself. It, too, is a barred door."

"Yes — for it is only flight in another form, with confession and disgrace. It would leave those women lonely and without a protector or any hope of further happiness in this life."

"Then it is as I believed. All doors are barred that seem to lead out of this trouble. I must remain. Is it not so?"

"It certainly is so. We have viewed the situation on all sides.⁷ It is a curiously complicated position. It is like one of those chess problems where the king seems to have plenty of exits at his disposal, but when one comes to examine the matter he finds that the king is only safe where he stands — to move is to be check-mated."

"Yes," said Dexter with a dreary sigh, "I stand upon my last square, and here I must remain."

"I wish the task before you were easier. But there is nothing easy about it; one knows that too well."

"I can begin it, and I will begin it — no man could be safe in promising to go through with it."

"I like better to hear you talk like that than to boast. Now let me suggest something. Do not tax your powers too far. Do not take Hugh's room."

"I would not sleep in it a night under any consideration. Every object in it would bring him before me — and not in life, but as I saw him last."

"And that would ill refresh you for next day's task in the mourning household. You must remain our guest for some days yet."

"I shall be grateful if that can be! The days will tax my fortitude to the utmost stretch; unless the nights brought respite and oblivion I should break down. But you know they expect me. What shall I say? Find me a way out."

"It is easy. It is well understood that you are not to go there until I and my wife can be here again. This dreadful news will retard Mrs. Griswold's recovery, and I shall be with her, of course. Now that is all settled."

"It is a great gain. It lightens my task."

"Now be of good courage. These first days are going to be the hardest. If you weather them it will be easier sailing afterward."

Dexter rose and walked the floor nervously, muttering —

"Ah, you have said it, indeed! These first days! The finding of the body! *I* must go and tell them! May some merciful gossip spare me that! The public excitement, the clamor of the village tongues! The inquest! I must be there and look upon my work! I must bear home the verdict! The funeral! I must support them there, I must be their solace, their comforter; I must soothe them with soft lies out of a guilty heart! O, one needs the shoulders of a Hercules to carry burdens like these, one needs the double-faced guile of the devil to play my part!" He calmed himself with a great effort, sat down, and said resignedly, "It is over, now — I am a fool — go on." [8]

The Judge said —

"The days that follow will be easier. Mind, you will be often moved to confess. Be on your guard; to confess will be to destroy those poor people's happiness utterly. You can become more and more to them every day, if you keep your secret. You will be their stay and their comfort; having you, they will learn to bear the loss you have unintentionally caused them, and by and by they will cease to feel it. When the day arrives that you stand at the altar with Clara Burnside, nobody there will be unhappy, nobody there will be otherwise than joyous." [9]

"Except me — for the secret will rise up against me there, once more, and accuse me."

"Of what? Of nothing. You will see that the keeping of that secret has made two people rich with happiness whom its betrayal would have burdened with misery for life. But if you shall still have any weak misgivings, no matter: You must suffer the penance of silence for the sake of those women. The secret *must* be kept."

The yellow glow of the tallow candles was paling in the fresh new light of the day, now; the household were astir; footsteps were growing frequent in the streets; the village was waking up. Dexter thanked the Judge for his wise counsel and his encouragement, and ascended to his room with a heavy heart. He sat down and wrote a brief letter to his mother in which he shared with her his fearful secret. He sealed and directed it, called Toby and told him to mail it.

Toby retired to a private place and unsealed it before the mucilage had had time to dry. Then he put it into a blank envelop and pocketed it, purposing to get it directed to Arkansas as soon as he could collect and add to it enough more manuscript to make a respectable letter of it — for Jim and his mother complained when his letters were brief.

Dexter tried to snatch an hour's sleep, but he found it impossible. As long as his eyes were open, he was drowsy; the moment he closed them he was broad awake, his brain a whirl of harassing thoughts and flitting images. At breakfast he was silent, absent-minded, and without appetite. He went out, and strolled down the street, dreamy, dreary, and feeling old and worn. But a change soon came. Rumor had begun to stir. He presently found himself accosted at every turn, by inquisitive villagers. When one goes to a strange city, the question "Is this your first visit to our city?" seems innocent enough; but it begins to madden him when it is an hour old and has been answered thirty or forty times. The question "Have you any idea what has become of Burnside?" became such a persecution to Dexter before he had walked half a mile, that he finally fled to the woods to get away from it. It smote him like an accusation. The horror of it had grown with every repetition, until he had come to believe that in a little while longer it would either drive him mad or to confession. It was noon before he could gather courage enough to go to Mrs. Burnside's.

But he had less to bear there than he had expected. Comforters were coming and going, all the time. That is, the visitors came disguised as comforters, but their real business was to inquire. Dexter mainly spent the afternoon apart with Clara. She was trying to believe that Hugh was only keeping up one of his "pets" a trifle longer than usual, but would presently be delivered of it and might be ex-

125

pected to step into the house at any moment. She was succeeding pretty well in her effort, though it had to be forced somewhat.

Dexter was at his post again in the evening, and new relays of comforters and inquirers were at theirs, also. Clara still kept up her spirits, but the forcing grew hourly more apparent. Her eyes, instead of wandering fitfully to the door with a pretense of having no particular object in doing it, got the habit of turning swiftly and anxiously to it, now, at every sound, and without any dissembling. The ill disguised despondency in her face deepened with every added disappointment. Still she talked on with a fictitious cheeriness that went to Dexter's heart. But his miserable evening drew toward its close at last. The visitors were all gone; Mrs. Burnside kissed Clara good-night and shook hands with Dexter, but did not trust herself to speak, at the moment. She bent her gray head, as she moved away, and Dexter saw her put up her handkerchief. When she reached the rear door, she turned and said in a voice that trembled a little —

"Leave the light burning, children — I will wait up for him, he will be tired and hungry, poor boy."

A sudden faintness went to Dexter's heart, and his pulse missed a beat. The moment the mother was gone, Clara turned a hopeless face upon him, and said —

"Something tells me he will never come again. . . . . . There — say nothing — not a word. I should break down. I must keep up, for my mother's sake. Talk of other things. Talk, talk, keep talking. Get me away from this formless, boding horror!"

As Dexter was wending homeward at midnight, he stopped in a dark angle to take a last compassionate glance in the direction of the twinkling light in the Burnside windows. Three men brushed past him, and one of them said in a voice which he recognized —

"My hands are cut to the bone, and I am all fagged out with lassoing the wrong cattle and hanging on to them. Maybe we'll fail, in this job, but if we do, there's another ready to our hand. If this young fellow stays disappeared another day, there'll be a reward for him."

A second voice said —

"And another for the party that helped him disappear. Both in our line."

Dexter shuddered, and said to himself, "Every chance remark refers to *him*.[10] I am never to get away from this awful business. And now ill fortune has sent these detectives, far from their beat, just in the nick of time, to hunt me down. There is no hope for a man so clothed in toils and fetters as I am."

When he reached home he found Milly sitting solitary in the parlor, dry-eyed, white as marble, with her gaze fixed on vacancy. She was in a dead apathy of terror. On the floor near her lay a blurred little printed page, garnished with a moving array of fantastic display-lines —

Extra!

All about the Sudden and Mysterious Disappearance and Probable Bloody Assassination of the late Mr. Hugh Burnside, of this Village!

Dexter sighed, resignedly. He realized that his labors for the day, as a comforter, were not over yet.

Chapter [9]

DURING the next four days Dexter suffered all the tortures that such a situation as his might naturally be expected to yield. He saw, too, that in one detail, he and the Judge had made a mistake. That was in the provision they had made for relieving Dexter of duty as a consoler for a part of each day by removing him from the presence of the Burnsides. A very great mistake — it only provided double duty for him. When he had borne all he seemed able to bear at the Burnside homestead, he always found poor Milly sitting up, waiting for solace. He had to soothe her down for the night, with coaxings, comfortings and melancholy ballads, and shore her up in the morning to support the burden of the day.

His tortures never abated; they grew, constantly. Out of doors he could not walk a block without being questioned and commiserated. He saw the excitement of the village rise, and spread, and swell, hour by hour, until all other interests were swallowed up in it, buried out of sight. If ever by any chance, another subject was spoken of by any creature, Dexter never had the luck to hear the blessed words.

He had to go daily (to keep up appearances) and help the citizens beat the woods and drag the stream for the missing man — but there was one spot which he never searched, neither did he advise any-body else to search there. And after each search he had to go to the Burnside home and see two hopeless faces look the inquiry, "Is he found?" — an inquiry which he never had to answer in words. Every night he had to undergo the same ordeal with Milly.

Mrs. Burnside wished to offer, the third day, a reward of a thousand dollars for any information that would lead to the discovery of her son's . . . . . . but there she broke down and cried bitterly. She finally sobbed out, to Dexter —

"You know what I mean — I cannot speak the dreadful word." [1]

It was as dreadful a word to Dexter, to write. He tried hard to persuade her to let him advertise simply for her son, and stop at that; Clara pleaded with her also, but to no purpose; grief, fear, sleeplessness, and the wear of racking thought, followed at last by the death of all hope, had brought her to an unnatural state, a sort of gloomy self-aggrandizement where she found a painful pleasure in fondling her woes and making the worst of them; so, lifted above the earth and its paltrinesses, she moved in a cloudland of sombre exaltation, and from this height would not see her son otherwise than dead, nor have the fact called by any modifying name.

It cost Dexter a pang to add to the advertisement the lacking word "remains," but he had to do it.

Why the body was not found, was a most perplexing mystery to Dexter. However, he always said to himself, "The finding it is only a question of time; I am too elaborately and painstakingly pursued by ill luck to hope to be spared such peculiarly lacerating tortures as the discovery, the inquest and the funeral."

The weight of his woes was growing heavier and heavier. A brooding melancholy settled down upon him which he found it almost impossible to shake off, even in the presence of the three mourners whom it was his business to cheer. — The deeper his dejection grew, the more it endeared him to these mourners and the more and more they lapped him in their hearts and poured out the riches of their affection upon him. So their very tenderness was a pain to him, since it came from such a grievous misunderstanding of the cause of his dejection. When they said, "Poor Hale, how you loved him, how you mourn him! how merciful of God to have sent you to us!" it wrung him with such anguish, and it made him so hate himself and loathe the shackles that bound him to his double-dealing office, that all his vigilance and all his strength of will were required to keep the devastating secret from leaping from his lips.

Late one night, after some such experience with the Burnsides — it was about the fifth or sixth day after Hugh's disappearance — Dexter said to himself as he dragged himself homeward, "If there is any comfort in knowing the whole extent of the program of torture I have got to endure, I have at least that comfort: my evil genius has reached her limit; she can invent nothing more."

But this was a mistake. He found Milly waiting, as usual; as usual, utterly smileless and miserable; but there was an added something about her look, now, — a hard, bitter, ungirlish something in the expression of her face, that attracted Dexter's instant attention. This soft young thing had cried away all her tears, and in the process a change had come over her. She had apparently changed into a woman — a woman with a purpose, too. Dexter perceived that she looked like her father, now, though she had never resembled any-body but her mother before. He sat down and took her hand. It was so cold it made him start. He said —

"Milly, you do not look like yourself; and you are cold. You must go to bed; you are not well."

"Never mind me," she said, "but listen. I have been thinking. I have made up my mind. You have tried hard to give me hopes, but there was something in your voice, something in your manner that — look me in the face and tell me whether you think he is dead or not!"

Dexter was surprised into confusion by this sudden and unex-pected assault. He showed it, and his eye fell before the girl's steady gaze. She said, calmly —

"That is enough. You believe he is dead. So do I."

Dexter hastened to recover his lost ground with a lame speech, but she tranquilly interrupted it and went on —

"Yes, you believe it, and I believe it. *Say* you believe it. . . . . . Why do you hesitate? Do you think I cannot bear it? Look at me."

She said it almost as disdainfully as her father might have done. Dexter raised his eyes and met her steady gaze for a moment, and then said, in a reluctant voice —

"It is useless to dissemble any longer. I believe he is dead."

The girl's face did not change. A period of silence followed which seemed long to Dexter; then Milly's face began to cloud, and presently she shot forth the thought that was in her mind with startling suddenness —

"He was murdered!"

The words almost took Dexter's breath away. He wondered if they had brought a guilty look to his face. Milly continued, without any stop —

"He is dead. He was murdered. I have thought it all out. Now I come to what I was going to say to you. His murderer must be found. His murderer *shall* be found. He shall be hunted night and day — he shall not escape. Will you do me a favor?"

Dexter was in a cold perspiration by this time. But he made shift to promise the favor.

"Very well," said Milly. "I am going to do you an honor which you deserve, for you have shown yourself a dear and faithful friend to him and to his memory. You shall help me hunt down the miscreant that murdered him!"

Dexter tried to stammer out his thanks, but they choked him. Milly continued —

"I am rich in my own right. I want to offer a thousand dollars reward for the discovery of the assassin — more, if you think best. Now —"

"I will write your father about it at once," said Dexter, eagerly, being aware that Judge Griswold would promptly squelch this new danger.

"No, not a word to him!" said Milly. "He would take it all on his own shoulders. What satisfaction would that be to me? I want to hunt this wretch down *myself*. I shall be jealous of all rewards but my own. I will spend every penny I possess but I will have him. I do not want this to get to my father's ears and be spoiled; therefore my reward for the apprehension of the assassin who took away my poor Hugh's life must be published and signed with your name as coming from *you*!"

This most unexpected denouement shook Dexter to his founda-
tions, and he said sadly to himself, "No, I was mistaken when I supposed the limit of invention had been reached, in the matter of
devising tortures for me. I, the murderer, must sign an advertisement
offering a reward for my own apprehension!" Then with a sigh, "No
mere journeyman is conducting my case; it is Satan in person." His
next thought brought a glimmer of cheer with it: "Well, at least she
does not suspect *me* — I was afraid she did."

He promised to write, sign, print, and publish the advertisement,
and then ventured to ask Milly if she suspected anybody in particular.

"Certainly I do. Crazy Hackett! Poor Hugh has lost his own life
because he saved mine. Hugh did not save a weakling or a traitor in
me.[2] Crazy Hackett will know this, presently."

Dexter tried to make the girl understand that the law does not
hold crazy people responsible for their acts, but this roused her
to such a burst of illogical and indignant disbelief in such an un-
righteous, idiotic and impossible thing, that he forebore to argue
the case.[3]

Dexter's instinct suggested to him that he was taking an unwise
contract upon himself. The thought crossed his mind, "If I am
ever found out I should die with shame to be confronted with
this advertisement." So he set to work to dissuade Milly from
her purpose. She listened gravely; he warmed to his subject,
and sailed along with increasing zeal and pleasure in the progress he was making, but in an unlucky moment, he forgot himself and stupidly threw out an argument born of his secret
knowledge —

"You see, Milly, it might have an odd look, coming from me, and
might cause rem—"

He caught a grave, surprised look in Milly's eyes, and stopped,
inwardly cursing his supernatural obtuseness. He said to himself, "It
is a true saying, 'Leave the guilty alone to say the incautious thing.'"
Milly regarded him a moment, then said —

"Odd? From you, his cousin, his nearest friend, in effect his brother-in-law?"

There was no answering that. Milly was inclined to pursue the matter, and things were growing uncomfortable for Dexter, when the lucky thought occurred to him of turning her attention to Crazy Hackett once more. This was effectual. While she unburdened her mind upon that text, Dexter re-gathered his composure, and so was able, when she had finished, to properly formulate a matter of importance that was in his mind. He told her she must allow him to reveal this matter to Clara, and to her mother, if necessary — and continued —

"Until the death is proven, it will be best for Clara to do everything she can to keep her hopes alive. I am helping her all I can in this direction. This advertisement puts me in the position of not only believing him dead but murdered. How shall I explain? You see how awkward it is."

Milly did see. She answered promptly, and said —

"O, let her hope as long as she can! She can never suffer supremely until hope is gone. You shall tell her that it is only I that believe him dead and that he was murdered. You shall tell her that I am weak and foolish through grief, and my vagaries will not brook control. — Beg her to avoid talking with me about them. — Then tell her you do not believe he was murdered, tell her you do not believe he is dead, and you will see her hopes revive and her confidence return. I wish I were in your position!"

Dexter gasped out a "Why?"

"Because for her sake I could so dissemble a mere belief in his death as to make my hopeful words sound honest and full of cheer. Ah, I would give the world to be in your place. Happy you, who only *believe* he is dead — it leaves a blessed gap of uncertainty, a little rift in the black cloud-rack that the sun can come through! But put yourself in my place and see the difference — for I seem to *know* he is dead!"

In time Dexter escaped from this trying interview and sought the refuge of his room. He sat down, wearied with the toils and distresses of the day, and leaned his head in his hands. His spirits were at a very low ebb. He said —

"The further I go, the deeper I sink into the mire of duplicity. Every hour seems to add a new and more diabolical requirement to the list of frauds I am appointed to perpetrate. I am the unhappiest soul that cumbers the earth — yet observe the unjustness of my situation: the guiltiest criminal may end his miseries by suicide and welcome; but I, who am innocent, am denied it!"

Chapter [10]

CAPTAIN SIMON WHEELER was a man who had tried various occupations in life, but had fallen just a trifle short of success in all of them. He was of a hopeful, cheerful, easy-going nature; therefore his partial successes encouraged him to expect an entire and colossal success some day, instead of being to him an accumulation of evidences that the thing to be more confidently looked for was a conspicuous and unmistakable failure in the fulness of time.

Among other experiments, he had tried the small country show business in various forms, and had come out about even on each experiment. He did not know he was too ignorant of business and of men to succeed as a showman. He merely believed that the reason he had not made a fortune and a name was that he had not happened to get hold of the right kind of a show. So his confidence in himself was in no degree impaired. Ten years before our story opens, his last show had demonstrated itself to be only a copper mine instead of the gold mine he had bought it for. He cheerfully boxed it up and stored it away at the homestead in Guilford, for he was near his native village at the time.

The homestead consisted of a log dwelling and three or four log farm buildings, scattered about a small farm. One of the buildings, which was separated from the dwelling house by a tobacco field, was called the "negro quarter," for grandeur. A family of slaves had inhabited it, formerly, but Wheeler set them all free as soon as his father was dead, for he was an advanced thinker, in his groping way, and always had opinions of his own.

The Captain had profound religious views, and their breadth equaled their profundity. He did not get his system from the pulpit, but thought it out for himself, after methods of his own. One may get an idea of it from a dream which he professed to have had once,

137

and which he was very fond of telling about. Here it is, in his own language —[1]

"I dreampt I died. I s'posed, of course, I was going to lay quiet when the rattle went out of my throat, and not know any more than if I was asleep. But it wasn't so.[2] As I hove out the last gurgle, 'stead of settling down quiet, it was just as if I was shot off! — shot out of a gun, you understand! I whizzed along, head first, through the air, and when I looked back, in about a second, this earth was like a big, shining, brass ball, with maps engraved on it. But did it stay so? No, sir! It shrunk together as fast as a soap bubble that is hanging to a pipe when you take your mouth away from the stem and let the air slip out. In another second it was nothing but a bright spark — and then it winked out! I went whizzing right along, millions of miles a minute. Dark? Dark ain't no name for it! There wasn't a thing to be seen. You can't imagine the awfulness of it. Says I to myself, 'Knowing what I know, now, no friend of mine shall die with useless flowers in his hand if I can raise enough to buy him a lantern.' And cold? Nobody down here has any idea what real cold is.

"Well, pretty soon a great wave of gladness and gratitude went all through me, because I glimpsed a little wee shiny speck away yonder in the blackness. But did it stay a speck? No, sir. It seemed to start straight for me, swelling as it came. In the time it took me to breathe three breaths it had swelled till it filled up the whole heavens and sent off prodigious red-hot wagon-wheel rays that stretched millions of miles beyond. And hot? People down here don't know what hot is. I shut my eyes — I couldn't stand the glare. Then I felt a great breath of wind and a sudden sound like *whoosh*! and I knew I'd passed her. I opened my eyes, and there she was, away yonder behind, withering up, paling down, cooling off — another second and she was a twinkling speck — one more instant, and she was gone! Black again — black as ink — and I a-plowing along.

"Well, sir, I run across no end of these big suns — as many as a half a million of them, I judge, with oceans of blackness between them, which shows you what a big scale things are got up there on — and I saw little specks sometimes that I didn't come near to, and every now and then a comet with a tail that I was as much as ten seconds passing — one as much as fifteen or twenty, I reckon — which shows you that we hain't ever seen any comets down here but seedlings, as you may say — sprouts — mere little pup-comets, so to speak. *You* won't ever know anything about what He can do till you have seen one of them grand old comets that's been finished and got its growth — one of them old long-handled fellows that He sweeps the cobwebs out of the far corners of His universe with.

"In the course of time — I should say it was about seven years — not short of seven, I know, and I think it was upwards of it — my speed begun to slacken up, and I came in sight of a white speck away off yonder. As it grew and grew, and spread itself all over everywhere and took up all the room, it turned out to be the loveliest land you can imagine. The most beautiful trees and lakes and rivers — nothing down here like them — nothing that begins with them at all. And the soft air! and the fragrance! and the music that came from you couldn't tell where! Ah, that music! — you talk about music down here! It shows what you know about it.

"Well, I slacked up and slacked up, and by and by I landed. There was millions of people moving along — more different kinds of people, and more different kinds of clothes, and talking more different kinds of languages than I had ever heard of before. They were going toward a great high wall that you couldn't see the end of, away yonder in the plain. It was made of jewels, I reckon, because it dazzled you so you couldn't look steady at it. I joined in with these people and by and by we got to the wall. There was a glittering archway in it as much as a mile high, and under it was standing such a noble, beautiful Personage! — and with such a gentle face, when you could look at it. But you couldn't, much, because it shone so.

"I ranged up alongside the arch to watch and listen and find out what was agoing on, but I kept ruther shady, because I had old clothes on, but mainly because I was beginning to feel uneasy.[3] Says I to myself, 'This is heaven, I judge, and what if I've been preparing myself on a wrong system all this time!' I listened, and my spirits begun to drop pretty fast.

"The people were filing in, all the time, mind you, and I a-watching with all my eyes. A mild-faced old man's turn came and he stepped forward. He had on a shad-belly coat. The Beautiful Personage looked at him ever so kindly, and in a low voice that was the sweetest music you ever heard, he says to him —

" 'Name, please?'

" 'Abel Hopkins,' says the old man.

" 'Where from, please?'

" 'Philadelphia,' says the old man.

" 'Denomination, please?'

("That word made me shiver, I can tell you. I felt my religious system caving from under me.)

" 'Quaker,' says the old man.

" 'Papers, please?' says the Beautiful Personage.

("I felt some more of my system cave from under me, and my spirits went lower than ever.)

" 'The Beautiful Personage took the papers and run his eye over them, and then says to the old man —

" 'Correct. Do you see that band of people away in yonder, gathered together? Go there and spend a blissful eternity with them, for you have been a good servant, and great is your reward. But do not wander from that place, which has been set apart forever for your people.'

"The Quaker passed in and I glanced my eye in and saw millions and millions of human beings gathered in monstrous masses as far as I could see — each denomination in a bunch by itself.

"A wild-looking, black-skinned man stepped up next, with a striped robe on, and a turban. Says the Beautiful Personage —

" 'Name, please?'

" 'Hassan Ben Ali.'

" 'Where from, please?'

" 'The deserts of Arabia.'

" 'Denomination, please?'

" 'Mohammedan.'

" 'Papers, please?'

"He examined the papers, and says —

" 'Correct. Do you see that vast company of people under the palm trees away yonder? Join them and be happy forever. But do not wander from them and trespass upon the domains of the other redeemed.'

"Next an English Bishop got in; then a Chinaman that said he was a Bhuddist; then a Catholic priest from Spain and a Freewill Baptist from New Jersey, and next a Persian Fire-eater and after him a Scotch Presbyterian. Their papers were all right, and they were distributed around, where they belonged, and entered into their eternal rest.

"Not a soul had gone in on my system, yet. I had been a-hoping and hoping, feebler and feebler, but my heart was clear down and my hopes all gone, at last. I was feeling so mean and ashamed and low-spirited that I couldn't bear to look on at those people's good luck any longer; and I begun to be afraid I might be noticed and hauled up, presently, if I laid around there much longer. — So I slunk back and ducked my head and was just going to sneak off behind the crowd, when I couldn't help glancing back to get one more little glimpse of the Beautiful Personage so as to keep it in my memory always and be to me in the place of heaven — but I'd made a mistake. His eye was on me. His finger was up. I stopped in my tracks, and my legs trembled under me. — I was caught in the act. He beckoned with his finger, and I went forward — you see there wasn't any other way. The Beautiful Personage looked on me, a-trembling there, a moment or two, and then he says, low and sweet, the same as ever —

" 'Name, please?'

" 'Simon Wheeler, your honor,' says I, and tried to bow, and dropped my hat.

" 'Where from?' — just [as] mild and gentle as ever.

" 'I — well, I ain't from any particular place, your honor — been knocked about a good deal, mostly in the show business, your honor — because, on account of hard luck I couldn't help it — but I am sorry, and if your honor will let me go, just this once, I —'

" 'Denomination, please?'

"He said it just as ca'm and sweet as ever, and I bowed — and bowed again — and tried to get my hat, but it rolled between my feet, and I says — scared most to death — I says —

" 'I didn't know any better, your honor, but I was ignorant and wicked, and I didn't know the right way, your honor, and I went a-blundering along and loving everybody just alike, niggers and Injuns and Presbyterians and Irish, and taking to them more and more the further and further I went in my evil ways — and so . . . . . . so . . . . . . if your honor would *only* let me go back just this one time, I —'

" 'Papers?' says he, just as soft and gentle as ever.

"I had got my hat, but my fingers shook so I couldn't hold onto it and it dropped again. The perspiration was rolling down my face, and it didn't seem to me I could get breath enough together to live. When that awful question come, I just gave up everything, and dropped on my knees and says —

" 'Have pity on a poor ignorant foolish man, your honor, that has come in his wicked blindness without a denomination, without one scrap of a paper, without' —

" 'Rise up, Simon Wheeler! The gates of heaven stand wide to welcome you! Range its barred commonwealths as free as the angels, brother and comrade of all its nations and peoples, — for the whole broad realm of the blest is your home!' "

Captain Wheeler had a voice like a man-o'-warsman, and he always brought out that closing passage with the roar and crash of a thunder-peal.

As we were saying, Wheeler retired from the show business and set up as a small farmer on his little homestead; but he soon found that the cultivation of corn and tobacco was rather a monotonous occupation for one whose life had been so full of variety and activity as his. He began to grow restless, and presently fell to turning over new schemes in his mind. He looked upon it as a special providence that just at this unsettled time, when he was so certain to make a move soon, and so likely to make a wrong one, a book fell into his hands which showed him instantly and as clear as day what he was born for. He had a mission in this world — he had not a shadow of doubt about it — a great career was before him! He promptly banished all the crude schemes that were fermenting in his brain, and turned his whole attention to his "mission."

This book which located him securely and permanently when his anchors were dragging was entitled "Tales of a Detective." It became his Bible. He read and re-read it until he knew it by heart; he adopted its professional slang and buttered all his talk with it; he reverenced its shallow, windy hero as one who was inspired; he marveled over its cheap mysteries and trivial inventions and thought they were near to being miracles. Now this was all perfectly natural, for these reasons, to-wit: Captain Wheeler was country-born and village-bred; all his goings to and fro had been among backwoodsmen and villagers; he was almost without education and real experience of men and life, and this gave him a confidence, a self-appreciation and a deep knowingness which nothing but ignorance can afford — ignorance carefully selected, and boiled down and compacted to pemmican; he was very brave, he was a manly man, and void of meannesses and implacabilities; but at the same time he was as gentle-hearted as a girl, as simple-minded as a little child, and as easily seen through as glass. The capstone to his character was a fervid and romantic imagination — and this naturally made him a hero-worshiper and kept his head filled with dreams of some day being a hero himself.

All this is as we see Simon Wheeler. How did he see himself? Like all other villagers, he was a professed "student of character;" he believed he could cast his practised eye on the most inscrutable of men and read him like a book; he believed he had a consummate knowledge of men and life; he was proud to believe himself as vengeful and implacable as an Indian, and his constant divergences from this character he regarded as mere experiments to show himself what a supreme mastery his will held over the dearest appetites of his nature; he believed he was very deep, very wary, very wily, and gifted with a cunning that was capable of deceiving the most sagacious intellect that could be enlisted against it.

Therefore, we repeat, it was natural for this kindly, simple-natured, transparent old infant to fall down and worship that detective rubbish and its poor little tuppenny hero.

Captain Wheeler was right in one thing — he was a born detective. He had every quality that goes to make up the average detective: not the "booky" one, that brilliant, sagacious, all-seeing, all-divining creation of the great modern novelists, but the real detective, the one that exists in actual life.

The Captain's appetite increased with what it fed on. He sent for every detective book he could hear of. He devoured all these tales with avidity and accepted them as gospel truth. To him these detective heroes were actualities; and in time their names and their performances came to be quoted and referred to by him with the facility and the loving faith with which scholars quote the great names and recal the great deeds of history. He was another Don Quixotte, and his library of illustrious shams as honored, as valued, and as faithfully studied and believed in as was the Don's.

He established this library in one of the ground-floor rooms of the house called the "nigger quarter." He did not call this apartment his library; far from it: he called it the "Chief's Office;" and he loved to sit there alone, in great state, at particular hours, and receive imaginary "reports" from imaginary "inspectors" and other subordinates, detail couples and groups of these for special secret service for the next watch, issue general orders to others, and appoint various book-renowned shadows to go and "shadow" sundry suspected villains whom he dug out of his own brain and furnished their villainies to them from the same source.

In a room which communicated with the "office," the Captain kept a lot of old theatrical costumes, a melancholy relic of his old showing days. They began to gather value in his eyes as his detective mania grew; later, when he began to branch out as a detective himself and required disguises, they became his most precious possession. This room, the office, and one or two rooms on the upper floor, were sacred; the Captain kept their mysteries under lock and key. Even his wife came no nearer to this holy building than was necessary to the delivery of messages — which was not very near, for she had a long-range voice when she chose to elevate it. Mrs. Jenny Wheeler was as child-like and simple-hearted as her husband, and had as full a faith in his detective abilities and his great future as himself. There was not a lazy bone in Wheeler's body. With all his detecting he never allowed his little farm to run behind; he made it furnish a good and sufficient support for himself and his wife; there was plenty to eat and plenty to wear; if there was little money, it was no matter, for little was needed. If Mrs. Wheeler wanted something done, and Simon said he was "on duty," or had to receive a "report" or "issue orders" to a relief-watch, or go and "shadow" a "crib" or a "fence," or a "crossman," or "pipe" somebody suspected of "shoving the queer," she waited patiently and without a word, for she felt that these great official duties were paramount.

Hugh was given a large ground-floor room in the "nigger-quarter" which had formerly been the kitchen. It had a great fire-place in it, a comfortable bed, several old chairs and a table. The Captain charged

his wife never to come in sight of this tramp, for he was a "deep one"
and required lulling and sagacious treatment, else he would be sure
to take the alarm and decamp. He charged Hugh to keep the tobacco
field between himself and the house, because his wife "did not like
the expense of hired men and would want him sent away" — an
unnecessary warning, for Hugh had no mind to risk detection where
he could avoid it. He had small fear of the Captain's seeing through
his disguise, but he judged that it would be best to get used to being
a tramp, and easy in the costume of the character before displaying
himself too freely.

The Captain brought Hugh's meals to him at regular hours, and
used these opportunities to study his man. He talked to Hugh apparently at random, but with a deep purpose. He usually got a brand
new theory as to minor details, out of these conversations, but the big
bottom belief that this tramp was the murderer of Hugh Burnside
remained, fixed and unalterable in his mind. By practice, Hugh soon
achieved a change of voice; he felt secure, now, from discovery by
the Captain, though he had had but slight misgivings in that matter
before.

Hugh might have soon wearied of being a person who had mysteriously disappeared, romantic as the thing was; he might have soon
wearied of his ragged disguise and the trifling drudgeries his character of a tramp required of him; he might have soon wearied of his
monotonous life in and about the "nigger quarter;" all these things
might have soon lost the charm of their novelty and moved him to
bring his adventure to an end, but for a certain other and more
powerfully restraining interest. This was a strong curiosity he felt to
discover what the Captain's suspicions about him were. The old man
was watching him and pumping him — these things were certain.
The door which opened from the kitchen into the office was kept
locked; he detected slight sounds in the office at night. Was the Captain spying through the keyhole? — Once or twice when Hugh was
playing at wood-chopping he thought he heard a movement in the

bushes near at hand. When Hugh had been in the nigger quarter a couple of days he thought he would explore the building. He was surprised to find that the office and another room on the main floor, and two rooms overhead, were locked. Here was a mystery which must be solved.

When he heard the Captain leave the office by the outside door that evening, he dropped softly into his track. He saw him enter a little grove of peach trees a short distance away and seem to reach up and fumble about the trunk of one of them. It was not light enough for him to make out more than this, but he judged that the keys were being concealed. — He was not mistaken. The old man had dropped them into a shallow natural pocket in the crotch of the tree. It took Hugh some little time to find the right spot, but he succeeded at last, and carried off the prize. Five minutes later, he was in the office with a lighted candle. — He took a cursory glance at the books, and then a slate that hung against the wall over the desk caught his eye. At the top of it, rudely lettered in white paint, was this:

CHIEF'S HEADQUARTERS.

Underneath, written with a slate pencil, was this:

NIGHT-DUTY ORDERS.

Chief will be absent in villadge on special duty from 9 till midgnight.

Inspector Adams will shadow Nobby Bill and report to Chief.

Detective Barker will pipe the Jew fence for prigged * *thimbles,† props** and dummies.††*

* Stolen [MT]
† watches [MT]
** breast-pins [MT]
†† pocket-books [MT]

No change of duty for rest of force.

Reliefs rep't to Hedquarters at usual hours.

WHEELER,

Chief of Detective Dep't.

The names used above were those of famous detectives who figured in the Captain's favorite books.

Hugh went to his own quarters, now, to wait until 9 o'clock; for he did not doubt that the "Chief" would obey his own orders and go on special duty in the "villadge" at that hour.

When the proper time arrived he invaded the Captain's mysteries, candle in hand. He found the room adjoining the office full of cheap old theatrical costumes, and among them various odds and ends likely to be held precious by a professional of the Captain's sort. — The costumes depended from pegs in the wall, and the first dim flicker which the candle threw upon them produced rather a startling effect, for it turned them into hanged people swaying to and fro in the last agony. But as it was only their shadows that swayed, this ceased as soon as Hugh and the candle-flame stood still.

Each costume bore a label. One was "An Old Saler;" another "A Hiwayman;" another "A Nigger;" another, "Irish-woman" — and so forth and so on. Hugh recognized some of the costumes; he had seen Wheeler about the village in them on imaginary detective duty.

Here and there were the valuable specimens of detective bric-a-brac just referred to. One was labeled "Peace of the skelp of the half-breed that killed Conklin's hired man;" another, "Peace of the rope that hung Whitlow;" another, "Huff of the jakass that kicked Johnny Tompson in the hed of which he died and whom I bought when he was shot to get the huff;" another, "Brickbat which busted Archibald Skidmore Nickerson deceas'd;" another, "Left thum of a horse theef;"

148

another, "Part of second hand glove said to ben used by detective Larkin of St Louis as a clew to find out who rob'd the State Bank, but did not succeed, the burglar not wearing gloves that time;" another, "Shin of celebrated N. Y. detective;" another, "Bottle that had the asnic in it that Elizabeth Sapper took but was pumped out and nothing come of it;" "Part of a dog which bit deacon Hooker of which he died;" another, "Tooth out of a stranger supposed to ben murdered by hiwaymen." There were many more grisly gems in the collection, but we will leave the rest uncatalogued.

In one of the locked rooms upstairs Hugh found another museum like this one; when he unlocked its larger neighbor he came upon a spectacle which startled him for a moment. Through the flickering light and the dancing shadows he saw a swaying and bowing assemblage of pale and silent men and women, who were most gaudily and fantastically dressed. He stared, speechless, at these people a moment — then he perceived that they were only wax figures.

Hugh approached, and inspected the convention at his leisure. General Washington was there, duly labeled, stiff as a monument, and with ten years' dust on him. He imagined he was taking leave of his generals, no doubt, for his two hands were advanced suggestively; but as these two hands were now wire-bridged with cobwebs, ignorant persons would jump to the conclusion that he was holding yarn for Queen Elizabeth, who sat before him. The Duke of Wellington was there, with the stuffing sticking through his trousers where they were torn at the knee. Daniel Lambert was present, his mighty stomach a home for happy mice. Ajax was defying the lightning, and Lafayette had lost his props and was leaning against him, with a loose familiarity of attitude which hinted that he needed a lamp post and thought he had found one. Poor Louis XVI, in his tin crown, had fallen across the lap of the terrible Robespierre, who had a dagger in one hand, a horse pistol in the other, and an innocent caterpillar asleep on his chin. Around a coffin which had once been gaudy with cheap finery, stood some Romans holding imaginary handkerchiefs

149

to their eyes, and in the coffin lay imperial Caesar, in dusty magnificence. Murderers and pirates abounded, and there was a couple of very passable devils with Benedict Arnold in charge. —

During a couple of hours Hugh amused himself with re-grouping these figures in all sorts of absurd ways, and then retired, promising himself further entertainment with them when other excitements ran low.

Shortly after midnight the Captain arrived and paid him a visit. Hugh inquired what news was stirring.

"Well, there ain't anything stirring, these days, but the murder, of course, Trampy."

Hugh was interested. Said he, —

"What do they say about it?"

"All sorts of things. — They don't seem to know how to feel grieved enough about that poor young Burnside."

These were grateful tidings for Hugh. He hoped the subject would be enlarged upon. — The Captain presently went on, —

"You see, his mother advertised for his remains, two or three days ago, and that warmed up the general distress considerable."

[The manuscript breaks off about a third of the way down MS p 512, the expanded narrative having reached a point about halfway through the plot of the play on which it is based. In the play the story continues with a revelation of the various theories about the murder. As we have seen, Wheeler suspects the tramp (Hugh); the three detectives, balked in their efforts to capture Belford, turn their attention to the "murder." Baxter, for what to him are good and sufficient reasons, suspects Mrs Burnside of killing Hugh with a short-handled broad-axe; Billings, for similar reasons, suspects Clara of having brained Hugh with a stove-lid; and Bullet, for reasons no less cogent, points the finger of suspicion at Milly, who, he reasons, slew Hugh with a hymn book, a *Plymouth Collection*.

Belford's body (in the play, Dexter actually kills him by accident) is discovered; identified as Hugh's by the clothes, it is given an impressive funeral. While the ceremony is in progress in the church, Hugh (as tramp) confesses the "murder" to Wheeler, who plans a dramatic announcement of his solution to the crime. His triumph is ruined by the three detectives, who choose the grave-side ceremony for the final test of their theories. As the coffin is lowered into the grave, Baxter thrusts a broad-axe into Mrs Burnside's face, Billings suddenly swings a stove-lid up before Clara's eyes, and Bullet pushes a hymnal under Milly's nose. When each suspect starts violently at the display of the "murder weapon," she is immediately arrested, and haled off to be charged before the local justice.

When Mrs Burnside is formally charged with the crime, Tom Hooker, unable to see an innocent suffer, confesses to the murder. Lem wavers but finally "caves in" when Clara is charged: he confesses. The accusation of Milly by Bullet brings Dexter's confession. At this point in the proceedings, Wheeler, who has been trying to gain the floor, finally makes himself heard. He brings forth the tramp and charges him with the "murder." The tramp confesses, then strips off his disguise and reveals himself as the "murder victim." The lovers fall into each other's arms, and the curtain falls on general jubilation.

Twain apparently became dissatisfied with this ending and subsequently planned a different one for the novel in what is presented in Part II of this volume as Group C of the working notes. But even after considerable reflection, one cannot say that the new conclusion is to any appreciable degree less preposterous than the first one. — The Editor.]

20

(Mrs. G. doesn't know the
D's, but loves D because
her husband does — + pities
them.

lasted longer than I can
remember — it cannot
end till one house is ex-
tinct. When the sister of Charley
Hale
∧ Dexter's father married a Burnside, some weaklings im-
agined it was York & Lancaster wedded again, + the wars
of the roses done finished.
Wiser heads took into account
the fact that Edward Dexter
was an invalid, a prisoner
in his bed. He remained a
prisoner ten years. What did
he do then? The moment he
was on his legs he took his
gun + followed came to
Missouri — to this village,
madam!" Griswold
    Mrs. Burnside looked
up & gasped — up & gasped —
∧ "Came here? I never
knew it?"

Page 20 of the manuscript with the early form of Dexter's name

end-words. It crowds you
to make them rhyme, some-
times. But put it away. -
Don't read it now."

Milly, beaming with happiness & with pride in her poet,
~~Milly tucked it into her~~
Tucked the precious rubbish into her
bosom to keep company
with some spools, a thimble
& an assorted cargo of other
odds & ends. Then she dexterously
~~She craned~~
brought up from among these a something which
~~was that literary jewel~~
she did not exhibit. Her heart increased its beat almost
~~that might Now she said,~~
to a flutter, & she said, timidly, & watching
~~diffidently, & watching~~
Hugh's face wistfully —
"Do you like book-
marks, Hugh?"

"O, what an idea!"
laughed the burly youth.
"A man don't care for
such things. They're for
girls & old women. A body
might as well ask a man if
he likes doll-babies. Why?"

Page 130 of the manuscript with examples of major and minor revisions

2

Wheeler plays maniac. —
Charley plays keeper.
~~The Hamburg Sailor~~

No, let Wheeler, as a
Sailor, tell wonderful
sea-yarns to Tramp.

Were you ever on a canal?
I was in a Storm on
one, once?

His life with the Tram —
conversations, &c —
shall be the gem of the
book.

Suppose ~~Mrs~~ Charley dis-
misses + hides, + Cap'n
tells him his plans and
clews? Good! Charley
Sometimes sees Clara (who

Jack Belford – $500 reward.
dead or alive.
Hoxton
Old Humphrey, at Marly
Mrs. Mary Burnside
Mr. Edward Dexter (elder)
Boggsville, where jail is.
Maj. Hoskins, ~~bailiff~~ sheriff.
Guilford Torch of Civilization
Mrs. Ruth Griswold.
Old Mammy Betsy, can
Col. Whiting, Bayou
Noir Plantaⁿ Ark.
Bagley's Emporium
~~Billings~~ Baxter, little red-headed
quick-motioned person,
rapid speaker.
Billings, short, slow, dull looking
man, lifts fat finger,
pauses, – then? – nods head
3 times, saying "Um".
Bullet, long, lean man – ponders,
with finger at face – then asks 2?
of a single word.

PART II

SIMON WHEELER, DETECTIVE

The Working Notes

The Working Notes

THE THIRTEEN SHEETS of working notes fall into three fairly distinct major groups which I have designated A, B, and C, although it should be clearly understood that the grouping is entirely my own, inferred from the matter treated in each group. Italicized words or phrases enclosed in square brackets [ ] represent deletions; angle brackets ⟨ ⟩ enclose inserted words or phrases. In so far as practicable, the physical arrangement of the notes on the page has been preserved, in spirit if not in exact line-by-line form.

Group A

This group of notes is written in pencil on half-sheets of Crystal Lake Mills paper; the five pages were numbered 1 through 5 by Twain. Because the notes concern "Charley" Dexter, not Hale, they obviously belong to the very earliest stage of the 1877–78 period of composition and are related to the first thirty or so pages of the manuscript, those pages written before Twain changed the name from Charley to Hale. The name Charley is a direct carry-over from the play.

A-1

Hugh ⟨18 or 19⟩ is only giddy — his
mother & sister must never mourn in his
presence.
Only his sweetheart

Let him ask himself —
Do they mourn? *Am* I doing wrong?

He must be in a romantic pet against his ma
& s — they have said something that "hurt"
him. He is *so* sensitive & chuckle-headed.

Mrs Hugh is Ma
Clara is Cl. Spaulding [1]
Mill is a sappy sweet creature of 14 ⟨or 15⟩
with 2 long tails down her back

A-2

Wheeler plays maniac. — ⟨Charley plays keeper.⟩
[*Old humbug sailor*]
No, let Wheeler, *as* a sailor, tell wonderful sea-yarns to Tramp.

Were you ever on a canal? I was in a *storm* on one, once? [2]

His life with the Tram — conversations, &c — shall be the fun of the book.
Suppose [*Hug*] Charley disguises & hides, & Cap'n tells *him* his plans and clews? Good! Charley sometimes sees Clara (who

A-3

is brokenhearted) at a distance) — drops mysterious hints? — hey? *No*, guess not.

Hugh & Charley, at different times, see Clara & Milly walking with the new young minister getting consolation, & mistake their grateful glances for love.

Spread out on the *real* grief of Mrs. Hugh — make her find more comfort in her daughter Clara's brave & loving ministrations than anywhere else.

A-4

3 villains in the piece — those detectives.

The old woman is a good old soul, whose boarders, Tom & Lem lead her a tormented life. She misquotes Scripture, proverbs & everything else.

Charley is 30, Hugh 18 or 19.

Wheeler is married, but his wife stays at her [*daugh*] son-in-law's — sickness in the family.

Charley overhears Mrs. Hugh praying for the murderer or something like that.

A-5

Capn blames[?] his "You done it!" on Charley as first proposed.

⟨Guilford⟩ [3]

Mrs. Hugh & Clara [*too ill*] attend the funeral, but are not around when Hugh is.

Hugh visits home by night & leaves mysterious signs — wants to reveal himself, but 2 things are stronger — enjoyment of the pity his death occasions, & fear of ridicule.

Put in these editors & give some personal editorials.

Group B

This group consists of five half-sheets of Crystal Lake Mills paper, two of which contain matter on both sides of the sheet. Miscellaneous notes apparently written from time to time during the course of composition in 1877–78, the pages are unnumbered and therefore exhibit no clear evidence of sequence. The arrangement of the notes is entirely my own; the reasons for assigning each sheet to its particular place in the sequence are given in the separate headnotes.

B-1 and 2

[These two sheets are written in the same violet ink as the manuscript itself. The first sheet is unnumbered; Twain numbered the second "2." At first glance, the notes appear to be review notes similar to sheet C-1 of the notes for *Huckleberry Finn* (see Bernard DeVoto, *Mark Twain at Work* [Cambridge, Mass 1942] 72–74), but such a conclusion is improbable because the list of characters culminates with several projected for a portion of the manuscript never written. The notes were probably made sometime during the composition of the first eighty or so pages, a conclusion suggested by a comparison of names on the list with revisions in the text. The town visited by Mrs Griswold while Edward Dexter was in Guilford is, in the list, named Hoxton. On MS p 21 (see p 7), it was originally Otway, later revised to read Hoxton. In the notes, the jail is located in Boggsville; on MS p 80 (see p 25) Twain originally wrote Bullville, then cancelled "Bull" and inserted "Boggs." On the other hand, Major Hoskins is identified, on MS p 80, as sheriff with no evidence of revision; in the notes Twain first wrote "jailer" and then revised it to read "sheriff." The revisions establish coordinates, as it were, which "fix" the composition of the note concurrently with MS p 80.

B-2 is written on the reverse of what was apparently the beginning of p 2 of a business letter. Also numbered 2, the reverse contains the words "ceive them from me as cash." About midway down the page under the Wheeler notes, appears the numeral 78E, and under that 75" (i e, 75E).]

B-1

Jack Belford — $500 reward, dead or alive.

Hoxton

Old Humphrey, at Marley

Mrs. Mary Burnside

Mr. Edward Dexter (elder)

Boggsville, where jail is.

Maj. Hoskins, [*jailer*] sheriff.

Guilford Torch of Civilization

Mrs. Ruth Griswold.

Old Mammy Betsy, care Col. Whiting, Bayou
     Noir Planta^n Ark.

Bagley's Emporium

[*Billings*] Baxter, little red-headed quick-
     motioned person, rapid speaker.

Billings, short, slow, dull looking man, lifts
     fat finger, pauses, — then? — nods head
     3 times, saying "Um."

Bullet, long, lean man — ponders, with finger
    at face — then asks ?s of a single word.
Bob Tufts detec [4]

B–2

Crazy Hackett
Happy Winny
Sappy
Holy Jacobs.

B-3

[These notes are written in pencil on a half-sheet discarded from some other manuscript. Page 3 of the manuscript from which it came, it is half-filled with the following aphorisms written in the same violet ink as the *Simon Wheeler* manuscript:

    The offender never pardons.
    Praise a fair day at night.
    Take heed of an ox before, an ass behind, & a [*rascal*] knave on
        all sides.
    Short reckonings make long friends. <old reckonings breed new
        disputes.>
    Nothing comes out of the sack but what was in it.

These sayings are similar to the one written in the margin of MS p 116 (see p 39) and possibly represent a collection of proverbs intended for the use of Mrs Higgins (see second note, A-4).

    Upside down and diagonally in the upper right corner of the sheet appears the following:

    25000
      10
    ―――
    25000

The second digit of the sum or remainder is somewhat blurred but is fairly definitely a 5. One wonders if Twain used that sort of arithmetic in his business affairs.

    The Wheeler notes are written across the bottom half of the sheet at right angles to the discarded text. They deal with events described in chapters 3 and 4, and, since they are obviously jottings made in haste, they probably represent notes made while Twain was composing that portion of the manuscript.]

Meet W
Note to Barnes

Letter fm mother
Hugh's girl.
⟨Toby "loses" note to⟩
Destroy will?

⟨Here introduce Toby wanting a letter copied
out of R. W.⟩ Toby sends to his mother the
letter in wh Dex begs leave to come & explain,
& does the same with [*Milly*] Clara's letter to
Dex in wh she says now or never. So next time
they meet they don't speak. By & by they try
writing once more with the same result.

B-4 and 5

[These notes are in pencil on both sides of a half-sheet on which Twain
originally had written and then discarded seven lines of text for MS p 203
(see p 61). The discarded lines read:

everything but silence & thought. They were beginning to regret
their [*solemn*] resolutions of renunciation; both were ashamed of
this, but neither made confession.

The notes project events for the latter portion of chapter 4.]

B-4

Mrs. B's satisfaction
Toby says Hugh & Milly sick kit to hot
brick
Hale & Clara together increasingly — bliss
perfect — endless lally-gagging — pictures
& incidents — or talk of theirs of how poor
& empty the world was before & how inno-
cently they took this & that laughably
absurd & insipid state of things for happiness — how inexperienced they were, indeed! They hunt for solitudinous places &

he reads poetry while she gloats upon him,
praises his reading & knits.
Mrs. B. "now don't get your feet wet— or do
[*not*] be careful with the gun,

B-5

for you have become very precious. Clara —
now *do* be careful — & don't be gone long.
  Button off — here Clara, sew it on.
  Clara — There — You are *so* hard on your
clothes — I just sewed that on a day or two
ago — (love pat) — There, go 'long. (Heart
sings for joy.) Laughs idiotically at the least
trifle — joy bubbling always.
  Toby gets him to copy letter beginning, "I
think it better that we part, though it rends
my heart to say it &c" to send to Mam in Ark
— Hale gives him one for Clara of a different
tenor, begging that next time they meet she
show by her manner if she is willing to let
him try to explain & make up. But the latter
letter is on pretty paper & looks prettiest
every way — so Toby exchanges & [*gi*] gives
the *former* to Clara. Toby says he delivered it.
That note makes permanent breach — especially as Clara's note asking if he really feels
so, is sent to Ark.
  H & Milly quarrel twice a day

B-6

[Written in violent ink on a half-sheet of Crystal Lake Mills paper, the same
ink and paper as the manuscript itself and the other notes, these notes are
therefore from the 1877–78 period of composition. Because they project

events beyond the point where the manuscript breaks off, they were evidently made just before Twain abandoned the story, either just before sailing for Europe in 1878 or during his European tour of 1878–79.]

⟨Hugh burglarizes clothes.⟩ [5]
Toby to give Mrs. Dexter's letter to Clara.

Dexter to explain offering [6] reward for Hugh & keep Clara believing he may not be dead.

Hugh to see that offer.

Detectives to shadow [*Craz H*] ⟨3 women⟩ & scoff at Craz Haz being the one.

Hugh reads "ad" for remains — his mother's. It is 3 days before Milly's.

Milly goes secretly to detectives about Crazy —they don't believe. It confirms their belief in *her* guilt.

[*Dex will exp*]
Hugh worried about his mother & sister, because of the ad. Inquires of Cap, who tells him who Hugh is, & that the mother & sister only sham distress.

Group C

The notes of Group C are of a much later date than either the manuscript or the previous notes. Written in black ink on three sheets of paper numbered 1 through 3 by Twain, they contain Twain's last projection for the conclusion of the story. The paper on which they are written is a very light blue, medium weight laid paper with horizontal chain lines. Although the sheets are similar in size, 5½″ by 8⅞″, to the half-sheets of Crystal Lake Mills paper previously used, these sheets are not half-sheets, i.e.

full sheets torn in half; the edges are trimmed, and bits of gum clinging to a sample of similar paper in MTP, Berkeley, indicate the paper came in tablets. This paper was used extensively by Twain in the late 1880s and early 1890s for correspondence. It also appears in the manuscript of *A Connecticut Yankee* and the dramatized version of *The Prince and the Pauper.*

C-1

Wheeler has got the murderer in the person of Hugh the tramp, & is waiting for sufficient evidence, which come by & by — for Hugh will find out the above & will confess to Wheeler — W. thinks the $1000 reward secure.

Hugh goes out when he chooses, leaving a dummy asleep to represent him.

To his own family & to Milly he is a deaf & dumb old woman.

Clara knows Dexter for the murderer by his confession to his mother, beginning, "Dearest, I have killed Hugh Burnside. Wait till I come & explain all. Pray for (over)[7] Your miserable son, Hale.

She determines to not let on. If he is a true man he will tell her — as being her due — & will prove it was an accident, then she will stand by him against the world. She has to suffer dumb heart-break, for no hint brings him to confession.

Meantime he knows his letter has miscarried or he would hear from his mother — & meantime *she* is not worrying, knowing him to be in love & busy.

163

C-2

Milly thinks Crazy Hackett is guilty.

⟨Dexter pretends to be shadowing him. Reports to her.⟩

The [*crazy*] half-blind old woman comes & sits around eating her alms & overhearing her lamentings.

Bullet thinks Dexter did it to get all of Humphrey's money.

⟨Half-blind woman heaves Robespierre in on top of Wash. Pumps Toby.⟩

Baxter thinks Milly did it out of jealousy, she being his sweetheart; [*thinks* [*her*] ⟨Dexter⟩ *$1000 reward is Dexter's*] The half blind deaf & dumb old woman (Hugh) overhears him questioning Toby & thinks he suspects Toby — so Hugh fetches General Washington & throws him down unused well — Baxter can dimly descry it — heaves down a bucket of chloride of lime to make the body keep — heaves straw on top of that — & waits in confidence for further evidence, shadowing all the village girls (or old Miss Griswold) seeking for the [one?] Milly was jealous of.

Bucket [8] thinks Miss Griswold did it to supplant Milly. Pumps Toby. Heaves Julius Caesar in on top of Robespierre.

[*Wheeler*] Hugh dumps Louis XVI down on top of Caesar [⟨*shows*⟩] & confesses to Wheeler that after concealing Hugh's body in the woods he went & got it at night & threw it in that well to cast suspicion upon Milly's father — who, ⟨this⟩ tramp had heard, was ferociously opposed to the match. Wheeler slips at night through the high weeds of that disused great garden with sparkle-lantern, lowers it with a string, as the others had done, gets chloride of lime — great trade in it of late — heaves it down, weeds on top of it.

C-3

Hugh, with hurdy-gurdy, & disguised out of all recognition; Judge Griswold; Milly; Dexter; & Miss Griswold are all arrested at the same time & brought with Sheriffs & all the village — with Clara & her mother — to the old well, & the bodies are fetched up, one by one — the detectives maintaining every time that the wax figures are mere blinds & the real corpse is down there yet — till at last, when Milly lets go some peculiarly strenuous wish that it was all a dream & she could die happy if she could but see him once more, Hugh theatrically sheds his disguise & plunges into her arms — then Dexter into Clara's.

I guess we had better go back & make the judge privately believe Dexter did it to carry out the feud & entirely against his desire & feeling & only from a lofty sense of duty. Which lifts D. to the very summit of human perfection in the judge's eyes; & thinks him all the nobler for concealing the deed in order to save the women suffering, whereas a lower spirit would want to *include* them in the suffering to make the vengeance the more comprehensive.

At the end he is willing to be glad his daughter's Savior wasn't killed, & he still loves Dexter but does *not* revere him any longer.

Toby's letters must always *help* the confusion — even *cause* it.

PART III

SIMON WHEELER, DETECTIVE

The Run-Away Horse Episode

The Run-Away Horse Episode

ON AUGUST 23 1877 the Clemens family entertained a large number of family friends, relations, and attending servants from Elmira, N. Y., at their nearby summer retreat, Quarry Farm. In the group was Ida Langdon, wife of Charles Langdon, Livy's brother; Ida was driving a new and spirited gray horse. At sunset, the gray was harnessed to the barouche, and Ida drove from the yard, taking with her her daughter, Julia, and the nursemaid, Norah. Once in the road and headed downhill, the gray quickly increased the pace, despite all that Ida could do, and soon was a full-fledged run-away. Before the spectators could realize what was happening, the barouche plunged down the steepening grade of the road and disappeared from sight around a curve. Twain and Theodore Crane, husband of Livy's elder sister, Susie, ran in pursuit, expecting to find nothing but injury or death at the foot of the hill. Instead they found that the runaway had been stopped by John T. Lewis, the hired man, who was on his way up the hill to the farm. The incident, especially Lewis' alertness and prowess, greatly impressed Twain. On August 25–27 he wrote two extensive accounts, one to William Dean Howells (see *Mark Twain-Howells Letters* [Cambridge, Mass 1960] 1 194–199), the other (reprinted below from the original in the Berg Collection) to Dr John Brown. As we have seen, he also worked the incident into the fabric of *Simon Wheeler, Detective* upon his return to Hartford.

Dr John Brown was an Edinburgh physician and, at the time Twain met him in 1873, an author of some reputation whose fame rested on the highly popular *Rab and His Friend*, published in 1859. When the Clemens family arrived in Edinburgh during their 1873 tour of England and Scotland, Livy was so exhausted by the social excitements of London and the fatigues of travel that she needed medical attention. Twain sought out Dr Brown and secured his services. Dr Brown not only attended Mrs Clemens, whom he soon restored to health and spirits, but also became a close friend and companion of the Clemenses, visiting at their hotel, entertaining them at his home, and escorting them about Edinburgh. One of his special delights was playing with little Susie Clemens, whom he called "Megalopis."

Although Twain never saw him again (the plan to visit him in 1878–79 miscarried), he maintained a fairly regular correspondence with him until his death in 1882.

Quarry Farm
Elmira, N. Y., Aug. 25/77.

Dear Doctor John:

I thought I ought to make a sort of record of it: the pleasantest way to do that would be to write it to somebody; *but* that somebody might let it leak into print, and that we wish to avoid. . . . . . There is Dr. John — he is safe — so let us tell Dr. John about it.

Day before yesterday was a fine summer day away up here on the summit. Aunt Marsh and Cousin May Marsh were here visiting sister Susie Crane and Livy (my wife, you may remember) at our farm house. By and by mother Langdon (who is Livy's mother), came up the hill in the barouche with Norah the nurse-maid and little Jervis (Charley Langdon's little boy) — Timothy the coach-man driving. Behind these came Charley's wife and little girl in the buggy, with the new, young, spry gray horse — a high-stepper. Theodore Crane arrived a little later.

Our two cubs, Susie ("Megalopis") and Clara, were on hand with their nurse Rosa. I was on hand too. Susie Crane's trio of colored servants ditto — these being Josie, housemaid; Aunty Cord, cook, aged 62, turbaned, very tall, very broad, very fine every way (see some account of her in "A True Story Just as I Heard It" in my collected Sketches); and the laundress Chocklate (as Clara calls her — she can't say Charlotte), still taller, still more majestic of proportions, turbaned, very black, straight as an Indian — age 24 — a superb creature to look upon. Then there was the farmer's wife (colored) and her little girl Susan. Wasn't it a good audience to get up an excitement before? — good excitable, inflammable material?

Lewis was still down town, 3 miles away, with his two-horse wagon, to get a load of manure. Lewis is the farmer (colored). He is of mighty frame and muscle, stocky, stooping, ungainly, has a good manly face and a clear eye. Age about 45 or 47, and the most picturesque of men, when he sits in his fluttering work-day rags, humped forward into a bunch, with his aged slouch hat mashed down over his ears and neck. It is a spectacle to make the broken-hearted smile.

Lewis has worked mighty hard and remained mighty poor. At the end of each whole year's toil he can't show a gain of fifty dollars (£ 10.) — He had borrowed money of the Cranes till he owed them $700 — and he being conscientious and honest, imagine what it was to him to have to carry this stubborn, hopeless load year in and year out.

Well, sunset came, and Ida the young and comely, (Charley Langdon's wife) and her little Julia and the nursemaid Norah, drove out at the upper gate behind the new gray horse and started down the long hill — the barouche receiving its load under the porte-cochère, and all the "Quarry Farm" tribe, white and black, grouped upon the grass in front. Ida was seen to turn her face toward us across the fence and intervening lawn— Theodore waved good-bye to her, for he did not know that her sign was a speechless appeal for help.

The next moment Livy said, "Ida's driving too fast down hill!" She followed it with a sort of scream, "Her horse is running away!"

We could see 200 yards down that descent. The buggy seemed to fly. It would strike obstructions and apparently spring the height of a man from the ground.

Theodore and I left the shrieking crowd behind and ran down the hill bareheaded and shouting. A neighbor appeared at his gate — a tenth of a second too late! — the buggy vanished past him like a thought. My last glimpse showed it for one instant, far down the descent, springing high in the air out of a cloud of dust, and then it disappeared. As I flew down the road, my impulse was to

171

shut my eyes as I turned them to the right or left, and so delay for a moment the ghastly spectacle of mutilation and death I was expecting.

I ran on and on, still spared this spectacle, but saying to myself "I shall see it at the turn of the road; they never can pass that turn alive." When I came in sight of that turn I saw two wagons there bunched together — one of them full of people. I said, "Just so — they are staring petrified at the remains."

But when I got amongst that bunch, there sat Ida in her buggy and nobody hurt, not even the horse or the vehicle! Ida was pale but serene. As I came tearing down, she smiled back over her shoulder at me and said, "Well, you're *alive* yet, *aren't* you?" A miracle had been performed — nothing less.

You see, Lewis-the-prodigious, humped upon his front seat, had been toiling up, on his load of manure; he saw the frantic horse plunging down the hill toward him, on a full gallop, throwing his fore-feet breast-high at every jump. So Lewis turned his team diagonally across the road just at the "turn," thus forming a V with the fence — the running horse could not escape that, but must enter it. Then Lewis sprang to the ground and stood in this V. He gathered his vast strength, and with a perfect Creedmoor aim he siezed the gray horse's bit as he plunged by, and fetched him up standing!

It was down hill, mind you; ten feet *further* down hill neither Lewis nor any other man could have saved them, for they would have been on the abrupt "turn," then. But how this miracle was ever accomplished at all, by human strength, generalship and accuracy, is clear beyond my comprehension — and grows more so the more I go and examine the ground and try to believe it was actually done. I know one thing *well*; if Lewis had missed his aim he would have been killed on the spot in the trap he had made for himself, and we should have found the rest of the remains away down at the bottom of the steep ravine.

Ten minutes later Theodore and I arrived opposite the house with the servants straggling after us, and shouted to the distracted group on the porch, "Everybody safe!"

Believe it? Why how *could* they? They knew the road perfectly. We might as well have said it to people who had seen their friends go over Niagara.

However, we convinced them; and then, instead of saying something, or going on crying, they grew very still — words could not express it, I suppose.

Nobody could do anything that night, or sleep, either; but there was a deal of moving talk, with long pauses between — pictures of that flying carriage, these pauses represented — this picture intruded itself all the time and disjointed the talk.

But yesterday evening late, when Lewis arrived from down town, he found his supper spread, and some presents of books there, with very complimentary writings on the fly leaves, and certain very complimentary letters, and divers and sundry bank notes of dignified denomination pinned to these letters and fly-leaves — and one said, among other things, (signed by the Cranes), "We cancel four hundred dollars of your indebtedness to us," &c, &c.

(The end whereof is not yet, of course, for Charley Langdon is out West and will arrive ignorant of all these things to-day.)

The supper room had been kept locked and imposingly secret and mysterious until Lewis should arrive; but around that part of the house were gathered Lewis's wife and child, Chocklate, Josie, Aunty Cord and our Rosa, canvassing things and waiting impatiently. They were all on hand when the curtain went up.

Now Aunty Cord is a violent Methodist, and Lewis an implacable "Dunker Baptist." These two are inveterate religious disputants. — The revealments having been made, Aunty Cord said with effusion —

"*Now* let folks go on saying there ain't no God! Lewis, the Lord sent you there to stop that horse."

Says Lewis —

"Then who sent the *horse* there in sich a shape?"

But I want to call your attention to one thing. When Lewis arrived the other evening, after saving those lives by a feat which I think is the most marvelous of any I can call to mind — when he arrived, hunched up on his manure wagon and as grotesquely picturesque as usual, every body wanted to go and see how he looked. They came back and said he was beautiful. It was *so*, too — and yet he would have *photographed* exactly as he would have done any day these past 7 years that he has occupied this farm.

Aug. 27.

P. S. — Our little romance in real life is happily and satisfactorily completed. Charley has come, listened, acted — and now John T. Lewis has ceased to consider himself as belonging to that class called "the poor."

It has been known, during some years, that it was Lewis's purpose to buy a thirty-dollar silver watch some day, if he ever got where he could afford it. To-day Ida has given him a new, sumptuous gold Swiss stem-winding stop-watch; and if any scoffer shall say "Behold this thing is out of character," there is an inscription within, which will silence him; for it will teach him that this wearer aggrandizes the watch, not the watch the wearer.

I was asked, beforehand, if this would be a wise gift, and I said, "Yes, the very wisest of all; I know the colored race, and I know that in Lewis's eyes this fine toy will throw the other more valuable testimonials far away into the shade. If he lived in England, the Humane Society would give him a gold medal as costly as this watch, and nobody would say 'It is out of character.' If Lewis chose to wear a town clock, who would become it better?"

Lewis has sound common sense, and is not going to be spoiled. The instant he found himself possessed of money, he forgot himself in a plan to make his old father comfortable, who is wretchedly poor, and lives down in Maryland, 500 miles away. His next act, on the spot, was the proffer to the Cranes of the three hundred dollars of his remaining indebtedness to them. This was put off by them to the indefinite future, for he is not going to be allowed to pay that at all, though he doesn't know it.

A letter of acknowledgment from Lewis contains a sentence which raises it to the dignity of literature:

"But I beg to say, humbly, that inasmuch as divine providence saw fit to use me as a instrument for the saving of those presshious lives, the honner conferd upon me was greater than the feat performed."

Good-bye, dear Doctor. You must tell the family, and the Judge, and Mr. Barclay about our great black hero, whom we are so proud of.

Ever lovingly Yours,

Saml. L. Clemens

Notes

Notes

INTRODUCTION, pages xi–xxxv

[1] In the Introduction, the quotations from the novels are taken from the Author's National Edition of Mark Twain's Writings (N Y, Harper & Bros 1899–1910): vol 16, *A Connecticut Yankee in King Arthur's Court* (*CY*); and vol 13, *The Adventures of Huckleberry Finn* (*HF*).

[1a] Typescript Notebook 30 (II), p 32 (entry for Monday, June 1 1896), The Mark Twain Papers, The General Library, University of California, Berkeley (hereafter designated MTP).

[2] SLC to Olivia Clemens, Bloemfontein, South Africa, June 1 1896 (original in MTP).

[3] In TS Notebook 27, p 35 (MTP), under the entry for November 4 1894 Twain lists a number of suggestions for readings, among which is "Si Wheeler's arrival in heaven."

[4] At the top of MS p 433, Twain wrote "Gillette's SS speech," a reference to William Gillette's play *Secret Service*, produced in 1895.

[5] SLC to Howells, Elmira, June 27 1877 (*Mark Twain-Howells Letters* [Cambridge, Mass 1960] I 184: hereafter *MT-HL*). One should remember that Twain habitually used half-sheets of paper. Fifty-four pages, then, would equal twenty-seven full sheets of manuscript.

[6] SLC to Howells, August 29 1877 (*MT-HL* I 200).

[7] Original in MTP. The key word, "detecting," like the rest of the note, is in Reade's inimitable scribble and almost illegible. The first three letters, "det," are clear, but the remainder may be either "ecting" or "ailing." Since "detailing" makes no sense in the context, "detecting" seems the logical choice.

[8] Original in MTP.

[9] Original in MTP.

[10] *MT-HL* I 187.

[11] *MT-HL* I 187–188.

[12] *MT-HL* I 188–189. Twain's assertion that the ms contained over 300 pages is an estimate. The actual ms in the MTP runs to 292 pages with, however, additions on the reverse of a great many pages which would, in the aggregate, bring the total well over 300 pages.

[13] The certificate is preserved in Twain's business scrapbook for 1872–78, p 21, MTP. According to Twain, the title was chosen after Livy objected to the first title, *Balaam Ass* (*MT-HL* I 189), but, since Twain nowhere else refers to the play in this manner,

179

INTRODUCTION, pages xv–xxxv

the comment probably is another instance of Twain's and Howells' jokes about their supposed henpecked status.

[14] Original in Yale University Library.

[15] *Ah Sin,* written in collaboration with Bret Harte, was first performed on May 7 1877 at the National Theatre in Washington. It opened for its disastrous New York run at Daly's Fifth Avenue Theatre on July 31.

[16] SLC to Howells, Elmira, August 29 1877 (*MT-HL* I 200).

[17] Russell to SLC, August 25 and 28 1877, originals in MTP. According to Russell's note of August 25, Twain had by this time changed the title from *Simon Wheeler, The Amateur Detective* to *Clews.*

[18] *MT-HL* I 207 (copyright © 1960 by Mildred Howells and John Mead Howells). Captain Edgar Wakeman was the captain of the *America,* on which Twain sailed from San Francisco to the Isthmus in 1866. Twain used him as the model for Captain Blakeley in *Roughing It,* Captain Hurricane Jones in "Some Rambling Notes of an Idle Excursion," and Captain Stormfield in "Extract from Captain Stormfield's Visit to Heaven."

[19] Original in the Berg Collection, The New York Public Library.

[20] See *Mark Twain's Notebook,* ed A. B. Paine (New York 1935) 129.

[21] *Mark Twain to Mrs. Fairbanks,* ed Dixon Wecter (San Marino 1949) 218.

[22] Original in MTP.

[23] For an account of this event, see Twain's letter to Dr John Brown dated from Elmira, August 25–27 1877, reprinted in Part III. Another account addressed to Howells appears in *MT-HL* I 194–199.

[24] The Clemens family departed from Hartford on Wednesday, March 27 1878.

[25] *MT-HL* I 246. The burlesque chapter written for *A Tramp Abroad* was excised and later used as the title piece for *The Stolen White Elephant,* published in 1882.

[26] *MT-HL* I 269.

[27] TS Notebook 25, p 44, MTP. Frederick J. Hall, partner in Charles L. Webster & Co, Twain's publishing firm, became its manager in 1889 when Webster withdrew.

[28] TS Notebook 27, p 35, MTP.

[29] *MT-HL* II 674–675.

[30] Orion Clemens to Elisha Bliss, Jr, Keokuk, February 1 1877 (original in MTP).

[31] Andrew Chatto to Moncure D. Conway, London, January 31 1877 (original in Justin G. Turner Collection, Los Angeles; typescript in MTP).

32 *MT-HL* I 167.

33 This device proved of only temporary value, because in June 1878 Belford Brothers bought the *Canadian Monthly* and merged it with *Belford's Monthly*.

34 TS Notebook 12, p 2, MTP. If Twain did write such an episode it has since disappeared; it is not, of course, in *A Tramp Abroad*, nor has it survived in the discarded portions of the ms preserved in MTP.

35 See Walter Blair, "When Was *Huckleberry Finn* Written?" *American Literature* xxx (March 1958) 12; Walter Blair, *Mark Twain & Huck Finn* (Berkeley and Los Angeles 1960) 209, 214, 224–225, 234, 250, and 271; and Franklin R. Rogers, *Mark Twain's Burlesque Patterns* (Dallas Tex 1960) 132–135.

36 TS Notebook 28a, I, p 35, MTP.

37 Rogers, *Mark Twain's Burlesque Patterns* 134–135.

38 Paine No 259, p 48 and 49, MTP.

39 The episode was based upon the Smarr-Owsley shooting in Hannibal, January 1845. For the details of this affair see Walter Blair, *Mark Twain & Huck Finn* 307–308.

SIMON WHEELER, DETECTIVE

In the following Notes, words printed in italics within square brackets are words deleted in the MS. Prior deletions within a later deletion are enclosed by further pairs of square brackets.

PART I, Chapter 1, pages 3–10

1 Above this phrase, at the top of MS p 2, Twain has noted in parentheses "not Saturday but Monday," apparently referring to the excised passage following the next paragraph (see note 3); the shift in time from Saturday to Monday seems to have no special significance except that Monday would allow time for the Guilford papers, weeklies issued on Friday, to reach Drytown for Hale Dexter's perusal upon his arrival there as related in chapter 2.

2 . . . woods and hills, [*shady valleys, overhung by pictur*] lay before him. (Above "woods and hills," at the top of MS p 3, Twain has written in parenthesis "*moonlight, now.*")

3 Following this paragraph, on MS p 3–4, Twain has deleted one paragraph:

> It was a Saturday afternoon in summer, and the sun was sinking fast. The villagers were out in force; the weather was too fine to be wasted. Groups and couples, in the lightest of summer raiment, were distributed along the bank of the stream, from the village all the way up into the gorge, a mile and a half away — for this was the favorite promenade. Some sat in the shade of the rocks and trees, some walked. Some gossiped, some courted, some romped, some dozed or knitted or mused, according to age, sex or disposition.

PART I, Chapter 1, pages 3–10

⁴ This paragraph, on MS p 4, originally began:

> Along the bank of this stream, from the village far up into the gorge was a broad and well worn footway, which in places stretched. . . .

⁵ Following this paragraph, on MS p 12–13, Twain has deleted one paragraph:

> For a month there had been a guest in the house — Charley Dexter, aged twenty-four or twenty-five; dark, compact, muscular, manly, a spirted fellow, intelligent and educated. [*He was from a Missouri town some fifty mi*] His home was in Kentucky, [*but he was latterly from*] but for some months had been visiting various families of relatives and old friends of his parents in several parts of Missouri. He had spent more than two months in Guilford, with his aunt the widow Burnside, before extending his visit to the Griswolds, where he was to remain as long. He was not related to the Griswolds, but Mrs. Griswold and his mother had been school mates in girlhood and devoted friends and neighbors in early married life. During the three months and upwards which he had now spent in Guilford, Mrs. Griswold had grown to be as fond of him as if he had been her son, and to treat him accordingly.

Note that originally Dexter's name was Charley; in the next few pages of the MS, Twain has gone through the text striking out "Charley" wherever it appears and substituting "Hale."

⁶ Above this clause, at the top of MS p 20, Twain has noted parenthetically "Mrs. G. doesn't know the D's, but loves D because her husband does — and pities him." The suggestion was undoubtedly a result of the deletion reproduced in note 5, but it was not acted upon as the subsequent text will show.

⁷ Having some difficulty in keeping the Burnsides and Griswolds clear in his mind, Twain first wrote "Mrs. Burnside" and later corrected himself (MS p 20).

⁸ Twain originally named the town Otway and changed it to Hoxton in a subsequent revision (MS p 21). Both names are fictitious.

⁹ Along the margin beside this sentence, Twain wrote the word "Explain," apparently intending to return to this passage and expand it (MS p 23). The point which needed explanation, as indicated by a vertical stroke in the margin, is Dexter's use of an alias "for better security."

¹⁰ Twain started to write "Burnside" and then corrected himself (MS p 26).

¹¹ Beside this and the following three paragraphs, MS p 31, Twain has drawn a vertical line in the margin and written the word "kill."

PART I, Chapter 2, pages 14–25

¹ ". . . kindly point —"

[*"Point the way? It wouldn't do any good. You couldn't go in a beeline. It's*]

"Point the way? I will. . . ." (MS p 44)

2 During the composition, Twain originally began MS p 54 with the following: "frankness that if you have enjoyed [*the jaunt*] this half hour nearly as much as I have" and then, apparently dissatisfied, turned the sheet over and wrote the present text.

3 ". . . his name! [*I deserve to never see him again. He would have told me in an instant. Now I've lost her for good.*"] A woman wouldn't have forgotten such a thing." (MS p 56)

4 . . . middle of a sentence, [*with* —

"*I suppose he is just passing through the country — not going to stop.*"]

brightening hopefully as she spoke —

"Now suppose Mr. . . ." (Recto and Verso MS p 57)

5 After "*Nothing!*" Twain originally wrote and later cancelled: Then to herself: "That failed." (Verso MS p 57)

6 ". . . asked him! [*That sex is so stupid!*"] (MS p 63)

7 This meditation was inserted during a later revision of the text at a time when Twain had forgotten the name of the old man in question. In writing the insert Twain here and in the next sentence left blanks to be filled in but never filled them (Verso MS p 75).

8 Originally "Bullville" (MS p 80).

PART I, Chapter 3, pages 28–32

1 This reference to the California gold rush, of course, places the events of the story in the very late 1840s or early 1850s.

2 Opposite this clause, in the margin of MS p 94, Twain has drawn a short line and noted "kill former." The reference is to the use of the same descriptive clause, "the light of battle was in his eye," at the opening of the Judge's explanation of the feud to his wife in chapter 1.

3 "What is your plan?"

[*"I have formed none."*

"*You will give him a full and equal chance with yourself?*"

"*Sir!*"

[*"There — you must pardon it. It expressed more than I meant.*]

"*Good. You* ARE *a Dexter. I know it now. Don't be offended. I had only the merest shade of a misgiving — it is gone, now.*"

"*What gave it you?*"

"*A sentence in*]

"I have formed none. . . ." (MS p 95)

4 Above this sentence, at the top of MS p 96, Twain has noted "Maiden sister of 40," a reference to Martha Griswold, who is introduced a few paragraphs later.

PART I, Chapter 3, page 32

5 Twain has written in the margin of MS p 100 "Refer to sick sister in earlier chap." Since no such reference appears in the previous pages, Twain apparently abandoned the novel before acting upon this instruction.

6 Above this phrase, at the top of MS p 101, Twain has noted in parentheses "Last part of Chap. before A¹." The note makes little sense. The reference to "A¹" is to the opening page of the next chapter, MS p 104, which is labeled A¹ in the upper left corner.

7 ... the matter. [*Toby is shrewd and reliable. He shall serve in my place.*] (MS p 102)

Twain replaced Toby with the Judge's friend, Major Barnes, for the obvious reason that it would hardly be consistent, in portraying an affair of honor such as this between two Southern gentlemen, to provide Dexter with a Negro slave for a second. Major Barnes, not only because of his social position but also because of his military rank, is much more appropriate for the office.

PART I, Chapter [4], pages 35–69

1 Originally Twain formed two thoughts in Dexter's mind; the paragraph before revision, on MS p 112, read as follows:

The tremendous surprise of the situation had thrown Dexter's mind into a state of chaos. Only two thoughts took form and shape in this confusion. One was, "Thank God, the time has come and gone, and I shall never be a murderer, now —" The other was, "I shall see her again."

2 "... welcome, sir; [*I am glad to see you again, sir.*] Mother. ..." (MS p 112)

3 Above this, on the left side of the top margin, MS p 116, Twain has written "Better to be a stalled ox and feed on the vapors of a dungeon" (continued in the bottom margin) "vault than gain the whole world and lose thine own soul, as the saying is." The right side of the top margin bears the notations "*Dam*-mascus blades" and "*Hell*-en's B." These two notes are of interest because they are jokes used in "The 1,002nd Night." Once, in exasperation, King Shahriyar exclaims, "O, *Dam*——ascene liverwort. . . !" On another occasion, the King begins, "O, Hel——" When Scherezade breaks in with a horrified "Sire!" he continues, "——en's Babies. . . ." *Helen's Babies* is a novel by John Habberton which enjoyed a tremendous popularity after its publication in 1876.

4 "... vivid way," [*said the guilty Dexter, nearly aground for something to say.*] gasped Dexter. (MS p 118)

5 ... odds and ends. [*She cried over that literary drivel that night. Now she said diffidently, and watching*] Then she dexterously. . . . (MS p 130)

6 At the top of MS p 140, appears the faint notation "Work in the glass eyes?" and beneath that "Wheelers do it." The reference to glass eyes suggests that Twain had in mind for this novel another version of Jim Blaine's story in *Roughing It* about Miss Jefferson and Miss Wagner (Vol II, chap 12).

Farther down the page, the text was written over the following almost illegible pencilled notes:

> Meet[?] W . . .
>
> . . . . .
>
> Note to Barnes
> letter from mother
> Hugh's girl

[7] Here Twain accidentally repeated "heavy-heartedness" instead of writing "spitefulness" (MS p 152).

[8] This title and the subsequent letters which Hale copies for Toby are apparently creations of Twain's imagination. The purpose, of course, is to burlesque the books of model letters printed and circulated in large numbers during the latter half of the nineteenth century.

[9] At the top of MS p 169, Twain has written "7-up——", apparently a reference to the card game, and beneath that, faintly, "corn shucking."

[10] Originally Twain left a blank for the name of the paper. In a finer pen with black ink, presumably at a later date, he filled in *Torch of* and left the remainder blank, apparently unable to remember the full title (MS p 173).

[11]. . . wending homeward, [*silently pondering over the sudden change in the Burnside weather, and wond*] and Clara. . . . (MS p 181)

[12] This paragraph, on MS p 183, was written over the following pencilled notes:

> Carries off flowers
>
>   poem
> Hugh's heroic day dream
> Dex & Milly at home
> Absent from Clara 2 days

[13] One page of the notes accompanying the novel is written on a discarded MS p 203 on which Twain originally concluded this paragraph in the following manner:

> . . . everything but silence and thought. They were beginning to regret their [*solemn*] resolutions of renunciation; both were ashamed of this, but neither made confession.

[14] . . . perfect until [*he should save Milly's life in some blood-curdling way. His opportunity came presently when he was least expecting it.*] that lack. . . . (MS p 227–228)

[15] Twain originally began the next paragraph "The slow and tiresome journey was accomplished in due course," then struck out what he had written and began again in greater detail (MS p 230).

[16] . . . to read, [*but really to watch the road for Hugh's carriage.*] but her mind. . . . (MS p 233)

PART I, Chapter [4], pages 74–82

[17] Here again, Twain left a blank for the name of the paper. Later with a much finer pen and black ink, he filled in *Torch of* but omitted *Civilization* (MS p 240).

[18] On MS p 244, Twain left a blank to be filled in later with the proper name. Although there are two weeklies published in Guilford and Twain has quoted from both, I have chosen *Torch of Civilization* here because neither in the text nor in the notes does Twain give a title for the other paper and, further, in the case of previous blanks Twain has consistently supplied that title.

[19] In the upper left corner of MS p 262, Twain has written "Follows Miss Sanning," apparently projecting an episode which he never developed.

[20] Originally Twain wrote, ". . . make Miss Martha an' Milly pack right up an' tuck 'em away a-boomin'." But at the end of the chapter, at the top of MS p 270, Twain noted to himself, "Milly does not go to D. town." In accordance with this note, he went back and altered this passage (MS p 264).

[21] After "[Name]" on MS p 269, there is a note in an apparently different hand: "Note over." The note on Verso MS p 269 is "Finish chapter from page 270 B [1]." See chapter 3, note 6.

PART I, Chapter [6], pages 91–92

[1] At the top of MS p 297, Twain has written "Wheeler shall *play drunk* like Garrick." David Garrick had a gift for simulating drunkenness which made his portrayal of Sir John Brute in Vanbrugh's *Provok'd Wife* his favorite and most renowned comic role. A spectator describes Garrick's performance in the following fashion:

"In the beginning, he wears his wig straight, and one sees the full, round face. Afterwards, when he comes home quite drunk, his face looks like the moon of a few days before the last quarter, nearly half of it being obscured by the wig. The part which one does see is flushed and greasy, yet it is extremely friendly, and thus makes up for the loss of the other half. . . . He enters his wife's room, and to her anxious inquiry what is the matter with him, replies 'as sound as a roach, wife.' Yet he does not stir from the doorpost, against which he leans as heavily as if he wanted to rub his back on it. He then becomes in turn brutal, tipsily wise, and again friendly, all to the loud applause of the audience. In the scene where he falls asleep he amazed me. The way in which, with closed eyes, swimming head, and pallid face, he quarrels with his wife, and melting his r's and l's into one — into a sort of dialect of medials — now abuses, now falters out scraps of morality; then the way in which he moves his lips, so that one cannot tell whether he is chewing, or tasting something, or speaking — all this as much exceeded my expectation as anything else I have seen this remarkable man do. I wish you could hear him say 'pre-ro-ga-tive' in this part. It is only after two or three efforts that he is able to get as far as the third syllable" (quoted in Margaret Barton, *Garrick* [New York, Macmillan 1949] 62–63).

[2] This is, of course, another version of the quip used in *The Prince and the Pauper* (chapter 14). While listening to the Archbishop of Canterbury's report on preparations for Henry VIII's funeral, Tom Canty whispers to Lord Hertford:

"What day did he say the burial hath been appointed for?"

"The 16th of the coming month, my liege."

" 'Tis a strange folly. Will he keep?"

PART I, Chapter [7], pages 97–112

[1] This chapter begins on MS p 319 on what was originally to be page 5 of some other ms, possibly an earlier draft of this novel. The page contained just one line, a fragment of a sentence: "O I was pretty unfairly," which Twain crossed out.

[2] In the margin of MS p 328, beside the last portion of this paragraph, that is, from "Ah, there was no crime" to the end, Twain has written "Describe this instead of talking here[?]."

[3] At the top of MS p 331, Twain has noted "Capt. tackles 2 drug clerks, Hale, Tom and Lem."

[4] Opposite this and the following sentence, along the margin of MS p 333, Twain has written "Break this up more."

[5] This sentence, which begins at the bottom of MS p 334 and concludes in the top margin of MS p 336 renumbered 335, replaces an extensive deletion which begins at the bottom of MS p 334 and extends to the bottom of the original MS p 335:

"Therefore, remain where you are. Make yourself a comfort to them."

"I? I cannot go near them. [*They would*] I, comfort them? I, talk with them about this awful thing, with this grisly secret in my heart? They would speak of his 'assassin' — that is the word they would use. They would wonder to see me labor in my talk; they would marvel to see me always struggling to get away from the subject. I should go mad! Put yourself in my place."

Judge Griswold had to confess that the case was more difficult than it had seemed before. Presently Dexter said, with something like a groan —

This revision leaves the present manuscript with no page numbered 336 as Twain has noted on the reverse of the cancelled MS p 335.

[6] ". . . kind of a cow. [*There's money in her, too. Old Barnum*] Now I'll tell you. . . ." (MS p 350)

[7] Above this paragraph, at the top of MS p 356, Twain has written two notes: "He avoids taking up quarters at Mrs. B's" and "Clara has made his room fine."

[8] At the top of MS p 376, Twain has noted parenthetically "detective library and wardrobe," a suggestion which is acted upon later in the detailed description of Wheeler's "headquarters."

[9] Hugh had [*matured his plans for a romantic, mysterious disappearance*] been thinking diligently. . . . (MS p 378)

PART I, Chapter [8], pages 119–127

1 In the top left corner of MS p 400 Twain began a note "Stray dog poi or," which he crossed out. Shifting to the top right corner, he wrote, "Wolf poisoned Dr. calls bones human. Only 1 or 2 left — spinal column — can't account for tail."

2 The first part of this chapter, MS p 400–410, has been substantially expanded from an earlier draft, for MS p 410, originally numbered 406, begins with two paragraphs, deleted in the revision, which originally immediately followed this paragraph:

> It was well for Dexter that the candle light was dim: none saw the effect of this speech upon him. He stammered out his thanks and a protest against dislodging Hugh, but Mrs. Burnside said —
>
> "No, Hugh will not mind it, it will gratify him. Besides, it is all settled and we won't have it any other way." [See also note 3.]

3 Following this paragraph, which concludes MS p 409, Twain has inserted p 406–409 of an earlier draft renumbered 410–413. The material thus inserted embraces the following nine paragraphs.

4 Then Dexter [turned] [turned a lusterless eye upon the Judge, and said, with a heavy sigh —

"You have seen, you have heard. Their restored] said in a voice. . . . (renumbered MS p 411–412)

5 ". . . at an end. [You see how they are going to suffer. Shall they bear the whole burden of a calamity which nothing but my criminal heedlessness has brought upon them? I will not desert, but stand my ground, do my best to help them, and live through these horrors that will begin for me to-day if I can.] I realize now. . . ." (renumbered MS p 412–413)

6 You have chosen [the manly part. I do not say it as a compliment;] rightly, I feel sure. — (renumbered MS p 413)

7 ". . . on all sides. [To move is to be checkmated.] It is a curiously. . . ." (MS p 416)

Twain rejected the briefer metaphor in favor of the more extended simile which completes the paragraph.

8 Now attributed to Dexter, this speech is an expansion of the deleted first portion of the Judge's speech which follows. The excised portion, given below, begins MS p 422, originally numbered 412 (see note 9):

> [only generalized your course?"] These first days are going to be the hardest. The finding of the body, the public excitement, the inquest, the funeral, — if you can endure these first days all is safe; those that follow will grow gradually easier. [By and by, they] Mind, you will be often moved. . . .

9 This and the following three paragraphs are on MS p 412–414 of an earlier draft renumbered 422–424.

10 At the top of MS p 433, Twain has written "Gillette's SS speech." William Gillette was a young man from Hartford who appeared in John T. Raymond's dramatic pro-

duction of *The Gilded Age* at the Hartford Opera House in January 1875. Paine, in describing the cast, includes "a Hartford young man, who would one day be about as well known to playgoers as any playwright or actor that America has produced. His name was William Gillette, and it was largely due to Mark Twain that the author of *Secret Service* and of the dramatic 'Sherlock Holmes' got a fair public start. Clemens and his wife loaned Gillette the three thousand dollars which tided him through his period of dramatic education. Their faith in his ability was justified" (A. B. Paine, *Mark Twain, A Biography* [New York 1912] I 539).

PART I, Chapter [9], pages 129–133

[1] The following paragraph is on a new MS p 439. At the bottom of MS p 438 a deleted passage begins which continues on the original p 439, now renumbered 439½:

> So [*Dexter*] he added to the advertisement the word "remains." Clara sat by, watching, but said nothing. That is, aloud — though to herself she said: "This is the death of hope; he made no protest against that word. His good generous heart has made him say his hopeful things out of pity for us. But now I know that he, too, believes the poor boy is dead. I will be silent, for he is suffering much for our sakes, poor Hale!"
>
> Yes, much more than she imagined.

The next paragraph of the present text, beginning "It cost Dexter" is inserted in the paragraph break between "poor Hale!" and "Yes, much more" of the deleted passage. Above the word "remains," in the top margin of MS p 439½, Twain wrote the following note, also deleted: "*No, he protests vigorously.*"

[2] "... traitor in me. [*I will never rest until* [*I have brought*] *his murderer has answered for his crime.*"] Crazy Hackett will know. . . ." (MS p 450)

[3] The following passage, at the bottom of MS p 451, has been deleted at this point:

> When Judge Griswold saw Dexter's advertisement, he wrote —
>
> "It will help to throw the dogs of the law off the scent. It was a bold and ingenious conception, but I am not glad you have done it. In

The abrupt halt in mid-sentence and an abrupt change in handwriting and pen between MS p 451 and 452 strongly suggest that MS p 451 with its deleted passage concludes a portion of an earlier draft. MS p 452 to the conclusion of the chapter, all similar in handwriting and pen, would be then a later revision.

PART I, Chapter [10], pages 138–140

[1] The obvious connection between the following account of Simon Wheeler's dream visit to heaven and "Extracts from Captain Stormfield's Visit to Heaven" helps to date the composition of the earliest surviving draft of the latter. Twain first began the development of this motif in San Francisco in 1868 in a now lost sketch of Captain Wakeman's visit to heaven. Dissatisfied with the result, he abandoned it. In 1872 or '73 he tried a new approach which again failed to satisfy him. The next step in the

PART I, Chapter [10], pages 138–140

evolution of the Wakeman-Stormfield story is Si Wheeler's narrative, which apparently is simply a reshaping and possibly a condensation of the 1872–73 Wakeman-Stormfield narrative. The reshaping to pad the Wheeler novel apparently led Twain to a new plan for a separate Wakeman-Stormfield story which he outlined to Howells during Howells' visit to Hartford, March 6–7 1878. Howells encouraged him to go ahead and urged him to make the narrative a separate publication, not a magazine sketch (see SLC to Orion, March 23 1878, in *Mark Twain's Letters*, ed A. B. Paine [New York, c 1917] I 323).

The first surviving draft of the Wakeman-Stormfield story, in which the central character is named Captain Hurricane Jones, is written in violet ink on Crystal Lake Mills stationery, a paper also used in the MSS of the Wheeler play and novel. The name of the central character suggests that the draft was written after "Some Rambling Notes of an Idle Excursion" (early 1877). According to Walter Blair's study, the violet ink was used at Hartford from late November, 1876, to mid-June, 1880, and sporadically in Europe in 1878–79; the paper was used from 1876 to 1880 ("When Was *Huckleberry Finn* Written?" *AL* xxx [March 1958] 7 and 9–10). These facts make it clear that the earliest surviving draft of the Wakeman-Stormfield story cannot be the 1872 or '73 version which Twain described to Orion; it must be instead the version proposed to Howells March 6–7 1878. Consequently, it must have been written in Europe in 1878–79 or in Hartford between November 1879 and June 1880.

2 Along the margin of MS p 463, beside the opening of this narrative, Twain has written, "Knock out " " marks" (knock out quotation marks).

3 I was beginning to [*feel*] *be afraid I had missed a connection somewhere and fetched up at the wrong place.* [*My*] I listened, and my spirits. . . . (MS p 471)

PART II, The Working Notes, pages 155–164

1 Clara Spaulding, later Mrs John B. Stanchfield, was Olivia Clemens' girlhood friend from Elmira. A frequent visitor both at Quarry Farm, the Clemens' summer retreat near Elmira, and at Hartford, she was also Mrs Clemens' companion on the 1873 trip to England and during 1878–79 European tour.

2 Possibly Twain meant to include something similar to the ballad of storm and shipwreck on the Erie Canal, "The Aged Pilot Man," in *Roughing It*, II chapter x.

3 Inserted in violet ink.

4 Written along lower half of left margin.

5 Scribbled in top margin.

6 Above "offering" Twain has written the figures "455."

7 Despite the "over" nothing appears on the reverse of the sheet.

8 Twain has apparently forgotten that in the manuscript the third detective is named Billings, or he had determined upon a change.

Minor Revisions

The more extensive or significant revisions and deletions in the manuscript are given in the Notes to the text. Below are listed the less extensive
revisions, keyed to the page and line of the present edition and the cor-
responding page in the manuscript.

The following types of deletions or revisions have not been indicated:
those which represent mere slips of the pen (usually words partially
written); those which fail to illuminate Twain's choice of words or in-
telligibly register a change in thought; and three substitutions of pronouns
for names to avoid awkward repetition.

In the list below, an arrow bracket precedes the revised word or words.

p 3:4–5 [MS p 1]: where nothing ever happened > where the telegraph intruded
      not.
p 3:9 [MS p 2]: at all > either
p 3:11–12 [MS p 2]: Ossian was > Ossian and Thaddeus of Warsaw were
p 3:22 [MS p 4]: winding across > stealing through

p 4:6 [MS p 6]: nothing > no power
p 4:12 [MS p 7]: ears > head
p 4:12–13 [MS p 7]: as by brackets > as one keeps curtains back by brackets
p 4:20 [MS p 8]: its true and only sensible > what he called its only warrantable
p 4:21 [MS p 8]: might fall > and fell
p 4:26–27 [MS p 8]: but he ought > but there an end
p 4:28 [[MS p 9]: all sorts of people > everybody, indiscriminately
p 4:30 [MS p 9]: killed > clubbed
p 4:31 [MS p 9]: waitress and another > chambermaid and another

p 5:16 [MS p 11]: lashed to> tied at
p 5:28 [MS p 14]: and her life > whose life
p 5:30 [MS p 14]: and a good deal of the pluck > and the pluck

p 6:2 [MS p 15]: coquettishly, so nice > coquettishly, which
p 6:3 [MS p 15]: very pretty > pretty
p 6:7 [MS p 15]: all day, with young Dexter, taking > all day, taking

p 6:23 [MS p 17]: "It is young Charley D > "It is Mrs. Burnside's nephew
p 6:23 [MS p 17]: Charley > Hale

p 7:7 [MS p 19]: work > deed
p 7:14 [MS p 20]: Charley > Hale
p 7:16 [MS p 20]: done > finished
p 7:19 [MS p 20]: followed > came to
p 7:24–25 [MS p 21]: killed my sister's husband > warned my sister's husband and called him out and killed him.
p 7:30 [MS p 21–22]: — I never > — so wounded

p 9:10 [MS p 26]: without > forgetting
p 9:12 [MS p 27]: Presently he was a fine > Presently he said —
p 9:16 [MS p 27]: a generation > three generations
p 9:30 [MS p 29]: waylaid me > met me unexpectedly

p 10:14 [MS p 31]: "It is close by. > "Is the old man any better?"
p 10:16, 25, 26 [MS p 31]: Charles > Hale

p 11:6–7 [MS p 33]: — now I notice it, there are > now that I observe it closer there are
p 11:9 [MS p 33]: Charles > Hale
p 11:30 [MS p 36]: sat > walked the floor

p 13:21 [MS p 40]: heard > glanced rearward and saw
p 13:22 [MS p 40]: which was a welcome sight > a welcome sight
p 13:28 [MS p 41]: very handsome > handsome

p 14:2 [MS p 41]: that sort > the sort

p 15:21 [MS p 47]: deep in > active

p 17:15–16 [MS p 53]: so when I get hold of a > but with you it's different
p 17:27 [MS p 55]: vexed spur-stab > spur-stab
p 17:29 [MS p 55]: had something of vexation > expressed a trifle of vexation

p 18:4 [MS p 56]: blundering absurdity > blunder
p 18:7 [MS p 56]: young fellow > chap
p 18:7 [MS p 56]: fool > numscull

p 18:10 [MS p 56–57]: Said the former > The latter

p 18:11 [MS p 57]: listened > listening without hearing

p 18:32 [MS p 58]: The first thing he did was to > He looked around and said —

p 19:20 [MS p 59]: Blister > Burn

p 20:27 [MS p 64]: put up > arrived

p 21:1, 3 [MS p 64]: four > three

p 21:6 [MS p 65]: benches and bottles lay wrecked > benches lay wrecked

p 21:16 [MS p 66]: And down went the inquirer > He had his hands full in a moment.

p 21:19 [MS p 66]: shams. > imitations!

p 21:22 [MS p 66]: sledge-like > vigorous

p 21:22–23 [MS p 67]: " 'Nough!" > for quarter

p 21:27 [MS p 67]: Dexter went > The landlord

p 22:8 [MS p 69]: Benton > Ozark-way

p 23:26 [MS p 74]: you ain't abed > you're around

p 24:11 [MS p 75]: "This *is* the oddest fish I have come across yet," > "This *is* an odd fish,"

p 24:14 [MS p 75]: Nothing but that young girl > Of that young girl

p 24:16 [MS p 76]: music > the distant murmur of music

p 24:20 [MS p 76]: read > decipherable

p 24:24 [MS p 77]: dreary paragraphs > paragraphs

p 24:25 [MS p 77]: exasperating > infuriating

p 25:22–28 [MS p 82]: public ear with > refined and > long-outraged public ear

p 27:4 [MS p 83]: Mrs. Dexter > Mrs. Griswold

p 27:11 [MS p 84]: "Yes, mother said, 'Ruth (meaning you) will expect a shadow > "Yes, mother said she would have to certify me to you

p 27:17 [MS p 85]: the Lambs always lions > the Strongs always weak

p 28:4 [MS p 86]: child > daughter

p 28:20 [MS p 88]: that not being his way > or even in a fluid state p 29:3 [MS p 90]: lasting > deep

p 29:4 [MS p 90]: revealing > betraying

p 29:7 [MS p 90]: half-past nine > ten

p 29:18 [MS p 91]: came forward in his grave > stately way > moved forward, held

p 29:23–24 [MS p 92]: The Judge said — > There was a brief silence. Then the Judge's spoon stopped stirring; he looked up and said with solemnity —

p 30:17 [MS p 94]: animation > life

p 30:26 [MS p 96]: well > right

p 31:12 [MS p 97]: Judge > gentlemen

p 31:22–23 [MS p 98]: pocket > reticule

p 31:25 [MS p 99]: "I didn't notice. Ah, here it is." > "I didn't notice."

p 32:10 [MS p 100]: only > favor > only sister

p 33:1 [MS p 104]: drafting > he drafted

p 33:2 [MS p 104]: writing > he wrote

p 33:6–7 [MS p 105]: vaguely floating > floating, vague

p 33:25 [MS p 107]: armed himself > ordered Toby to carry Judge Griswold's note to Major Barnes, then armed himself

p 33:27 [MS p 107]: guileless > foolish

p 33:29 [MS p 107]: The blood rushed to his face > His cheeks burned

p 35:30 [MS p 114]: the warmth of blood > the blood

p 37:6 [MS p 119]: man's heart > man's guilty heart > man's heart

p 37:6 [MS p 119]: cloven, and his release is swift, but > cloven, but

p 37:6 [MS p 119]: his wife's > his innocent wife's > his wife's

p 37:22 [MS p 120]: dismally > nervously

p 37:29 [MS p 121]: feeling rather cornered > nearly aground for a reply

p 39:11 [MS p 126]: to have > to see

p 40:4 [MS p 129]: rot > drivel

p 40:11–12 [MS p 130]: Milly tucked it into her bosom > Milly, beaming with happiness and with pride in her poet, tucked the precious rubbish into her bosom

p 40:27 [MS p 131]: enveloped > put

p 41:29 [MS p 135]: separated > punctuated

p 45:33 [MS p 150]: happy > gladsome and gay

p 46:10 [MS p 151]: said Dexter to himself > said Dexter
p 46:12 [MS p 151]: a lunatic > a maniac
p 46:19 [Verso MS p 152]: have had chosen himself > have chosen him
p 46:23 [Verso MS p 152]: gloominess > heavy-heartedness
p 46:28 [Recto MS p 152]: good — not > mollifyingly

p 47:7 [Verso MS p 153]: and is nearly at > but has not quite swung to

p 48:2 [MS p 155½]: give it to him!" > do it!"
p 48:3 [MS p 155½]: embrace > hug
p 48:9 [MS p 156]: annoy > gall
p 48:9 [MS p 156]: rather as if he were a > in a zealous torrent
p 48:23 [Verso MS p 158]: bowling down > filling away on
p 48:23 [Verso MS p 158]: in a wind > with a wind
p 48:29 [MS p 159]: pages > leaves

p 49:8 [MS p 161]: in places > sometimes
p 49:11 [MS p 161]: can > kin
p 49:12 [MS p 161]: awful > mons'us
p 49:21 [MS p 162]: funny > curus

p 50:4 [MS p 164]: now > at present
p 50:8 [MS p 164]: you shall > thou shalt
p 50:9 [MS p 164]: a hundred-fold > a double and treble
p 50:13 [MS p 165]: the moth doth not > moths do not
p 50:16–18 [MS p 165]: Ain't dem words lovely an' don' > Don't dem words taste good in you' mouf! don't dey 'mind you of suckin' a sugar-rag when you was little? an' don't
p 50:19–20 [MS p 165–166]: O yes, dat's de one, King Sol'mon > King Sol'mon

p 51:26 [MS p 170]: nestled > buried

p 52:10–11 [MS p 172]: that evening > than the Griswold supper
p 52:15 [MS p 173]: offensive > not gracious, or even civil
p 52:19 [MS p 173]: young fellows > striplings
p 52:29 [MS p 174]: soft sigh > sigh

p 53:8 [MS p 175]: pleasant — and unexpected! > pleasant!

p 53:19–20 [MS p 176]: began an animated chat with them > to their grateful surprise began to pour out upon them an animated badinage

p 53:32 [MS p 178]: Clar > The girl

p 54:1 [MS p 178]: neglectfulness > folly

p 54:12 [MS p 179]: shame > remorse > shame

p 54:14 [MS p 179]: Clara > Milly

p 54:21 [MS p 180]: broken heart > blistered heart

p 54:22 [MS p 180–181]: parlor lights were out > joker and his friend

p 54:32 [MS p 182]: quickly > with a quick interest

p 55:6 [MS p 182]: This amiable creature > The dismal poet

p 55:10 [MS p 183]: Mill > Clara

p 56:7 [MS p 185]: What are you waiting for?" "Nothing." > Ah, I do not deserve such devotion!

p 56:8 [MS p 185]: Hugh heaved a soulful sigh > He came and kissed her tenderly, heaved a sigh

p 56:13–14 [MS p 185]: put out the lights and retired > and carried them to her chamber

p 56:19 [MS p 186]: too full of thought for speech > full of thought

p 56:27 [MS p 187]: grotesquely blind > blind

p 56:27 [MS p 187]: her age!" Then he said aloud — > her age!"

p 57:24 [MS p 189]: destined > a-going

p 57:25 [MS p 189]: fear not > don't be afeard

p 57:26–27 [MS p 190]: one who watches > there's one that's a-watching

p 57:28 [MS p 190]: meat > beefsteak

p 60:8 [MS p 197]: preferred > was full of

p 60:9 [MS p 198]: Here was a new bond of sympathy > Dexter felt nearer

p 60:27 [MS p 200]: When Hugh gave the flowers > Hugh found his sister

p 61:18 [Verso MS p 203]: under the moon > in the twilight

p 61:18 [Verso MS p 203]: eight > seven

p 62:12 [MS p 205]: Hugh's gloomy > the black misery of

p 62:27 [MS p 206]: "I, too > "Me, too.

p 62:27 [MS p 207]: it would be > for now he should have

p 63:4 [MS p 208]: beaming > alive

p 63:9 [MS p 209]: mind > brain

p 63:12 [MS p 209]: In another moment she said — "Now sit down and try to be contented while > Let us condense

p 64:10 [MS p 212]: this couple > they

p 64:12 [MS p 213]: circumstance > thing

p 64:29 [MS p 215]: transfixed with astonishment while > transfixed, while

p 65:21 [MS p 217]: "Look here! are you > "Are you

p 66:10 [MS p 220]: memorable evening > most memorable evening of her life,

p 67:7 [MS p 223]: a love-box in return > her requiting love-box as a grace

p 68:2 [MS p 226]: savage > pauper's

p 68:4 [MS p 226]: is a fair specimen of > suggests

p 68:5 [MS p 227]: inspect > contemplate

p 68:7 [MS p 227]: to realize > to get a realizing sense

p 68:8 [MS p 227]: height > altitude

p 68:8–9 [MS p 227]: believing > honestly believing

p 68:15 [MS p 228]: The family > She had

p 69:16 [MS p 232]: tried to make > made

p 70:9 [MS p 235]: the venturesome child > her

p 70:11–12 [MS p 235]: an appealing glance at the group > toward the group an appealing glance for help

p 70:14 [MS p 236]: after him > in his wake

p 70:30 [MS p 238]: pathetic sign > dumb expression

p 71:4 [MS p 238]: * and stopped bef > with its curtains all closed, and stopped before

p 71:19 [MS p 230a]: comprehended > grasped

p 72:6 [MS p 232a]: barring it and forming > so that the wagon formed

p 72:8–9 [MS p 233a]: and as the mad horse plunge > braced his big frame firmly

p 72:9 [MS p 233a]: mad horse > horse

* After p 239 in the MS, the sequence p 230a–239a has been inserted.

p 72:22–23 [MS p 234a]:   He had felt before that it > The one lack which he had felt before was supplied. That is to say, he had been conscious that his happiness

p 73:7 [MS p 235a]:   Then Tom Hooker and the reporter of the rival sheet > The two village papers
p 73:10 [MS p 235a]:   the thing > it
p 73:10 [MS p 235a]:   approach to the thing > likeness
p 73:31 [MS p 237a]:   wolf gorge > Hill Cottage

p 74:7 [MS p 240]:   across > athwart
p 74:12 [MS p 241]:   together with the cracker > the cracker
p 74:13 [MS p 241]:   clothes > raiment
p 74:21 [MS p 242]:   those brief periods > the earliest part

p 75:3 [MS p 243]:   a new state > a very advanced stage

p 76:5 [MS p 248]:   bent > staggering
p 76:32 [MS p 251]:   very mischief > mischief

p 77:12 [MS p 252]:   Dexter's > this last
p 77:29 [MS p 254]:   something > paregoric

p 78:15 [MS p 256]:   Billings > Baxter

p 79:23 [MS p 259]:   Bullet > Billings

p 80:4 [MS p 260]:   seemed > appeared

p 83:2 [MS p 270]:   arrive at any satisfactory > understand
p 83:7 [MS p 271]:   She managed to find out that Mrs. Griswold's sister > so she finally gave up and went to sleep.

p 84:2 [MS p 274]:   I > we
p 84:5 [MS p 274]:   I > we
p 84:11 [MS p 275]:   a strange > an unusual

p 85:3 [MS p 278]:   imploring accusing look > imploring look
p 85:15 [MS p 279]:   know > imagine

p 87:2 [MS p 280]:   fellows > druggist clerks

p 87:4 [MS p 280]: transpired > happened

p 87:18 [MS p 282]: "Hang'd > "Dog'd

p 87:25 [MS p 283]: steps > yards

p 87:25–26 [MS p 283]: then began to reel slightly and stagger > to a grassy open in the hazels

p 87:27 [MS p 283]: I feel it at my vitals. > How drowsy I am!

p 88:23 [MS p 286]: I knew > I wonder

p 88:27 [MS p 286]: sulk > slink

p 88:30 [MS p 287]: on this log > here

p 89:1 [MS p 287]: the big log > Hugh's big frame

p 89:10 [MS p 288]: You bet your life! > Don't you forget it!

p 89:17 [MS p 289]: the poles > a train

p 90:3 [MS p 293]: strolling along — no staggering along is the better word > strolling along.

p 90:7 [MS p 293]: entirely transformed > transformed

p 90:8 [MS p 293]: youth > young fellow

p 90:11 [MS p 294]: actually stagger > stagger

p 90:14 [MS p 294]: at the front of > about

p 92:26–27 [MS p 304]: the widow > Mrs. Higgins's

p 93:15 [MS p 306]: Sackett > Lem

p 93:27 [MS p 307]: what are you doing with him? > how does he come to be with you?

p 94:26 [MS p 310]: as pitch, you numscull — > as pitch

p 94:30 [MS p 311]: found him, you flat-head! > found him.

p 95:20 [MS p 313]: O my goodness! That is you did > O my goodness!"

p 95:28 [MS p 314]: "Nor I — bec > "So do I, Tom — because

p 96:8 [MS p 316]: Finally Tom said — > The young fellows

p 96:16 [MS p 317]: A detective > Its a track

p 97:14 [MS p 321]: Lem Sackett > is to mysteriously

p 98:11 [MS p 324]: Mine for yours? > Clothes, you mean?

p 98:26 [MS p 325–326]: river path, grinding The Last Rose of Summer > "Lover's Roost"

p 98:32 [MS p 326]: let him come to bag his game > I'm out of luck again

p 99:4–5 [MS p 327]: the one sur > the one true-aimed shot

p 99:6–7 [MS p 327]: moving > shadowy

p 99:22–23 [MS p 329]: he came sudd > for he could hardly

p 99:23 [MS p 329]: emerged > found

p 100:5 [MS p 331]: O, not for a moment. > You only did your duty.

p 100:19 [MS p 333]: it > you

p 101:6 [MS p 335]: could not > saw

p 101:7 [MS p 335]: nothing > no suggestion

p 101:27 [MS p 339]: assent > gratified assent

p 102:1 [MS p 339]: figures > dimensions

p 103:1 [MS p 343]: always sends > sends

p 103:20 [MS p 345]: Bob Tufts the detective > Bob Tufts

p 103:22 [MS p 345]: but > then

p 104:21 [MS p 349]: about > while

p 105:4 [MS p 351]: Illinois. No come > Illinois."

p 105:10 [MS p 352]: put > scared

p 105:19 [MS p 353]: will not > is not

p 109:13 [MS p 368]: was it most > we want to

p 109:22 [MS p 369]: "Jenny it was > "The author of his

p 111:13 [MS p 375]: again, this sin-seared > again. Let others

p 112:2 [MS p 377]: All that > 'Twasn't

p 112:7 [MS p 378]: Any very satisfactory > Any satisfactory

p 112:10 [MS p 379]: So > Wherefore

p 112:15 [MS p 379]: had reached > reached

p 112:32 [MS p 381]: wondering at and thought > wondering and said

p 113:6 [MS p 382]:   He pointed with his > He indicated the direction
p 113:28 [MS p 384]:   asked > said

p 114:1 [MS p 385]:   Watching him furtively > He considered a moment

p 117:9 [MS p 396]:   quarter > half

p 119:6 [MS p 400–401]:   Mrs. Burnside began in a > There was a trying time
p 119:29 [MS p 402]:   presently > at length

p 120:9 [MS p 404]:   unnecessary > unwarrantable
p 120:16 [MS p 405]:   but when its subsidence was followed by this > but this

p 121:16 [MS p 409]:   love > value
p 121:17 [MS p 409]:   I find that loss > Loss
p 121:20 [MS p 409]:   again, poor old boy! > again!
p 121:27–28 [MS p 411]:   without one > with hardly a

p 122:5 [MS p 412]:   theorizing > confusion in my mind
p 122:6 [MS p 412]:   Before they came, I thought > I had thought
p 122:9 [MS p 413]:   crystalized > clarified
p 122:9 [MS p 413]:   only > far more
p 122:10 [MS p 413]:   approaching horrors > siege of horrors
p 122:13 [MS p 414]:   am > feel

p 123:4 [MS p 416]:   To move is to be checkmated. > It is a curiously complicated
                          position.
p 123:7 [MS p 417]:   instantly checkmated > checkmated
p 123:22 [MS p 418]:   so grateful > grateful

p 124:21 [MS p 423]:   stifled secret > secret
p 124:23–24 [MS p 423]:   that that secret > that the keeping of that secret

p 125:17 [MS p 426]:   first goes > goes first > goes

p 126:3 [MS p 428]:   Hugh > Dexter
p 126:14 [MS p 430]:   until she was > at the moment
p 126:21 [MS p 431]:   said in a dead voice > said

p 127:10 [MS p 433]:   eyes > gaze

p 127:12 [MS p 433]: with fantastic display lines > with a moving array of fantastic

p 127:19 [MS p 434]: suppressed a groan > sighed, resignedly

p 129:2 [MS p 435]: can be imagined > might be expected > such a situation

p 129:6 [MS p 436]: insured him > provided

p 129:10 [MS p 436]: give > shore her up

p 130:4 [MS p 439]: racking and ceaseless > racking

p 130:4 [MS p 439]: had resulted in > followed at last by

p 130:30–31 [MS p 441]: awful > devastating

p 131:2 [MS p 442]: suf > torture

p 131:8 [MS p 442½]: attention, and made him shiver besides. > attention.

p 131:18 [MS p 443]: been thinking > made up my mind.

p 131:23 [MS p 443]: His eye > He showed it, and his eye

p 131:25 [MS p 444]: sufficient > enough

p 131:26 [MS p 444]: tried > hastened

p 131:27 [MS p 444]: calmly > tranquilly

p 131:31 [MS p 444]: gaze > steady gaze

p 132:1 [MS p 445]: There was > A period

p 132:7 [MS p 445]: He wondered > Milly continued

p 133:6 [MS p 449]: the devil > Satan

p 133:12 [MS p 450]: I will never rest > Hugh did not save

p 133:16 [MS p 451]: indignation > and indignant disbelief

p 133:24 [MS p 452]: went > sailed

p 133:26 [MS p 452]: based upon > born of

p 134:1 [MS p 453]: Are you not his cousin, are you not his nearest friend > From you, his cousin, his nearest friend

p 134:8 [MS p 454]: to get away gracefully when she had finished. Arrived at his room > when she had finished, to properly formulate

p 134:12–13 [MS p 455]: to do her b > to do everything she can

p 135:8 [MS p 458]: injustice > unjustness

p 137:5 [MS p 459]: having > being

p 137:7 [MS p 460]: shining and conspicuous > conspicuous

p 137:17 [MS p 461]: cheerily > cheerfully
p 137:23 [MS p 462]: grandly called > called
p 137:24 [MS p 462]: as soon as > Wheeler set them all free as soon as
p 137:30 [MS p 462]: one night > once

p 138:1–2 [MS p 463]: Said he — > Here it is in his own language —
p 138:26–27 [MS p 466]: heard a sudden > felt a great

p 139:8 [MS p 468]: ones > comets
p 139:11 [MS p 468]: By and by > In the course of time

p 140:25 [MS p 473]: good and faithful > good

p 142:12 [MS p 479]: reach > get
p 142:15 [MS p 479]: didn't have > went
p 142:30–31 [MS p 481]: receive > welcome
p 142:31 [MS p 481–482]: you, the whole broad realm of the blest > you!
p 142:32 [MS p 482]: citizens > nations and peoples

p 143:7 [MS p 483]: a man > one
p 143:24 [MS p 485]: country-reared > country-born

p 144:9 [MS p 487]: diver > constant divergences
p 144:10 [MS p 487]: keep > show
p 144:15 [MS p 488]: This kind > Therefore, we repeat it was natural for this kindly
p 144:24 [MS p 489]: accepted > devoured
p 144:25–26 [MS p 489]: heroes > detective heroes
p 144:29 [MS p 489]: recount > recal[l]

p 145:4 [MS p 490]: issue > detail
p 145:5 [MS p 490]: give > issue
p 145:6 [MS p 491]: imaginaries > shadows
p 145:18 [MS p 492]: put it > elevate
p 145:33 [MS p 494]: and several pieces of old furniture > several old chairs and a
                      table

p 146:14 [MS p 496]: out of these > as to minor details, out of these
p 146:18 [MS p 497]: small > slight
p 146:27 [MS p 498]: his > a strong

p 147:4 [MS p 499]: were locked > and two rooms overhead were locked.

p 147:9–10 [MS p 500]: too dusky > not light enough

p 148:28 [MS p 505]: killed > shot

p 149:1 [MS p 506]: of whom > of which

p 149:19 [MS p 508]: He had his two hands advanced > He imagined he was taking leave